FAST & Reckless

A RACING HEARTS NOVEL

FAST & Reckless

AMANDA WEAVER

SLOWBURN
A zando IMPRINT

NEW YORK

zando

Copyright © 2024 by Amanda Weaver

Slowburn is an imprint of Zando.
zandoprojects.com

First Edition: September 2024

Design by Neuwirth & Associates, Inc.
Cover design by Caroline Johnson

Library of Congress Control Number: 2024937605

978-1-63893-186-7 (Paperback)
978-1-63893-187-4 (ebook)

10 9 8 7 6 5 4 3 2 1
Manufactured in the United States of America

FOR MATT, ALWAYS

FAST & Reckless

PROLOGUE

Will Hawley downshifted, desperately attempting to hang on to his car as the laws of physics tried to rip it off the track. But the shimmy in the back tires foretold disaster. He could feel himself losing control . . . the sickening lurch in his head, and in his gut.

This was a reckoning. Barreling toward him at three hundred kilometers an hour.

Will took three shuddering breaths, trying to slow his racing heart.

Focus.

But it was too late.

The downforce, the tire pressure, the fuel load . . . it was all going sideways. Will lost his sense of the horizon, unable to tell which way was up.

It's over.

There was nothing left to do as a cascade of failures ripped through the race car and threw it into an uncontrolled spin across the track. Will's existence was reduced to a blur of color, burning tires, and a deafening roar as the car careened into a wall and crumpled around his body.

Will felt a ringing in his ears as his vision briefly faded to black. Only one thought pierced the fog: This was the last time he'd ever be on a Formula One track.

Because his career was fucking *over*.

Mira raced down the hallway of Lennox Motorsport, rubbing her thumb over the surface of her employee ID like a talisman. She glanced down at her new job title again.

Miranda Wentworth
Executive Assistant, Lennox Motorsport

This was real. She was back.

Mira stopped outside Penelope Farnham's open office door. "I did it," she whispered, overcome with emotion.

A woman, tall, angular, and about Mira's age, poked her head out of the office and raked her eyes over Mira with a lightning-fast glance. "You're Miranda? The new Pen?"

"I guess so? Yes. I am. And Mira's fine."

"I'm Violet, from PR," the woman said over her shoulder as she brushed past. "And you're supposed to follow me."

Mira hurried down the hallway after her. "But I'm supposed to find Penelope—"

"Yeah, well, this morning Pen's doctor told her she was absolutely *not* allowed to leave bed until her due date."

"Oh. She's not coming?" As intimidated as Mira had been at the prospect of meeting Pen in the flesh, not having her here to show her the ropes was infinitely scarier.

Penelope's doctor-ordered bed rest had led to Mira's last-minute hire, just weeks from the start of the Formula One season. Pen was, to put it mildly, a little freaked out about turning her job over to some total newbie from America. As Mira quickly packed up in LA and prepared to fly out to England, Pen had texted nonstop with instructions. Mira had already filled three notepads. And now it seemed like the job was about to become one hundred percent more terrifying.

Mira finally managed to catch up to Violet's long-legged stride and gave her long, tousled jet-black hair, pale skin, on-point winged eyeliner, shredded jeans, and battered leather motorcycle jacket a quick once-over. She radiated "cool girl" right down to her slick English accent. Mira tried not to be intimidated. "Simone's not in PR anymore?"

Violet shot her a quick glance. "Right. You already know your way around Lennox, don't you?"

"It's been a long time," Mira said, her stomach swooping with nerves. But if anyone was expecting that hot mess of a girl she'd been, they were in for a disappointment. That Miranda was gone forever, and *this* Miranda wasn't going to make a single slip.

"Don't worry, Simone's still here. I'm her assistant. She's out at the test track for press day. We're starting there." Violet hip-checked a door and ushered Mira outside, where a golf cart was parked haphazardly on the grass. "Hop in."

As Mira slid into the passenger side, Violet popped behind the wheel and slammed her foot on the gas pedal, sending the cart rocketing forward. Approaching the track, Mira could hear the unmistakable sound of state-of-the-art automotive perfection roaring across the asphalt. Forgetting all her professional cool, her heart began to beat faster. *This* was what she'd missed. The track, the cars, the *sound.*

"Were there a lot of upgrades to the car this season?" Mira asked.

"Oh yeah. It's a whole new car, really. It's on the track for the first time today, so things are a bit mad around here."

"Not the best time to be starting."

"It never is," Violet said with a grin. "Welcome to Lennox."

Violet braked with a spray of gravel at the edge of the track, and Mira stumbled out, unable to take her eyes off the streak of blue just coming out of a hairpin turn.

"It's beautiful." Her fingers tangled in the chain-link fence separating her from the track as the car hit the far curve, and she could see it properly for the first time.

Last year's livery design had been too blocky and broken up, obscuring the elegance of the car's design. This year was a huge improvement, solid Lennox royal blue with just a single slash of silver up the side, highlighting the car's aerodynamic perfection, low to the ground and sleek as a knife.

The car sped toward the next curve and she could feel the power of its engine. Anticipation had her toes curling inside her sensible black pumps, and her chest thrummed in time with the engine. Here came the turn.

The car kept accelerating far past when her own instincts would have told her to brake. Just when it seemed inevitable that the car would careen into the wall, the whine of the engine dropped as the driver downshifted. It powered through the curve at a speed that felt physically impossible.

She let out a gasp as it sped away, down the straight, as if the car had sucked the breath clean out of her lungs. "Holy shit," she murmured as her grip on the fence went slack. "That's some driver."

Violet chuckled. "Just you wait. Come on, let's go introduce you to everybody before he comes off the track."

She hurried after Violet, buzzing from her first close encounter with Formula One in seven years. For so long she'd been relegated to watching the races on her laptop in LA. But nothing could replace being here on the track, seeing it, *feeling* it.

As hard as coming back was going to be, it was what she wanted more than anything. If she could do this—successfully manage a season at Lennox—maybe she could parlay that into a career in racing management.

"Today's just a press day," Violet was explaining as they made their way to the pit lane. "So we can get some promotional footage of the car. They don't even have decent tires on it yet."

She remembered this part. FIA regulations forbade them to do much before official testing in Bahrain, but even a day like today, ostensibly just for press shots, was a chance to gather information about the car.

In the garage bay off the pit lane, Lennox's second car was being readied for the track, surrounded by a dozen mechanics in blue jackets. As she and Violet approached, they paused, sizing up the new arrival.

"Mira, this is the pit crew. Crew, this is Mira, Pen's replacement."

"We have names, Violet," a young Middle Eastern guy groused with a wink.

"And Mira will dutifully learn them all, Omar, but we don't have time today. Where's Harry?"

Omar turned and shouted over his shoulder. "Harry, Violet's here to harass you."

Harry . . . Mira's heart gave a twist. None of the crew had been around long enough to remember her. She had a fresh slate with them. But Harry . . .

A familiar old voice growled from behind the far side of the car. "I've got no time for press nonsense today."

Harry might have looked and sounded like a gruff gnome of a man, but when she'd been a curious little kid with a love of racing, Harry had indulged her, letting her hang around the race bay and patiently answering her endless questions. She hadn't seen him since . . . well, everything—and if he looked at her differently now, she might just shrivel up and die.

"Come out, Harry," Violet crooned. "I promise I won't bite. Look, I've brought along someone new for you to growl at. It's Mira, Pen's replacement."

At once, Harry's grizzled gray head popped up from behind the car. "Mira?"

The unmistakable joy in his eyes made her weak with relief. Her smile was genuine as she raised a hand in greeting. "Hi, Harry."

Harry scooted out from behind the car with surprising speed and agility for a man his age. "Come let me get a look at you, girl." He seized her by the shoulders, his eyes skating over her face. "All grown-up now, aren't you? Give us a hug, then."

He folded her into a firm embrace, and her eyes pricked with tears. She hadn't known how much Harry's warm welcome would matter to her until now.

"It's really good to see you again, Harry. So how's the car this year?"

His eyes lit up with enthusiasm, but as he opened his mouth to reply, a voice cut across the hum of the pit lane.

"Harry, what the hell! Are your engineers fucking idiots?"

Harry's eyes shot heavenward, and he let out a long-suffering sigh.

Mira turned to look in the direction of the voice and stifled a gasp. The first car had just come off the track and its driver was descending on them like an approaching thunderstorm.

Her eyes registered many things all at once. He was taller than she expected. And hotter—oh . . . *so* hot. His blue race suit was unzipped to the waist, the sleeves tied around his hips, revealing a thin white Nomex undershirt that hugged every inch of his upper body. His tousled dark hair—nearly black—looked far too good for having just been flattened under a helmet, and his thick dark brows were furrowed in anger.

But his eyes . . . his eyes were absolutely electric. She could tell they were bright blue even at a distance, and the intensity of his gaze gave her chills even when it wasn't directed at her. And then there were his cheekbones, his jawline, his chin . . . bone structure that beautiful should be illegal, especially when combined with the long legs and the broad shoulders and the tapered waist, and . . . *god.*

She dropped her eyes, embarrassed to realize that her face was hot and her body had gone all fluttery. No no *no.* She was absolutely *not* allowed to feel this white-hot flare of attraction just minutes into her first day, and certainly not for a driver, of all people. Maybe he was just some test driver, someone she'd encounter once, then never see again—

"Problem, Will?" Harry said as he approached, and Mira's heart sank.

Will. He was Will Hawley, Lennox's new driver.

Which meant he was about to become a very prominent part of her work life.

Well, that extremely inconvenient blast of physical attraction was going straight into a trunk, padlocked, and dumped into the depths of the ocean, because there was *no way*. Not ever. He was one thousand percent off-limits for a million different reasons.

To keep her eyes away from him, she flipped to a page of notes at the front of her notepad, everything she'd hurriedly compiled about the team on her flight over. Will Hawley was almost as new here as she was. Lennox had planned to keep both of last season's drivers, but then Phillipe Deschamps injured his shoulder. He'd had surgery during the offseason, but his recovery hadn't gone well. Just a few weeks ago he announced that he was retiring, and the hunt for his replacement began.

There had been loads of media speculation about who would be chosen, and everybody went bananas when they announced they were signing Will Hawley. The sport seemed pretty divided on him. Half thought he had more raw talent than anybody who'd ever gotten behind the wheel. The other half thought he was a hot mess whose off-track bullshit canceled out any promise he might have.

Either way, though, he was danger. The words were written all over that gorgeous face in big capital letters. And if there was one thing Mira was good at these days, it was steering clear of anything dangerous.

When Will stormed into the garage bay, it was clear he was interrupting something. For one, Harry was hugging some woman, which was weird all on its own. Harry was not a hugger. Violet from PR was hovering just behind them, smiling. Also weird. Nothing made Violet smile, except maybe pulling the wings off flies. Well, whatever he'd walked in on could wait. He was there to drive and if he couldn't do that, they were all fucked.

"Excuse me, but could you please try caring about your fucking jobs for a moment?" Will snapped. With a sigh, Harry met his gaze. "We have a problem. A big fucking problem. That is *not* the car I had in the simulator."

Harry pressed his lips together and put his hands in his pockets, turning to face Will fully. "I know."

Will blinked, his brain trying to catch up. Was this a joke? He'd been practicing for weeks, memorizing every *inch* of the car, and Harry just . . . forgot to tell him it would be changing? Renewed anger flushed through his chest. "You *know?* This is intentional? What kind of bullshit is this? You put me in one car in the simulator and I get something completely different out on the track? How the fuck am I supposed to be ready for Bahrain if this is the bullshit I'm going to have to deal with? When are you going to get around to building the car I've been testing in the sim?"

"Can't be helped, Will. We've got a lot to do to get the cars ready for Bahrain, and that's how we have to allocate the resources. Decision's come from the top."

The team principal, then. This was his decision.

"That son of a bitch," Will growled.

Behind Harry, Violet sniggered and glanced at that new woman Harry had inexplicably *hugged*, who was ducking her head to smother her own smirk. He shot a look at her, trying to figure out who she was and what he was missing. Blond hair pulled back into a high ponytail, black wool coat, black trousers, sensible black heels . . . some new office worker, maybe? Lennox was a big organization. He certainly didn't know everybody yet. But why was she here in the pit, hugging Harry?

Just then, her eyes lifted to his and he blinked in surprise. She was prettier than he'd first registered, with a face like one of those Disney Princesses—high cheekbones, a nose just shy of being pert, and lush lips—and eyes that dominated her face. Large and dark green, fringed by thick, feathery lashes, with arched eyebrows several shades darker than her hair. *Very* pretty. And much younger than that office drone outfit let on. Early twenties, he'd guess.

He very much wanted to know what this girl looked like when she wasn't on duty. With that blond hair let loose and a whole lot less clothing, maybe. A different sort of heat rushed through him, the kind he usually reserved for off the track. But he was in the middle of a serious work problem, so that was, unfortunately, going to have to wait.

"Look, Will, it can't be helped," Harry said, snapping him back to the present. "It's going to be Matteo's specs for a little while."

"I can't believe this! What's the point of signing me if I'm not going to be supported?" Apparently he'd be dealing with a car designed and built for Matteo Gatone, Lennox's other driver, who was the team veteran and took priority.

Lacing his fingers behind his neck, Will groaned and let his head fall back, staring at the flat gray winter sky overhead. This was a disaster. The racing world was going to give him exactly one race to prove himself before they made up their minds about him, and he was going to be hamstrung by his car. Fucking fabulous. So much for his triumphant return to F1.

"But what about all the work we've been doing in the simulator? We had it dialed in. You saw my stats." He'd spent *hours* in the simulator generating data for the engineers. What was the bloody point if they were going to throw all that info out the window when it came to the actual car?

"It's going to take time, and we don't have a lot of that right now. Matteo's times are fine in the car as is, so we had to shift priorities. We'll update your brake ducts next chance we get," Harry said.

"When?" Will demanded. He was finally about to get another chance behind the wheel in Formula One, and if his equipment wasn't up to scratch, he was going to be fighting with one hand tied behind his back.

Harry held his hands up to placate him. "You'll have it by Melbourne."

Will blinked, absorbing that crushing blow. "That's the second race of the season."

"Will, sorry," Violet suddenly interjected. "But I'm going to have to steal Harry away. Time to get Matteo's car out there."

"We're in the middle of something, Violet," Will said, through gritted teeth. "You know, about the *racing* we do around here? A bit important."

"Melbourne is weeks away, which means *you* can wait. Today's about pictures." Violet smiled smugly at him before looping an arm around Harry's shoulders and steering him away.

"No worries, I'm just a bloody *driver*," he called after her. "Happy to wait."

Violet stuck up two middle fingers over her shoulder, still walking away.

Well fuck you too, he thought.

"Excuse me, Mr. Hawley?"

It was the new girl again. She was flipping through a notepad filled with dense, tiny writing so he gave her a closer perusal. Long neck, creamy skin, hint of pink on those cheekbones, looked fit under that coat. Forget pretty. She was *hot*. He probably shouldn't go there. She was a Lennox employee, and he kept his after-hours pursuits separate from work. But he might make an exception for this one.

He'd worked very hard to purge any reckless vices that got in the way of his driving. Thank god sex wasn't one of those vices.

He smiled and leaned in. "What do you need?"

She held up a finger to silence him, never looking up from her notepad. "Hang on . . ." she muttered. American. That was interesting. Not too many of them around Formula One. "I had a note about you somewhere, I swear."

Will knew he'd had problems in the past with, erm . . . overconfidence. More than one scathing sporting op-ed had described him as cocky and self-important. But . . . *seriously?* She was working for a Formula One team and didn't already know who he was? Racing groupies were usually tripping over themselves to get him to notice them. Could this girl be at least a *tiny* bit impressed to meet him? A little blushing and stammering wouldn't hurt.

He edged closer to her. In her distraction, she didn't seem to notice. "Perhaps you'll find me in there under 'extremely hot, talented team driver'?" he teased, pretending to peer over the edge of her notepad.

Her eyes snapped up to his, and his smile dropped off his face. Whatever flirtatious comment he'd planned next melted clean out of his head and all he could do was look at her. That face, those eyes . . .

"I know who you are," she said quietly. And that ice-cold tone of voice said she very much didn't *care* who he was. *Okay . . .*

"Ah, I see Will's already introduced himself." Violet had finished up with Harry and was striding back in their direction. As a rule, he tried to avoid Violet, as she was almost always annoyed with him. Then again, Violet seemed annoyed with everyone, all the time.

"We haven't actually met," Will said, flashing a smile at the new girl again. Not so much as a hint of a smile from her in return.

"Will, this is Mira. She's here to replace Pen. Mira, this is Will Hawley." Violet waved a hand carelessly in his direction. "Just signed on as a driver. He's rumored to be *really* hot and talented. I guess we'll see." Violet winked at him.

Mira. Pretty name to go with the pretty face. And replacing Pen. That meant he'd be seeing quite a lot of her. Not such a hardship.

"Yeah," she murmured, one corner of her mouth finally tugging up ever so slightly. "I clocked the driver part."

He was used to Violet treating him like shit. That was part of her *quirky personality*. But Mira seemed equally unimpressed. Maybe she just didn't understand racing all that well. After all, she was American.

"Well, as you're still learning the ropes of Formula One," he said, as gently as he could. "If you've got any questions, I'd be happy to help you out."

She cleared her throat and dropped her eyes back to her notepad, fiddling with her pen. "Got it, Mr. Hawley," she said coolly. "I'll keep that in mind."

Mira's eyes slid sideways to Violet, who smothered a chuckle. Will got the uncomfortable feeling that they were having a laugh at his expense, although he couldn't sort out why, which annoyed him to no end. Violet was probably just enjoying watching him get shot down. She loved watching other people squirm.

"Okay, then, Mira," Violet said, hooking her arm with her own. "We'd better get you back to the office. I'm sure Pen's left a lengthy list for you."

Violet began to tow her away, but Mira stopped short and spun back toward him. "Dinner tonight!"

Well, maybe the flirting had worked after all. "Sounds great," he said.

She was still scanning her notes and entirely missed his triumphant smile. "There's a dinner tonight for department heads, to celebrate the start of the season. Vincenzo's at eight. Penelope said you'd know the place."

He shifted his weight from the balls of his feet to his heels as his smile faded. Heat spread up the back of his neck as he tried to recover. "I do. Will I see you there?"

She scowled. "Of course. It's my job."

Then she turned her back on him and disappeared with Violet. Considering he'd just been behind the wheel of a Formula One car for the first time in three years, it was baffling that in this moment, he wasn't thinking about the car at all. Had she just . . . *dismissed* him? That was not something he was used to from women. Whatever anybody might say about him, he was hard to ignore. But he'd see her again tonight. And he was nothing if not determined.

Mira tugged at the hem of her charcoal-gray sheath dress. Was it too short? Maybe she should have worn pants. Something serious and professional and—

The restaurant door opened and Simone came into the vestibule with Violet right behind her.

"Simone, hi again," Mira said.

The older blond woman, looking smooth as silk in head-to-toe ivory, smiled. "Already hard at work, Mira?"

"I wanted to start putting names to faces. Pen said I need to know every person in the company personally."

Simone gave a subtle roll of her eyes on her way past. "That certainly sounds like something Pen would say."

"Finally," Violet said. "Someone at one of these things I actually want to talk to. Save you a seat inside?"

Violet had ended up taking her around the rest of the factory that afternoon, and they'd had a good time together. The past few years had been pretty isolating, by Mira's own choice, but she'd still been lonely. Spending all your free time with your mother was just sad. Hanging out with someone her own age might be fun.

"Sure thing. I'll be in soon."

After Violet had gone through, Mira pulled out her cheat sheet of dinner guests to see who was still missing. Just then the front door opened, bringing in a gust of cold night air.

"Hello, again."

Her heart sank. *Him.*

When she looked up, the door was closing behind him, and he was tugging off his thin leather driving gloves with his teeth as he peered down at her.

She took a deep breath. "Good, you finally made it. We've got a private room in back. It's just through there and to the right."

He shrugged his expensive leather jacket off with sensuous, nearly feline grace. Underneath, he wore all black, a dress shirt open at the neck and slim-fitting trousers. *Uff* . . . even out of his racing uniform he was so beautiful. His hair was an artless riot of dark waves that probably always looked that good with minimal effort. She tried her best to keep her eyes away from his mouth. Those lips were sinfully pretty.

"Mira. It's Mira, right?"

She jerked her gaze back up to his eyes. "Yeah?" she said cautiously.

Slinging the jacket over one arm and stuffing his hands in his pockets, he leaned back on his heels. "You caught me in the middle of something at the track today. We didn't get a chance to talk."

"Talk?"

He took a step closer and a slow, wicked grin unfurled across his face. "To get to know each other a little better."

He was deadly. Yeah, he was aggressive and overconfident and brash, but just being near someone so . . . *passionate* was kind of exhilarating. He made her feel . . . alive—some combination of nerves and excitement she hadn't felt in a long time. And she honestly couldn't tell if it was his driving that made her feel like that or just . . . *him.*

"I didn't realize we needed to get to know each other," she said slowly, feeling her way through his conversation. She thought she was getting a vibe from him, but it might just be in her imagination. He was probably like this with everyone. Guys like him usually were.

He took a step closer to her and her whole body went on alert. Well, she was human. There were very few people who would not respond to the looming presence of someone like Will Hawley. There was just so *much* of him, and it was all so hot and so close, and he smelled really, really good.

"Listen," he said lowly. His posh English accent slid slowly over her like melted chocolate over ice cream. "These sorts of dinners tend to be a little dull, but they never go very late. Why don't we grab a drink afterward? Let me welcome you to the team properly."

And there it was. Her instincts weren't wrong. There was no question in her mind that welcoming her *properly* would involve a lot more than drinks. Her nerves fired. Part of her wanted to know what would happen if she said yes, and for one split second, she found herself leaning in to him, closer to that gorgeous face, that smooth-as-silk accent, that delicious scent . . .

No.

Not this time. Mira pulled back and managed to mumble, "I have a lot of work to do."

His voice dropped into a timbre that had her hands curling into fists. "Tonight? Really?"

She didn't mean to look at his mouth, but somehow her eyes snagged on those lips as they curled into a smile, and she imagined what it would feel like to—

She took a hasty step back. "We'd better—um . . . they're waiting for us."

She turned, intending to head into the restaurant and far away from him, but then she felt it . . . his hand closing gently around her wrist.

"Hey, don't run off yet," he murmured.

She felt electrified from head to toe, excruciatingly aware of every beautiful inch of him right behind her. She could almost *feel* the heat of his body. The hairs on the back of her neck prickled, and then the sensation flowed downward, along her spine and out through her limbs, like molten gold.

He was barely touching her, a loose grip she could have broken out of in an instant. But the heat of his palm, the electric brush of his fingertips against the sensitive skin of her inner wrist, froze her in place.

Like one of those dumb rabbits who freeze in front of a snake. Except she was no dumb bunny, not anymore, and no snake was going to hold her in his thrall.

She shook her arm free with far more force than needed and it threw her off-balance. She stumbled. Will jerked backward too, both hands raised, either to reach for her or fend her off, she wasn't sure which. Didn't matter.

"Look, Mr. Hawley," she snapped, her voice nowhere near as strong as she would have liked. She pressed her palm to her chest to steady herself. "I'm sure you're used to every woman you meet melting into a puddle at your feet, but that's not going to happen with me. No drinks or anything else you might be offering."

His expression sobered and he opened his mouth to say something but she didn't want to hear what it was. Every second she spent alone with him was one more second than she should. "They're waiting for you. You'd better get in there before you're late."

Without waiting for a response, she turned on her heel and strode into the restaurant. This time he made no move to stop her. She never did that, confront someone. Her nerves felt jangly and raw. But now it was done. She'd made herself clear and Will Hawley would surely stay a mile away from her from now on. Which was good. For the rest of the night, she'd be reminding herself that that was a good thing.

"Everything all right?" Violet asked as Mira slid into the seat she'd saved for her.

"Fine!" she said brightly. The last thing anyone needed to know was that the new driver was hitting on her. She'd be out on her ass and back in LA before morning.

She blew out a trembling breath, refusing to look toward the doorway, even when she heard Will entering the room and greeting others. When Violet set a glass of red wine in front of her, she gratefully took a sip. Okay, she was off to a bit of a rocky start, but she'd handled it. She would continue to handle it. There was no way she'd let Will Hawley get under her skin and distract her from the job she'd come here to do.

Will absently responded to the friendly hellos and gentle teasing of the Lennox team as he made his way to his seat in the private dining room—the last one to arrive. His eyes were fixed on Mira, all the way at the other end of the table, between Violet and Natalia, the team principal's girlfriend. Natalia was leaning in, telling Mira something. How did the new girl know everybody already? Hugging Harry, sharing chats with Natalia? Didn't she start today?

And more importantly, what had happened back there? He hadn't been the least bit subtle in asking her out, but the anger in her pushback had surprised him. Had he done something wrong? Offended her or scared her in some way? The longer he thought about it, the worse he felt. Stupid dick moves like that were supposed to be in his past. Well, fine. Pen's replacement might be the best-looking thing he'd laid eyes on in months, but she'd clearly declared herself off-limits. Understood.

He'd reached for his wineglass before he remembered that he'd be back in the simulator tomorrow to work through today's data. It was a critical part of his job, helping the engineers figure out what they needed to adjust before Bahrain.

He couldn't afford for his reflexes to be any less than a hundred percent, and these days, he had strict rules about alcohol consumption before racing, even if the car was virtual. He slid the glass away and switched to water.

At the head of the table, Paul, the team principal, stood to make his informal greeting, so he pulled his attention away from Mira and put it where it belonged, on his new boss.

"I won't go on too long, I just wanted to thank you all for your hard work in previous seasons to bring us to this moment, and to thank you in advance for the work you'll put in as this season progresses. Even under FIA restrictions, today was very informative, and we're very optimistic about this year's car. I hope at the end we have won another constructor's championship or maybe even a world driver's championship. Before I let you get on to dinner, I wanted to welcome our newcomers."

Paul looked down the table and met Will's gaze. "As you all know, we're fortunate to have William Hawley on board to drive alongside Matteo. I'm sure he'll do great things for us this season." That last bit was half reassuring, half threatening, just like Paul himself. He could be your best mate, easy, personable, friendly. But when Lennox Motorsport was on the line, he was a dragon. A dragon you *did not* want to cross.

His introduction was met with an enthusiastic round of applause from the table, one he hoped he could earn. Across the table, Matteo raised a glass to him. "In bocca al lupo," Matteo said. Will didn't speak Italian, but he recognized the phrase. *Into the wolf's mouth,* the Italian version of *break a leg,* meant to convey the opposite. But the spark in Matteo's eyes made him think maybe he was literally wishing him into the wolf.

Matteo was his teammate and partner, but also his rival, and they both knew it. Although he'd never won a world championship, Matteo had a generous handful of podium finishes to show for his nearly ten years at the top of the sport, and he'd spent most of those years driving for Lennox. He was their guy. They were always going to put Matteo's needs first. Unless Will proved that *he* deserved the team's resources and support.

"Some of you have known our other newcomer for years," Paul continued. "Others met her today as she toured the facility. I'm delighted to have my daughter, Miranda Wentworth, joining us to replace Penelope for the season. Mira," Paul said, pausing to smile down at her, "welcome aboard."

More applause greeted that announcement, but Will barely heard the cheers. Miranda Wentworth. *Mira* Wentworth. Paul's daughter. The team principal's *daughter*.

Fuck.

Oh, fuck.

Now that little inside joke Mira—*Miranda*—and Violet had exchanged earlier today made total sense. He'd offered to help her understand Formula One when her father was practically a living legend in the sport. They'd been laughing their asses off at him. And he'd entirely deserved it.

Then, as if insulting her intelligence regarding racing weren't bad enough, he'd asked her out. Her reaction to that made sense, too. Who the hell did he think he was, coming on to the team principal's *daughter*, for fuck's sake? No wonder she was so pissed off.

It was all he could do to keep a polite smile glued to his face while everyone at the table toasted both of them. His eyes flicked over to her, and as if she could sense his gaze on her, she stole a glance at him. Her grin remained fixed, but there was something in her eyes and the slight cock of her eyebrow that was knowing. She was enjoying this moment. In no small part, he imagined, because she'd just proven what a giant ass he was.

He wanted to disappear from the restaurant, find a bar, and drink until the embarrassment of the day faded from memory. But that was out of the question.

Paul had given him a chance to drive—his last real chance. If he blew it, an F1 world championship would likely stay forever out of reach. He'd spend his career like he had the last three years, bouncing around Indy Car, Formula E—every place but the top spot at a top Formula One team.

He shot one more look down the table at Mira, her profile outlined in gold from the candles dotting the table. She smiled up at her father, a bigger smile than she'd aimed in his direction, and a dimple appeared in her cheek that he hadn't seen before. That simmering attraction bubbled up a little hotter in his chest.

No. She was Paul's *daughter.* Anything involving Miranda Wentworth would be a mistake. From here on out, there would be no screwups. Will Hawley would be a model citizen and dream driver. Anything less could wind up costing him everything.

When her dad finished the introductions, David Weber, the head of engineering, got up to talk a bit about the new car. Mira chanced a look down the table at Will. He was listening to David with perfect professional interest. There wasn't even a hint of that smooth-talking seducer from a few minutes ago. He'd had no idea who she was, and in the split second before he'd recovered, it was obvious the news had shocked him. Good. Maybe that would scare him away once and for all.

"Super hot, right?"

Mira startled and looked at Violet. "What?"

Violet rolled her eyes. "Please. You're allowed to look. Everybody does. I mean, he's not my personal flavor of hot male. I like them a little scruffier and a lot more emotionally damaged. But I will concede, objectively, he's a snack."

"So what's his story anyway?" Even though she'd done her own research earlier, PR always knew the real dirt.

"Story?"

"I looked him up. The hashtags are . . . enlightening.

Violet sniggered. "'F1fuqboi' is my favorite."

"Aside from that, it seems like people think he's the biggest talent the sport has seen in a generation . . . or he's a walking train wreck."

"He's both, maybe?"

"Come on, Violet. Spill."

"You never heard about him?"

"I kind of stopped paying attention to racing while I was in college."

The truth was, it had hurt too much to follow racing while she'd been in exile. As much as she was digging for info on Will, she hoped Violet wouldn't pry into her reasons too much or go snooping for answers. Her mother had spent a fortune on some specialist to scrub the internet of most of the mentions of her, but stuff was still out there. And people had memories. Ask around and someone was sure to have gossip to share, true or not.

"Glad you decided to stop living under a rock." Violet laughed. "Okay, okay, Will showed up three years ago driving for Hansbach. They recruited him right out of their junior program. His first test-drive was legendary. For months, all anyone could talk about was this kid, Will Hawley, possibly the best driver the sport had seen since Senna. But he managed to blow it all up in a single season."

"So what'd he do? Drugs, partying, and women?"

"Mmm. Not the drugs, as far as I know. But definitely the partying and the women. You know how these guys are."

"Yes, I do," Mira muttered under her breath. *Boy*, did she know.

"He was young, talented, and famous."

"And stupid."

Violet took a sip of her wine. "Yeah. In the end, he was just really, really stupid."

"What happened during his first season?"

"His *only* season. He crashed out of a bunch of races. Lackluster finishes in the others. It was so bad that Hansbach cut him loose midseason. Just like that he went from being the next great racing talent to a spoiled posh boy who'd bought himself a ride."

"He's rich," Mira stated. "Of course." That should have been obvious the moment he'd opened his mouth. That accent was way too smooth for mere mortals.

Violet nodded. "His family owns an entire *bank*. But if Will was just some nepo baby buying his way in, your dad wouldn't have given him a chance."

She glanced at her father, where he sat at the head of the table, chatting with Natalia, all smiles and twinkling blue eyes. You'd never guess at the steel under that surface. Her father had little patience for anyone who proved to be a drag on his organization. Mira knew that from personal experience.

"So how did he get back to F1?"

"He's been driving solid races in Indy Car and Formula E. Not a breath of scandal, either. Then last year, toward the end of his Formula E season, he had a truly phenomenal race. The track was wet, the absolute worst conditions to race under. Half the field crashed out in the first half. But Will? Drove the ride of his life. He didn't just win; he put nearly thirty seconds between him and the nearest car, despite nearly skidding out himself half a dozen times. It was hard to ignore what he'd accomplished. Phillipe had just retired and there was a spot open. And from a PR perspective, I can't deny it's a good story. Everybody loves a good redemption arc."

"So you think he's redeemed?"

Violet shrugged again. "He's been fine so far, but we've been stuck out here in bloody Essex. Not a lot to tempt him."

Well, that explained why he'd taken such a sudden interest in her. *He was bored.* And Mira would do her best to be boring. Soon enough he'd be back at the center of the Formula One vortex, with plenty of much more attractive distractions to keep him busy. Doubtless he'd forget all about her. And that, she told herself firmly, would be for the best.

"Let's hope he can keep his shit together."

"For all our sakes," Violet said.

"What do you mean?"

"Your dad took quite a risk bringing him back to F1. If Will blows it in one season again, it won't look good for Paul, either. Especially at this particular junction in Lennox's history."

The details of Mira's past at Lennox might not be common knowledge, but the team's struggles for the past several years certainly were. After everything had blown up, there'd been years of upheavals and personnel changes, and only now were they starting to hit their stride again, fighting to reclaim the status they'd had before everything had gone so wrong.

Considering everything on the line for Lennox, she didn't even blame her dad for saying no the first time she'd called him and lobbied for Pen's job. Or the second and the third. But she'd stuck it out, because this job was more than just an incredible career opportunity. It was her chance to fix everything she'd messed up seven years ago, and that included her relationship with her father.

She looked back at Will. He was leaning forward, his shirt pulling taut across his shoulders and biceps, and his teeth glinting in the candlelight as he laughed at something Matteo said.

"I'm sure Dad knows what he's doing," she said with more confidence than she felt.

"Let's hope so," Violet replied. "Because this whole team is depending on him."

Lennox deserved to come back strong, which meant that charming hothead at the other end of the table needed to keep it together. So no matter how much he flirted, and no matter how that flirting made her feel, she was going to stay far, far away from him.

After dinner, she caught a ride back home with her dad and Natalia. Natalia had invited her to stay in their guesthouse, and with the Formula One season kicking off in less than three months, it made more sense than trying to find a place of her own in the tiny village near the Lennox factory.

From the back seat, she stole a glance at her dad's face in the rearview mirror. He had the same intensity behind the wheel of his personal car as he'd once had behind the wheel of a race car, where he'd gotten his start. That's when her mother had met him. The British race car driver and the American supermodel had a whirlwind romance and wedding, but shortly after Mira's birth, they realized a baby was about all they really had in common.

The split had been amicable, though, happening while she was still a toddler, and now they were on very good terms. Her mother and Natalia had even become friends, which made sense, considering how alike they were. Despite her lush Italian beauty, Natalia was no trophy girlfriend. She was a respected attorney. And Mira's mother might have gotten famous for her beauty, but after retiring from modeling, she'd worked herself to the bone building her successful organic skincare line from the ground up. She and Natalia definitely had a lot in common.

There'd been a time when Mira had resented Natalia's place in her father's life, but seven years ago, when she'd desperately needed help, Natalia had been there for her without reservation, so now she adored her. Besides, she suspected her father might have ultimately relented and given her Pen's job at Natalia's urging.

As if he could feel her eyes on him, her father glanced up at her in the rearview mirror and smiled briefly. He was in his midfifties now, with graying hair and lines bracketing his eyes, but he still exuded the energy of someone half his age.

"How did your first day go, Mira?" he asked.

Her face warmed remembering that scene with Will before dinner. If her dad found out about that, he'd have her on a plane back to LA by midnight. Thankfully, she seemed to have scared Will off. He hadn't come anywhere near her for the rest of the night.

"It was very . . . intense," she said at last.

"It's a shame Pen's not here to help with the transition."

"I'll get up to speed quickly, I promise. I've already started going over the passport and visa requirements, and I've updated the online employee calendar with all the pertinent deadlines for documents to be in, so everybody should have received an email notification about it this afternoon, and—"

"Don't let your father scare you, Mira," Natalia said, reaching out to lay her hand on her partner's arm. "I'm sure you'll be fine."

"There *is* a lot to learn," she conceded. "I know the sport, but it's different from this side." Her father met her eyes again in the mirror, and she didn't miss the concern in his gaze. "But I'm so excited and grateful for the opportunity. I won't let you down, Dad."

"Mira . . ." he began, then paused. "I'm sure you won't," he finished. She didn't quite believe him, but she'd prove it to him—and herself.

Although he'd stepped all over his own dick the night before with Mira, Will was determined to shake it off when he arrived at the Lennox factory the next morning. He was scheduled in the simulator to work through the data from yesterday's drives, and anything he could do to improve the car's performance had to be his sole focus.

That resolve was sorely tested when he entered the simulator room to find Mira waiting there for him. To be fair, Paul was the one waiting for him, and Mira was there because . . . well, it was her job. And he was *her father*. She was busy, diligently taking note of everything Paul and David said, so he took advantage of her distraction to check her out. He was only human, after all.

Her black trousers and blue jumper were just as conservative as the gray dress she'd been wearing last night, but frustratingly, that didn't stop him from finding her attractive. Nor did her ruthlessly slicked back blond hair. It just made him imagine what it would look like falling across her shoulders. Like the sensible black shoes made him wonder if she painted her toenails, and the clingy blue jumper made him wonder about the bra underneath and—

"Will?" He startled to attention to find Paul and David staring at him and got the feeling they'd said his name more than once. Which was why he needed to stop obsessing over a girl who'd turned him down not once, but twice, and was his boss's daughter.

"Ready for me, Paul?" Yes, please, put him in the simulator where he could focus on driving and block out everything else.

"We want to look at one more thing. Give us a minute?"

"Sure thing."

David pulled Paul over to a bank of computer monitors. Mira was about to follow, but he nudged her elbow. Time to clear the air.

"Listen, Mira, if I made you feel uncomfortable, I apologize."

"I'm fine," she replied briskly, focusing on her notepad again to avoid looking at him. It was filled with her writing, tiny and precise, with bullet points and proper headings. Her notes looked like someone's PhD paper. Like he wasn't already terrified of her.

"I didn't realize who you were or I'd never have—"

Now she looked at him, her head snapping up, those clear green eyes zeroing in on his. "Oh, so you're only sorry because my dad runs the team?"

"No, I—"

"If I was just the clueless intern you thought I was, then I'd be fair game?"

"I didn't say—"

"Because you can't just—"

"I said I was sorry, okay?" His voice was loud enough that Paul and David glanced back over their shoulders at them.

Mira's mouth snapped shut as she cast a nervous glance around the room. "You're right," he said. "I should have backed off, no matter who your father is. Consider it my own special kind of punishment that your father *happens* to be Paul Wentworth."

She fought to control her smile. "When you figured it out, your face was priceless."

"Yeah, yeah, I'm sure I sounded like a total wanker, offering to explain racing to you." He rubbed the back of his neck.

She held up her forefinger and thumb, a hair apart. "Maybe just this much of a wanker."

"Okay, so yeah, I made an ass of myself and then I asked you out, and I'm now living in fear of your father. Does that make us even?"

Now she smiled in earnest, the first real smile he'd seen directed at him. Her dimples even made an appearance. Ah, fuck, this was going to be hard.

"Fine, we're even," Mira said.

"Let's start over entirely." He held out his hand to her. "Hi, I'm Will Hawley. Welcome to Lennox Motorsport."

Tentatively she took his hand. Warm. Delicate fingers. Pleasant little tingle as their palms made contact.

Nope. Off-limits.

"Nice to meet you, Mr. Hawley. Miranda Wentworth. Pleasure working with you."

She began to slide her hand away, but he held on to it for another beat. "It's Will."

Their eyes met.

"Okay," she whispered. "Will."

There was *definitely* a spark there. He wasn't imagining it. But he also wasn't going to indulge in it.

He released her hand. "I'd better finish getting ready." He untied the sleeves of his race suit from around his waist and started shrugging into the top half. He didn't miss it, the lightning-fast once-over she gave his upper body in his skin-tight undershirt. And okay, maybe he slowed down and flexed a little bit.

She cleared her throat. "You're suiting up for the simulator?"

He grinned. "We're still dialing in my specs on the suit. I'm trying a different size today. Tighter."

"Tighter?" Mira replied.

"Ready, Will?" Paul called from across the room, cutting off his chance for further teasing.

"Yep. Let's get to it."

He was glad they were past the disaster of last night. And he could do this—simply be colleagues with someone as gorgeous as Mira. This was the new Will Hawley, professional through and through.

Off-limits. Off-limits. He repeated it like a mantra as he walked up the short flight of metal stairs to the platform where the partial car sat, elevated on its hydraulic legs. There were a couple of techs there, still fiddling with the wraparound monitors that would display the track, like the most expensive, immersive video game ever played.

He tugged his gloves on while Paul prepped him. "Pay attention to the downforce in there today."

"Bit of a mess yesterday."

"We saw that. David thinks he's sorted out how to reconnect the air structures at the back, so we can optimize the diffuser. We've added a monkey seat under the rear wing to help connect airflow from the diffuser. You ought to notice a big difference from yesterday, even accounting for those bricks for tires you were on."

"Got it. Where am I racing?"

"We're putting you in Melbourne," Paul called up the stairs. "Since that's when you'll have the new front brake duct installed."

He ignored the flare of irritation at that reminder. He would be driving the first race in Matteo's car. Fuck it. He'd drive the hell out it. He'd drive Matteo's car better than Matteo.

Omar handed him his helmet and he glanced down at the room below. Mira was still there, watching him get ready. He cast one more quick glance at Paul, David, and all the other techs milling around the room. Everyone was occupied elsewhere. So he looked back at Mira, grinned, and lifted two fingers to his forehead in a little salute. She bit her lip and dropped her eyes to her notebook. But she was smiling.

So was he as he pulled his helmet on and climbed into the simulator.

Press events generally fell to Simone and Violet to manage. But Simone had a full day of conference calls, leaving Violet in need of help managing a day of driver interviews in London. That was how Mira found herself in the back of a chauffeured sedan heading to London at a painfully early hour of the morning. In truth, she didn't mind spending the day with Violet. During her first weeks at Lennox, she'd been working her ass off, but whenever she'd run into Violet, she always ended up laughing for a least a few minutes out of the day.

"You are a saint," Mira muttered when Violet opened the back door and handed her a large takeout coffee.

She almost choked on her coffee when Violet joined her in the back seat. "What are you *wearing?*" She'd never seen Violet in anything other than shredded jeans, band T-shirts, and leather jackets. Today she was in a black skirt suit, and her black hair was slicked back into a low ponytail. She was even wearing a pair of tasteful diamond stud earrings.

"I pull it out for public events. Seems major media outlets don't trust you when you're wearing a T-shirt that says 'Fuck the Patriarchy.'"

"You look nice."

Violet shrugged like her suit was full of bugs. "I look like somebody's mum."

Mira took a moment to consider her next question. She didn't want to pry, but she and Violet were becoming friends. Friends asked personal questions, right?

"So," she ventured, "you don't exactly seem like the public relations type—"

Violet let out a loud bark of laughter. "You want to know how a girl like me ended up in a place like this?"

"Kind of."

Violet hesitated for just a beat. "I used to date this guy, the lead singer in a band."

"That makes much more sense."

"Yeah, but I wasn't cut out for the groupie thing, you know? Hanging around the studio so I could tell the guys how brilliant they are." She rolled her eyes. "So I started doing PR for the band kind of by accident, because I was bored. I'd go find club managers or reps from music websites and chat them up while the band set up. Turns out, I had some talent for it."

"So what happened to the guy?"

Violet chuckled wryly, and for the first time, Mira saw a flash of something approaching a soft side in Violet's expression. "He dumped me for one of those idiot groupies who hung around the studio and told him how brilliant he was."

"Oh, I'm sorry."

"Don't be. It was all very cliché." As quickly as that flash of vulnerability appeared, it was gone, and Mira got the distinct feeling that she shouldn't poke at it. "I definitely got the best part of the deal with the on-the-job training. I figured I'd learned some marketable skills so . . . I marketed them. I answered an advert for Simone's assistant and talked her into hiring me. I was already a racing fan, so it was a good fit. Turns out the job is pretty much the same as rock, just a different group of contacts. And fewer dodgy clubs with sticky floors. The drivers are definitely easier to manage than egomaniac wannabe rock stars."

Again, that door seemed locked tight, so she changed the subject. "How long is the drive to London?"

"With traffic, about an hour."

"I thought we didn't start until ten? Why are we leaving so early?"

"Because we have another stop to make. I didn't trust Will to get his arse up and to London on his own, so I told him we'd pop round and give him a lift."

"Lovely," Mira muttered.

Every time she'd crossed paths with him over the last few weeks—and that happened too often for comfort—it still gave her butterflies in her stomach, as much as she tried to squash them. And now she'd be forced into his presence for an entire day. She already felt nervous.

The car pulled to a stop in front of a quaint stone house, saved from being described as a "cottage" only because of its large size. It even had weathered stone walls and an honest-to-God thatched roof. It looked like something straight out of *The Holiday*.

Her eyes went wide as she took it all in. "Is this where he lives?"

If she had to guess, she'd have thought a sleek new penthouse condo, something with glass walls and brushed-chrome fixtures, very minimalist and male.

"He has a place in London," Violet replied through a yawn. "I think he's just renting this. Well, off you go. Fetch him."

"Me? Why me?"

"You're the wrangler. I'm PR."

"Wrangling talent is in your literal job description."

"You're new, which means I get to pull seniority and make you deal with it."

Mira frowned but didn't argue as she got out of the car and made her way up the stone walk to the front door to ring the bell. Silence. She rang it again. And waited. More silence.

This time, she raised a fist and pounded on the door, not stopping until she heard a muffled crash and a curse from inside. The door swung open, revealing a very rumpled and nearly naked Will.

Oh, no.

The body was just as flawless as she'd guessed—not that she'd spent *much* time imagining his body under his clothes. At least, she'd tried *very hard* not to imagine it. The reality was better than anything her imagination had cooked up, however— a nicely muscled chest tapering into a slim waist and hips, *thankfully* covered by boxer briefs. A delicious V of muscle ran down, down, down to a pretty significant bulge. He had one hand on his hip and the other braced on the doorframe. The muscles and tendons in his arms were flexed, a landscape of male upper-body beauty. His eyes were narrowed as he took her in from under a riot of wrecked dark hair.

Now her mind ran wild as she fantasized about running her palms along that jawline to feel the dark stubble dusting it, or tracing those abs to see if they felt as taut as they looked. And maybe sliding a hand under the waistband of those boxer briefs to see if that bulge felt as big and hard as promised.

"What the hell are you doing here at this hour?" Even his fresh-out-of-bed growl was hot.

She dragged her eyes back up to his and her mind back out of the gutter. She had to get him dressed and into the car. *Definitely* dressed. That part was imperative. "Press event? In London? Violet was sure you'd still be sleeping. I said, 'Absolutely not! Will knows how important this press event is! I'm sure he'll be on time and ready.'" She raised her eyebrows to emphasize her displeasure.

His head dropped back, and he groaned. "Fuuuuuuuuuck. Okay, what's the address?"

"Uh-uh. No way am I leaving you, Sleeping Beauty. You'll never show up on time. Now get dressed and let's go."

"But—"

"Go."

He opened his mouth to argue, but then gave up, turning and stalking away from the door, leaving it gaping open in what she could only assume was an invitation to come in. He was already headed down the hallway and a moment later, she heard the house's old pipes bang as he started the shower. When she rounded the corner into the living room, she was confronted with a blinding explosion of pink and floral, from the ruffled curtains to the tufted sofa. Crocheted doilies and china figurines of cats covered every flat surface.

"Nice place," she shouted.

From down the hall, she heard a door crack open. "It's not mine," he yelled over the sound of the water. "It was the only furnished house to let in this backwater."

"It suits you," she yelled back.

She heard him grumble an oath before the door slammed shut. Suppressing a smile, she turned in the direction she guessed the kitchen was. It looked mostly unused, but there were two wineglasses, both still half-filled, on the counter. Two? She took a step closer and the mystery was solved when the toe of her shoe snagged on a lacy pink bra that had been discarded on the floor.

Nice. Very on-brand, Will.

Whatever he got up to after-hours was his own business, she supposed. Although she was battling a totally inappropriate flash of envy for last night's faceless hookup. *Somebody* had gotten to indulge in all those fantasies she'd just been entertaining. Whoever she was, at least she was already gone. *That* would have been awkward.

He didn't have any real food in his kitchen, but she did find a Keurig, so she made a cup of coffee and dumped it into a travel mug (pink and floral, from the gift shop at Historic Melford Hall). Ten minutes later, he appeared in the doorway of the kitchen, freshly shaved and dressed in a thin black wool pullover and dark jeans. His hair was wet, but with one rake of his fingers through the thick dark waves, it arranged itself into a perfectly artful mess. Rude.

"Seriously? Ten minutes in the shower and you look like that? It isn't fair."

He grinned broadly. "Are you flirting with me, Mira? I thought we decided to keep things between us professional."

"Doesn't seem like you need me as an outlet for your charm." She pointed at the bra in the corner, where she'd kicked it.

He had the grace to look mildly embarrassed. "She was just—wait, did you just call me charming?" He leaned against the counter and a smug smile tugged at his lips.

"Nope. Turn it off," she said sharply. "Take your coffee and let's go."

He looked from the pink travel mug to her. "Am I supposed to drink out of that?"

"If you don't, I will," she said, shoving it into his chest anyway. "Now, come on. Violet's probably about to strangle you."

When they reached the car, Violet had already moved to the front seat with the driver, leaving the back for her and Will.

"Nice of you to join us, Will," Violet muttered as Mira and Will slid into the back seat. "Are we all set? Yes? Fine, wake me when we get there."

For several minutes, they sat in silence as the car rolled through the bare winter countryside. Mist hung low on rolling hills. Even after so much time away, it still felt comforting and familiar. Mira pulled her eyes away from the view to check in on Will, who was looking at her. The moment their eyes met, he looked away and took a sip out of the pink travel mug.

"What's your deal, Miranda Wentworth?" Will asked abruptly. "It's been weeks and I'm realizing I don't really know anything about you."

"No deal," she said, schooling her face into its best professional mask. "I'm every bit as boring as I seem."

He shook his head. "Nope. You grew up in Formula One. That's not boring."

"Only partly," she corrected. "My mother lives in Los Angeles. I also grew up there."

"Obviously."

"What's that supposed to mean?"

He gave her a bored look. "Your accent, love. It's a bit of a dead giveaway."

"I was born in London, actually. Dual citizenship. But yes, I spent most of my time in LA. Yours gives you away, too, you know."

Now it was his turn to bristle. "Gives away what?"

"Where'd you go to school? Eton? Or maybe Winchester or Harrow?"

Color tinted the tops of his remarkable cheekbones. She wouldn't call it a blush, exactly. It was more like his emotions betrayed him and laid a temporary claim to his face against his will.

"Harrow," he said, after a minute. "How—"

"I said I lived in the States most of the time, not all of it."

"Right. You spent enough time with your dad to pick out public school accents and fall in love with racing. Continue."

"That's it. I like racing."

"You haven't missed a single simulator session."

"Okay," she conceded. "I *love* racing."

"So?"

"So, what?"

"What happened? Seems the old-timers at Lennox know you from when you were a kid, but nobody's seen you in years. Where have you been?"

She shrugged dismissively to hide her discomfort and glanced out the window. "I was in college, then I was working."

"Where'd you go to college? Working where?"

Oh my god, he just wouldn't quit. "UCLA, business major, summa cum laude. Junior assistant at a payroll company. See? Nothing worth talking about."

That payroll job had been like purgatory. She was organized and efficient by nature, so the work was easy, but when her old boss told her she had a great future with the company, she'd wanted to cry, imagining spending the next thirty years there. It seemed like divine providence when she'd heard about Pen's leave a week later. She'd been desperate to escape, but escaping to Formula One was like a dream come true. And if coming back here also meant facing her nightmare? Well, every dream had a price.

"And this is the first time you've been back to England since you were a kid? Why? I mean, if *I* loved Formula One and *my* dad happened to be principal of one of the top teams in the sport, I'd have a hard time staying away."

Staying away for seven years had been nothing short of awful. But she wasn't about to share the reasons for her exile with him, no matter how hard he tried to weasel it out of her.

"I missed it," she said evenly, in a tone of voice that invited no further questions. Of course, Will was not a person who respected boundaries.

"Not very much, apparently, since you never came back."

"Hey," she said, rounding on him. "Let's talk about how a rich kid from Harrow ends up in Formula One. That's a story *I'd* like to hear."

He blinked, his dark blue eyes turning wary. "Lots of kids love racing. Lucky for me, I had the talent to do something about it." He was the one to look away this time, squirming and fixing his attention on the dull winter countryside sliding by outside. "Until I fucked up, anyway."

"I've heard."

He scoffed. "Yeah, pretty much everyone has at this point. Just so you know, I'm not that guy anymore."

"Good, because my dad took a big chance on you, and I'm glad to hear you're not a rich boy who's going to blow that chance at the first opportunity."

He looked back at her, all traces of humor gone. "I appreciate what he's doing, bringing me back like this. I wouldn't do that to Paul. Despite what you might think of me, Mira, I'm not that much of a jerk."

Now that she knew him a little better, she didn't think he was a jerk anymore. A little arrogant maybe, but he wasn't malicious. He was determined to succeed, that was obvious. And in that one way, she understood him completely.

"**A**t least they feed us."

Will looked up from stirring his coffee as Matteo approached the catering table and surveyed the options.

"No amount of shite food is worth this," Will grumbled, tossing his stir stick in the trash. "I hate these things."

Matteo was thirty, and probably staring down the twilight of his racing career, but he still carried himself with the confidence of a rock star. He gave a loose shrug as he plucked a handful of grapes from the fruit platter. "I don't mind them so much."

Maybe that was because Matteo was fielding nothing but softballs today, Will thought irritably.

He'd never loved pressers, but he used to be *good* at them. Just smile, just charm. It was second nature to him. But this round was different. He was eager to talk about the new car, about race strategy, about the Lennox team ... but that's not what they wanted Will Hawley to talk about. They wanted to talk about his fall from grace and his surprising shot at redemption. Simone and Violet had warned him that the redeemed bad boy narrative was like catnip to the press, but just the same, it left him feeling attacked and defensive. By the time they'd taken a break, he was snapping answers and knew he wasn't coming across as well as he needed to.

"I just hate the personal questions," he griped.

Matteo tossed a grape up in the air and caught it in his teeth. Show-off. Clapping Will on the shoulder, he grinned. "Just stay positive and smile," he said before heading back to his chair under the floodlights.

"Easy for you to say," Will muttered to himself. For Matteo, they kept the personal questions to polite inquiries about his two adorable little kids. He was the mature center of the Lennox racing team, the dependable pro, and that's how they treated him. Lennox's respected elder statesman. Will was the wild card, the hotheaded bad boy, the flashy angle they'd use to sell their stories. It didn't matter that he could talk about the new car's technological improvements until he was blue in the face, because nobody asked.

As he returned to the hot seat, he could see Violet prepping the next reporter. This one was a woman, bright red suit, lots of makeup, very blond.

Behind them, he caught sight of Mira, hovering outside the glare of the studio lights bathing the drivers. She'd set herself up answering emails on her tablet, but he noticed her eyes on him far more than on the screen. Which wasn't so bad. If he was reading her right, after that car ride, it felt like she might be warming to him a bit. Like maybe he wasn't quite the fuckup she'd assumed. And now he had the strangest urge to prove that to her.

His expression must have been thunderous, because she grinned widely, pointed to her mouth, and then mouthed *Smile*. Right. As pissed off as these interviews made him, he had a job to do. There was so much on the line, for both him and the team. He couldn't afford to let them down. And he didn't *want* to let Mira down.

By the time Violet ushered the Glamazon reporter over, he'd schooled his face into a polite smile.

"Will, this is Pippa Hollywell."

Of course it was. He reached out to shake her hand and gave her his best winning smile. Pippa's eyes lit up.

"Great meeting you, Will." She flashed him her own flirtatious smile. Okay, fine, if flirtation would get him through this interview looking halfway respectable, then he'd do it.

He gave her a small, intimate smile. "Nice meeting you, too, Miss Hollywell."

"Please . . . call me Pippa."

He smiled again as she settled into her chair and crossed her long legs. Her skirt rode halfway up her thighs. She didn't make a move to tug it back down. So that's how she was going to play this. Will settled back in his chair.

"Okay, *Pippa.*"

"Let's get started, shall we?"

"Let's," he agreed. *Oh, yes, let's.*

"So you're back in Formula One after two seasons in Formula E and Indy Car before that."

What a brilliant observation, Pippa. Absolutely no one's noted that yet, even though it's on my Wikipedia page. "That's correct," he replied evenly. He deserved a fucking medal for not laughing.

"Are you glad to be back?"

That was like asking "Are you glad to still be breathing?" No one in their right mind would answer with anything other than a resounding yes.

"Delighted." See how well he could behave?

"And you're back with a new team." Would this woman's brilliant observations never cease?

"Yes, that's true."

"How are you liking being part of the Lennox Motorsport organization?"

"It's great. I think Lennox is a really good fit for me as a driver. Our goals are very aligned." Simone had drilled that statement into his head during his media-training session. He could say it in his sleep now.

"Has the organization been welcoming to you?"

Now his eyes did slide over to look at Mira, and he couldn't help keeping his gaze pointedly on her when he said, "Very welcoming. I've been embraced by *everyone* at Lennox." A tiny smile tugged at the corners of her mouth, too, despite how hard she was fighting it. The satisfaction of cracking that frosty reserve of hers distracted him enough that Pippa's next question sailed right past his defenses.

"Do you think they're worried that you'll fall apart midseason like you did three years ago?"

"Pardon?"

Pippa shrugged as though to say, *Oops, I don't know where that question came from either*, recrossing her legs, once again leaving her skirt up around her thighs. If she thought a nice pair of legs and the tease of a crotch shot would distract him, she had grossly underestimated him. His eyes stayed firmly on her face.

"Well, you did have a rather well-documented public meltdown—"

"I think meltdown is overstating things a bit—"

"—that led to your abrupt dismissal from Hansbach three years ago. Have you tamed your demons?"

How the fuck was he supposed to respond to that? As he took a moment to process, Pippa flipped her sleek blond hair over her shoulder and smiled, leaning forward enough to give him a good view of her cleavage, if he were inclined to look.

He wasn't. Staring her down, he replied through clenched teeth. "I think my driving speaks for me. It certainly convinced Paul Wentworth."

Pippa chuckled softly. "Yes, he was rather enamored, wasn't he?"

"He was *impressed*," Will snapped. His knee began to bounce involuntarily.

"Of course he was," Pippa cooed. "Enough to take an enormous risk and bring you aboard the team."

"Paul trusts in my abilities."

"I'm sure he does," Pippa said with a tiny pout and a false expression of understanding. "But does he trust you to control your more self-destructive tendencies?"

Will shifted forward in his seat. "Look, I might have made a few questionable choices in the past, but now I'm here to race."

"Hmm," Pippa said, fishing something out of her notebook. "And perhaps get loaded at a party or two?"

She held out a photograph, but Will refused to take it. He could already see it and he recognized the moment. It was from this past New Year's Eve. One night. He'd gone out for drinks exactly one bloody night in all the weeks he'd been at Lennox. Just pints with a couple of guys from the team to toast the New Year. He'd stopped at one and ended up driving Omar and Ian home when they'd both gotten hammered. Partway through the evening, he'd been recognized by a couple of inebriated female racing fans. They'd begged for a photo. How could he say no? He'd been a bit surprised when one dropped herself into his lap. Maybe a bit startled when the other kissed his cheek as she angled her phone at the three of them. They'd giggled their thanks and stumbled away, off to some other pub. All totally forgettable.

But there he was in that photo, squinting into the flash, looking half-wasted, one girl draped across his lap and the other hugging him around the neck and kissing his cheek. It looked awful, like those horrible paparazzi shots of him three years ago that cropped up every time he went out.

"Where the fuck did you—"

"*Okay*, we are all out of time!" Violet called in a high, forced singsong, stepping between him and Pippa. With one quick turn of her body, she bumped her hip into Pippa's hand, sending the photo falling to the floor. "Oops, let me just get that for you."

She scooped up the photo before Pippa could even reach for it, and it disappeared, secreted into Violet's pocket or her clipboard or somewhere. Pippa scowled. "If I could just—"

"We're on a *very* tight schedule today. I'm sure you understand." Violet slipped a hand under Pippa's arm, not-so-gently lifting her out of her chair.

Will didn't wait around to hear the rest of Pippa's protests as Violet steered her away. He was out of his chair, ripping off his mic, and storming across the studio in the opposite direction, toward his dressing room.

When he reached it, he slammed the door behind him. "Fuck! Bloody buggering fucking hell!" His voice bounced off the walls of the small space, echoing in the stillness. In two minutes, that witch had laid waste to everything he'd spent three years repairing. He might as well have been fresh off his dismissal from Hansbach, washed up at twenty-two and a fucking pariah.

"Will?"

"Can't anyone give me a moment of goddamned peace?" He spun around to find Mira standing just inside his dressing room.

Mira quietly shut the door and leaned back against it. Will was pacing the tight confines of his dressing room like an animal in a cage, his hands fisted into his hair.

"Fuck!" he roared again and slammed his hand against the chair, sending it clattering into the counter.

"Will, you need to lower your voice," she said evenly. "They can hear you out there."

"That was bullshit!" Will shouted, stabbing a finger in the direction of the studio. His eyes were wide, and his jaw was tight with fury. "It was New Year's Eve. I had one bloody pint and those girls asked me for a picture. Before I knew what was happening—"

"It's okay."

"—it's not like I downed a goddamned bottle of scotch—"

"I know."

"—and I've barely had more than a glass of fucking wine since then."

"Will, it's fine. I just wanted to make sure you were okay."

Just like that, the anger seemed to drain out of him. His eyes went flat and he slumped back on the dressing room counter.

He dropped his face into his hands. "Okay?" he muttered. "In two minutes one trashy journalist made me look like I'm just the same fuckup I've always been. Like the last three years didn't even happen."

A pang of empathy flared through her. She knew a thing or two about feeling like a fuckup. "I'm sorry."

He lifted his head, looking tired and utterly defeated. "It doesn't even matter. I mean, fuck it. They're all desperate to make me out to be the same immature screwup from three years ago. It's just hard to live things down sometimes, no matter how hard you try. So Pippa fucking Hobbyhorse thinks I'm a joke. So does everybody else. The press, the entire sport of racing, *you*."

"Hey." Maybe it was because the time she'd spent around him today had lowered her guard, or maybe it was just seeing him being so hard on himself, but she couldn't keep her distance from him when he was in this state. She crossed to him and put her hands on his shoulders. "Listen to me. Plenty of people believe in you. You wouldn't be here if they didn't."

He scoffed, so she pressed on.

"Everybody who saw you race in Formula E last season knows you have what it takes. Everybody on this team. My dad. Me."

Finally he turned his face to look at her. "You?" he said with a short, mirthless laugh. "When did lying to talent become your job?"

She shook his shoulders a little, or at least as much as that rock-hard body could be shaken. "Seriously, listen to me. I've been at every one of your simulator sessions. You're working harder than anybody I know. And you've got the most talent."

Will let out a long exhale, staring off into space like he was trying to believe everything she was telling him.

"Don't let her get to you," she said softly.

Then he was quiet, staring at her. And that's when she realized that her hands were still on his shoulders and his had found their way to her hips. And that she was nearly standing between his splayed legs, with less than a foot between them. She could see it in his eyes, the moment he realized it too.

Suddenly she was painfully aware of every tiny detail of him. His dark blue eyes, slightly shadowed under his heavy dark brows. His eyelashes that looked tipped with amber in the diffuse glow from the lights surrounding the mirror behind him. His high cheekbones sloping down to the hard line of his jaw.

His fingers tightened on her hips, and her body responded without her brain's input. Somehow she moved closer, standing between his thighs now. Her fingers had dug in, too, she realized, gripping his shoulders. His nearness, the ferocious intensity of his gaze on her face, made her throat and chest tight. And parts much lower, too. She licked her lips and his eyes finally left hers, dropping swiftly to her mouth and back up.

And then his face was drawing closer, never breaking the look, even as his head tilted, even as hers did. He was going to kiss her. She knew it and yet she couldn't bring herself to do anything that might stop him. He exhaled and she could feel his warm breath wash across her mouth. His hand slid up her back, his broad palm coming up to cup her neck, to hold her in place as he—

"Okay, sorted," Violet said briskly as she burst into the room. Her eyes were on her tablet so she missed Mira scrambling away from Will like he was on fire.

"I had a chat with Pippa's producer—" Violet continued, as Mira inhaled deeply and tried to clear the fog cluttering her brain. What the fuck had just happened? Or almost happened?

"—and I let it be known that if Pippa insisted on running her bullshit party boy story, their network was going to find their access to any and all Lennox events strictly curtailed. I think she'll choose wisely."

She finally looked up, eyes darting from Will to Mira and back again. "Everything okay?"

Okay? *Okay?* She'd just nearly kissed Will. He'd nearly kissed her. They'd both been absolutely about to kiss each other.

She chanced a glance at Will, but looking at him, you'd never have known that thirty seconds ago his mouth had nearly been on hers. He blew out a breath and scrubbed a hand over his face. "It's fine, Violet. Let them say what they're going to say. I can't stop them."

Mira's heart was still trying to beat its way out of her chest, but Will seemed perfectly at ease.

Hands on her hips, Violet glared at him. "No, you can't. But I can. I have to try, anyway. It's my job."

He gave her a weak smile. "I appreciate it. Thank you."

"You're welcome," she said with an overly saccharine tone. "So, are we done here?"

"Yes, please," he pleaded. "Let's get out of here."

Finally Mira found her voice, amazed to hear herself sounding so normal. "No, we can't. There are more interviews."

Violet glanced at her tablet. "Six more, to be exact."

Will looked pained. "Violet . . ."

"Hey, this is how you properly thank me for covering your ass back there. Get in there and behave yourself."

He groaned. "Got it."

"And smile," she said, turning and heading back out to the soundstage. "The ladies love you when you smile."

Mira gathered up the rest of her scattered wits and started to follow Violet out of the room. She heard him sigh behind her, but she didn't turn to look at him.

He was upset, that was all. She'd been there in front of him in a vulnerable moment and he'd . . . well, they'd . . . well, something almost happened that shouldn't have happened. But the important thing was, it *hadn't* happened. So they could carry on just as before. One thirty-second aberration wasn't the end of the world. Soon they'd be on the road, on the racing circuit, and Will was sure to forget all about it, and her. And by then, maybe she'd have figured out how to forget about it, too.

After the press interviews wrapped, Violet and Will decided they should grab some dinner before taking the car back to Chilton. Mira hadn't been to London in years, so she let Will and Violet pick the place. After a spirited debate, which was only settled because Will was paying and vetoed Violet, they ended up at a small brasserie not far from the television studio.

"It's cozy," Mira observed as they got settled. It was lit mainly by the votive candles on the table, and the walls were lined with an eclectic selection of old paintings and photos, all in mismatched gilt frames. Over the small bar in back, a chalkboard displayed the daily specials. A waitress with an undercut and a nose ring dropped off menus on her way to another table. It was hard to imagine this place being one of Will's favorites, but then again, he kept surprising her.

Will shrugged. "It's not far from my place. Good food."

"Where's your place?" Mira asked, telling herself she was just making polite conversation. In truth, she was wildly curious about his life outside of Lennox.

"Hackney, just north of here. I bought it . . ." He hesitated. "Three years ago. When I signed my Hansbach contract."

"I see," Violet teased. "It's your splashy Formula One driver den of iniquity."

Will shot her a look. "Not all that splashy, actually. It's just a flat in a converted old factory."

Okay, not quite the Death Star she'd imagined.

"What's good here?" Violet said, before Mira had heard nearly enough about Will's apartment.

He sighed. "Their pasta is brilliant, but my trainer will have my head if I eat it, so do it for me, please. At least I can smell it."

"Sounds good," Mira replied.

Violet was still examining the menu when her phone buzzed. She glanced at the face and frowned. "Order me the Bolognese and a big glass of red. I need to take this."

Then she slid out of her seat and made her way to the front door. Mira could see her out on the sidewalk as she took the call, looking more annoyed than normal.

"Wonder what that's about."

"I'm convinced Violet is secretly an elite assassin," Will said.

"Actually, I can totally picture that."

The waitress returned for their orders. She ordered for herself and Violet, while Will forlornly ordered the steamed salmon, no sauce. Now that she'd seen him—nearly *all* of him—it was hard to imagine that he could get *more* in shape, but the pressure to stay in peak physical condition was the same for drivers as for any other elite athletes, especially as the start of the season grew nearer.

When the waitress had deposited their drinks—wine for Violet and herself, sparkling water for Will—Mira glanced back toward Violet, but she was still outside on the phone. No help coming from that quarter. She was going to have to make conversation with Will on her own. Not that it was hard. He was surprisingly easy to talk to. And she was trying to forget any lingering weirdness from the afternoon, because he seemed fine. It probably wasn't even a big deal for him. He likely kissed random women all the time and then never thought about it again. He might have already forgotten it even happened. She wished she could.

"Do you think Violet really managed to kill Pippa's story?" he suddenly asked. His dark eyebrows were furrowed, casting his eyes into shadow. His uncertainty did a number on her, the same way it had that afternoon. It made her want to protect him, which was just ludicrous. Will Hawley hardly needed her as his defender.

"You're still thinking about that? Don't worry about it. It's all just bullshit gossip anyway."

"It's just—" He ran a hand across the back of his neck.

"What?"

"It's just . . . it's exhausting sometimes. Trying to live that shit down. Trying to prove to the whole world that I'm not the same anymore."

That hit her right in the solar plexus. "Don't I know it," she sighed, before she could catch herself.

He gave her a look. "I have a hard time imagining you've *ever* done anything you regretted, Mira. You're far too . . . cautious."

She almost told him he had no idea what he was talking about, but she bit back the words at the last minute. But it didn't matter, since her silence seemed to tip him off that he'd hit a nerve.

"What?" He sat up, leaning forward on his elbows. These tables were way too tiny, and he was way too close. "You have a *secret*. Tell me."

She sat back, crossing her arms over her chest. "There's nothing to tell."

"Look at you, all folded up like a crab. The hell there's not."

Just then the waitress arrived with their orders. Mira hoped the food would be enough to divert Will's attention, but when she looked up, he was still watching her from across the table.

"Does your big regret have anything to do with you disappearing for all these years?"

God, how on earth was he so perceptive? Will Hawley of all people? She glanced at the door, desperately hoping to see Violet returning, but she was still outside, pacing back and forth on the sidewalk, phone to her ear.

"It's not important. Ancient history at this point, anyway." She took a bite of her pasta, which was, as he'd promised, excellent.

"Can't be that ancient if it still bugs you." His voice was low and intimate, and it felt like they were alone in the soft gold circle of light cast by the candle flickering between them. That must have been why she opened that trunk full of her secrets, even if only a crack, and let some small part of it out.

She turned her wineglass in a circle before taking a sip. "I made a really stupid mistake when I was younger."

"Well, then you're in good company, because as it so happens, I'm a *pro* at stupid choices. There was a time when I might have held the world championship."

Despite the dread she felt about discussing her past, that made her laugh. "I'm pretty sure at one point in my life, we would have been on a race to the bottom."

"Did you kill a man just to watch him die? Or was it selling illegal arms to a fascist regime?"

"How'd you know?!" she said, with mock surprise. "No, nobody died. I just . . ." She closed her eyes and took a deep breath. "The last time I was at Lennox I was sixteen, traveling the circuit with my dad."

Will nodded. "Considering who your dad is, I figured you spent a lot of time on the track."

"I did. Which means I knew the rules. But whatever . . . I was a dumb teenager who thought she knew everything."

"Uh-oh. Sounds like the universe corrected you on that one?"

"Not the universe. Just a guy."

His eyes lit up with interest. "Ah. This is a love story."

Mira snorted in disgust. "It's *not* a love story."

Will raised his eyebrows. "No?"

"I got involved with someone I shouldn't have. I snuck around and lied to a lot of people to do it. I lied to my *dad.* Then it ended—badly, as you can probably guess—and everybody found out. I disappointed a lot of people, and I paid for it. Even worse, my *dad* paid for it, and the team paid for it."

"How?"

She shook her head. "I don't want to talk about it. What matters is that I really messed things up with him. And now I have a lot to make up for. I will never do something to put him in a position like that again."

"Hey." He reached across the table and laid his hand over hers. She froze, staring down at those long, elegant fingers, curled loosely over hers, and tried not to think about the rush of heat it sent to every last corner of her body. As suddenly as he'd touched her, his hand slid away again. "You were a kid. Kids make mistakes."

She blinked, still staring at her hand, where a moment ago, he'd been touching her. There had been a few guys since that early heartbreak, but none of them had managed to set her on fire with a casual brush of his fingers the way Will did. She'd completely lost her place in the conversation. But there he was across the table, as beautiful and unbothered as always, and she had to remind herself that while every look and touch he sent her way was enough to put her into heart failure, it was quite obviously not the same for him. She'd better remember that before she let him make a fool of her.

"I knew what I was doing," she said at last. Then she smiled wryly. "Or at least I thought I did."

"And you've been punishing yourself for this ever since?"

"I've been *learning* from it. There's a difference."

"Ah . . . it's all becoming clear now."

"What is?"

He waved his fork at her. "This uptight look of yours."

"What? I'm not—"

Will leaned forward, like he was telling her a secret. "Because it doesn't seem quite you. I get the feeling there's more to you than making those freakishly tidy lists of yours. Where did you learn to write like that anyway? It's not normal, Mira."

"It's not . . . my lists are . . . my handwriting isn't . . ."

"Mistakes sometimes make us better. I'm a better driver after the mistakes I made in my first year."

She speared a piece of rigatoni with more force than necessary. "Look, let's agree—you handle things your way, I handle things mine. Just as long as your way doesn't jeopardize Lennox, I won't give you a hard time about it."

In an instant, Will sobered. "I'd never harm the team. I hope you know that. I worked too hard to get back here."

She dropped her eyes to her plate, fiddling with her fork. "I know you did."

"I'm guessing you've been working hard to get back here, too?"

She nodded. "It's all I want."

"Really?" he said, leaning in and hitting her with that criminally hot mischievous grin again. "It's *all* you want?"

The butterflies in her stomach started up their fluttering again. His attention was a potent drug, and she was going to miss it when it was inevitably drawn off by other, more attractive, more available options. Because as much as she wanted to indulge in this feeling—a feeling she hadn't experienced in a very long time—she just couldn't.

"You are relentless," she murmured.

"You have no idea," he said in a low rumble that made her thighs clench. "And look, it worked."

"What are you talking about?"

"You're out with me."

"This doesn't count."

He looked around in fake confusion. "We're out. There's wine and candlelight. I'm pretty sure this counts."

"Whatever. You know what I mean."

He broke into a laugh. "I know, I know. But, Mira?"

"Yeah?"

He nudged forward again, so she leaned in, too. His face was just a few inches away, and she fought to keep her eyes on his, and not look at his mouth.

"Just so you know," he said quietly. "If you ever want to finish that kiss, I'm ready when you are."

She froze, heart pounding, heat pooling in all kinds of places. So he'd felt it too. The humor faded from his expression, and she knew from the heat in his steady gaze, that he was absolutely serious. Her mouth opened to reply, although she had no idea what she was going to say . . . what she *should* say . . . what she wanted to say. Because she wanted him, there was no denying that simple fact. She just couldn't have him.

"I—"

"Please tell me this is my wine."

Violet dropped heavily in her chair and seized the glass, taking a hefty swig.

Mira jerked back in her chair. "Um." She paused to clear her throat. "Everything okay?"

"What?"

"Your phone call?"

Violet shook her head. "Nothing. Just haunted by ghosts. You know how it is."

Oh, yes, she knew. And her own ghosts were just the reminder she needed to keep her head on straight. She'd just been dancing at the edge of a cliff with Will, but she absolutely refused to let herself be pulled over into the abyss.

A year of aerodynamic and mechanical design, months of planning, thousands of hours of work by hundreds of workers, and it all came down to testing in Bahrain, one week before the Bahrain Grand Prix. The top-secret planning and development would be secret no longer.

There would be no official winners after these three days on the track. The goal was to test the cars, make sure they were sound, and to generate data for the development teams back at the factories, so they could see if the cars they'd designed on computers and in wind tunnels were performing as predicted. But unofficially, a lot of prognosticating would happen in testing, and it would quickly become clear which teams had shown up with the cars and drivers to win this season, and which would face an uphill battle.

Adding to the pressure, the first race of the season was just over a week later. If there were any problems with the car, after testing there would only be six days to get it fixed before they had to be back on the track for qualifying.

Her father, the person in charge of the whole thing, was understandably on edge, but you'd never know it from looking at him. The sun was blinding as Mira hurried toward the garage at his side. He seemed so calm in the midst of the chaos.

"Mira, can you check in with David and make sure they're getting the data at the factory?"

"Already done. Video feed is good and all departments have confirmed they're receiving the telemetry."

"And can you make sure Ravinder's on headset? I want him listening in."

"He's on headset in the office, taking notes. I'll upload them to the server after the session."

"And did David send over those updated numbers—"

"Already programmed into the onboard computer."

He looked briefly at her without breaking his stride. "Well done, Mira."

She wanted to wallow in his praise, but there wasn't time. When they reached the garage, Matteo was already in his car so it was almost time to go. Omar handed Matteo his steering wheel and watched as Matteo clipped it into place and tested its functions. When Matteo's race engineer gave the go-ahead, Omar gave a thumbs-up and he fired the engine. The roar was immense. Mira could feel it in the ground under her feet, several meters away. Despite the nerves that came with testing, she couldn't help but feel a thrill, like this was the night before Christmas. It was almost here.

Then the mechanics around the car pulled back and Matteo headed out onto the track. Her father took up his spot in front of a bank of monitors, headphones on, feet braced apart, one hand curled under his mouth and the other arm crossed over his chest. His external calm was deceiving. His entire compact frame radiated coiled energy and intensity, and that steely gaze of his didn't miss a single detail.

He'd seemed so all-powerful when she was little, hardly the sort of warm, affectionate father to plop a little girl on his lap and read her bedtime stories. That wasn't Paul Wentworth's style. When she was older and started spending summers with him on the road, they'd finally established a genuine and affectionate bond, one that centered on the sport she'd grown to love as much as he did. Then she'd blown that to bits, and they'd been distant ever since. Now that she was on the circuit with him again, it was improving, but doing well in this job would go a long way.

Matteo's first lap was an installation lap as the engineers trackside and back at the factory poured through reams of real-time telemetry looking for anything the least bit awry. He circled back to the pits and shut it down for a systems check, and only after the team was completely satisfied that everything was screwed together properly did the mechanics fuel the car for a twenty-lap stint and refire the engine.

"Let's push into this turn," Paul said into his headset as Matteo neared the first complex of curves.

"He's never aggressive enough in the turns," Mira muttered under her breath.

Her father covered the microphone from his headset and murmured, "Exactly."

He looked over his shoulder and gave her a wink, and she had to smother her laugh with her hand.

No one was breathing as Matteo whipped into the turn, the car barely clinging to the blacktop. By the time he was powering out of the turn complex and into the straight, Mira felt nearly lightheaded.

Stats poured out on the monitors and she exhaled in relief and happiness. The numbers so far were great. For all the design and engineering done on paper and on computers, for all the hundreds of hours manufacturing and testing the parts, for the thousands of hours in the wind tunnel and the simulator, you never *really* knew what you had until you put it all together and got it out on the track. Matteo would have to do a lot more laps, and generate a lot more data before they had a handle on every aspect of the car, but right now, it looked really promising.

She touched her father's shoulder and held out a water bottle.

He slid his headphones off and cracked what had to be his first smile all day as he took it. "Natalia will thank you, Mira. She always worries that I forget to stay hydrated."

"That's because you do. Dad, this is phenomenal."

Paul glanced back at the bank of monitors, shots of Matteo out on the track and screens full of data. "Looks like we may have a winning car this year."

"I'm sure you do. Look at those sector times."

His smile grew wider as he scanned the telemetry. "I'm happy with that. Now let's see what Will can do in it."

Mira eyed the first stats of Matteo's performance. "He'll do better. He's a better driver."

Her father cocked one eyebrow. "Is he?"

"Dad, look at his simulator sessions."

"He's quick, I'll give you that."

"And you've built the strongest car in Lennox's history. Will's going to win the world championship."

"You think so?"

"I do. You think so, too. That's why you hired him."

Despite the tension of the day, he laughed. "You're right, Mira. Seems like I might have a winning team all around."

As he slid his headphones back into place and turned back to the monitors, she caught sight of Will standing behind him, and rolled her eyes. "I suppose you heard all of that?"

She'd been trying to stay so professional around him, but it was hard to maintain when that moment over dinner in London kept replaying in her mind . . . his face so close to hers as he made sure she knew he was still thinking about kissing her.

"That you think I'm the best driver on the grid? I wish I recorded it so I can play it back later when you try to deny it."

"You know that's what I think. Now you need to get out there and prove it to everybody else."

He grinned. "That's exactly what I intend to do."

WILL WAS ZIPPING UP his race suit, still smiling to himself remembering the way Mira had talked him up when she didn't know he was there, when Harry joined him. "Watch the braking into the turns until we can sort the reattachment issue," he said, without a word of greeting. "That way if it goes sideways at least you can bail on the corner. We've also switched you to the carbon-carbon brake pads you like, but you'll have no stopping power at all till they heat up, so mind the brake temps on your out lap."

Harry chattered on, listing every tiny facet of vehicle performance he was expected to provide feedback on. Will half-listened as he tugged his flame-resistant Nomex balaclava into place, over his head and up over his chin, until only his eyes were visible. Harry was just talking to vent the nervousness he'd never admit to. All the sage pieces of advice weren't going to matter much anyway when he was screaming into the first turn at three hundred kilometers an hour. Then he'd have nothing but his own instincts to get him through it.

The mechanics were still buzzing around, checking fittings and making microscopic adjustments. Paul clapped him on the shoulder.

"Take it easy out there. Let's just see what we have today."

"Will do, boss."

"Have a good ride." Typical understated Paul. That "have a good ride" somehow managed to mean "good luck," "don't fuck this up," and "you'd better make all my dreams come true" in four tiny words.

With that, Will headed to the car. Beata, the assistant who managed the drivers' kits, gave a last check to his suit, making sure all the closures were secure. It was lined with the same flame-resistant material as his gloves and balaclava, and could protect him from fire for eleven precious seconds, which could be the difference between life and death in a crash.

"HANS okay?" she asked.

"It's good. Thanks." The HANS would protect his neck in the case of major impact.

When she finished and gave him the thumbs-up, he took a second to breathe deeply and scan the track one more time.

Today wasn't about winning. As Paul had said, all he needed to do was go out and drive solidly, to provide plenty of data for the engineers.

But Will wanted more. The car wasn't even perfected yet, yet he still wanted to show the world that the car was the fastest on that track and that he was the fastest driver.

He hopped into the cockpit and slid down into position, the custom-fitted seat hugging him like a glove. Two mechanics went to work strapping him in so tightly he could barely move.

Omar handed in his steering wheel. "Good luck out there."
"Thanks, man."

He clipped the steering wheel into its column and waited for the thumbs-up from Omar.

"Time to go!" Omar shouted.

Will pressed the button to fire the engine and felt it roar to life, the power pulsing through his body like it was pumping his heart. God, there was no better feeling on earth. Well, maybe it felt better when he was going three hundred kilometers an hour.

The pit crew surrounding him high-fived, as pumped up to see the car's performance as he was. Now it was just him and the car. Time to see what they could do together. He pressed the throttle and the car shot forward.

Five moderate laps passed in a blur. He navigated back onto the track after fueling, listening to Paul and Tae chattering into his headset. As he neared the start/finish and everything still looked good, Tae gave him the go-ahead to open it up.

His adrenaline spiked as he shifted gears and let it go. The car screamed down the start/finish straight, gaining speed at an unfathomable pace. Will felt strapped to a rocket. As it neared the first turn, it felt as if everyone held their breath along with him. This was it. Clearly the new car had phenomenal speed in the straight, but could he manage that speed in the braking zones? He would, and he'd do it faster than Matteo had, dammit.

Smoke wisped up from the front wheel as the inside tire unloaded after braking into the turn. He released the brakes enough to let the wheel start to spin again. It felt as if he had far too much speed on entry, but he trusted his instincts.

Just when it seemed inevitable that he wouldn't make the apex, somehow the car arced inward, tires nicking the paint at the edge of the asphalt. As he rotated out of the slow speed corner, he rolled the throttle open and the car powered out of the turn like it was on fire.

Yes.

Now that he knew he had it, things really got fun. Dancing between throttle and brake, he continued to shed tenths of a second as the fuel burned off. The last awkward set of turns was a punishing 6G deceleration that threw him forward against the straps. His neck and arms ached as he fought the gravitational force.

Turn after turn, lap after lap, Will kept it in check, just barely, pushing the car and himself to the limit. He'd never worked harder to keep control of a car, but it was worth it. He felt unstoppable.

Will Hawley hadn't just come to polish his tarnished reputation. After three hard-fought years to get himself back to this place, he wasn't just here to keep a seat warm. He was here to win it all, and he wasn't settling for less.

And now the entire sport of Formula One knew it.

Mira rubbed at her eyes as the elevator descended to the hotel lobby. She needed caffeine and lots of it, as soon as possible. Testing had been an unqualified success for Lennox, but the first race of the season was a week away, so there was no time to revel in it. This morning, she was up early and headed back to the track to tackle the millions of issues sitting in her inbox.

The elevator doors dinged open and she squinted at the blinding light filling the lobby. She'd taken all of two steps when her eyes adjusted and locked on an imposing figure at the front desk.

No. Oh, no. From the second they'd left England for testing in Bahrain, she'd known this moment was inevitable. It had been seven years—a lifetime ago—but he wasn't dead, no matter how many times she'd wished he was. Even after she'd stopped pining, stopped grieving, she'd still reluctantly kept track of him.

So far, she'd been so careful, managing to avoid ever being in the same place at the same time as him, which was no small feat when they were circulating in the same small pool of people on the track. But he'd been staying in her hotel this whole week?

There was a time when just the sight of those broad shoulders and that shock of messy, red-gold hair had set her heart pounding. It was hammering now, too, but in a gut-churning combination of dread and panic. Getting to the hotel entrance would require walking right past him. Nope, not happening. Mira ducked to her left, through the door of the hotel restaurant off the lobby. She'd hide there until she was sure he was gone.

"Can I get you anything else, Mr. Hawley?"

At the mention of Will's name, she turned just in time to see a gorgeous, curvy waitress beaming down at Will as she handed him a cup of coffee. The waitress's bright smile flashed against her golden skin, a sleek mass of black hair twisted on the back of her head. Her black uniform dress fit her body far better than those things were supposed to.

She looked like she wanted to offer him a lot more than coffee, which wasn't surprising. They were out on the circuit now and Will was . . . well, he was Will. Anything—any*one*—he wanted would be his for the asking. That near-kiss between them back in London was about to be a distant memory . . . for him, anyway.

And that nightmare out in the lobby was all the reason she needed to make it a distant memory for herself as well.

She joined him once he was alone. "Morning." She nudged his foot—with slightly more force than necessary—in greeting.

He'd been raising his coffee to his mouth, and he had to juggle not to spill it. "For fuck's sake," he growled. "I almost spilled this."

She sank into the chair across from him. He was slouched in his chair, wearing his sunglasses, hair in disarray. He was heading back to London for some promo before the first race and had his roll-aboard suitcase with him, so she assumed he was just waiting for his driver to take him to the airport.

"I'm sure she would have brought you another one. Looks like she'd be happy to bring you anything you want."

He scowled behind his sunglasses. "You can stop at any time, you know."

She studied him in the morning light. Pale, unshaved, definitely not peak Will. "Hangover?"

"No, I'm not hungover. I just got in too late last night, considering how early my flight out is."

"Looks like you thoroughly enjoyed yourself, whatever you were doing." Was she fishing? It sounded like she was fishing.

"I'm off for over a week," he said, dragging his sunglasses off. "A couple of drinks isn't going to mess me up. I did *not* go on a bender, or engage in some drug-fueled orgy, or anything else you might be imagining."

Really, she couldn't blame him for celebrating a little. Will had thrown down a hell of a gauntlet in Bahrain. Matteo better watch his back.

"I don't think my imagination could keep up with you."

He hiked an eyebrow. "Want to try that out?"

"I'll pass, thanks."

He leaned back in his chair and stretched. "I promise you, Matteo is in much worse shape than me. And Rikkard got completely obliterated. He's going to be hungover for a week." He took a sip of his coffee and let out a small moan of pleasure. The sound had Mira clearing her throat as she looked away. If *coffee* could make him sound like that . . . No, she wouldn't even finish that thought.

"I bet."

"Like you've never had a bad morning after."

"It's been a while." *Forever.*

"Seriously, you didn't celebrate at *all* yesterday?"

She shook her head. "Too much to do."

He tipped his cup up and polished off his coffee before leaning back in his club chair. "Mira, you missed the most legendary party. It was on a freaking *private man-made island,* just off the coast. Oil money, of course. The house was insane. Infinity pool overlooking the Persian Gulf. They flew in David Chang to design the menu. I'm pretty sure I saw Jay-Z there."

"Sounds fun."

"It was. Even your dad and Natalia came. You should've been there. I bet you never left the track."

"I did," she protested.

"The hotel doesn't count."

She made no reply because he was right. All she'd seen of Bahrain so far was the hotel, the track, and the airport. Yesterday, while the rest of the team had been partying on a private island, she'd been at the office, updating the company calendars and sending out reminder emails about the week's upcoming deadlines. Even her *father* had partied harder than she had. Grim.

"You're about to spend months touring the world. Are you seriously going to work through the whole thing? Bahrain has amazing beaches and shopping, and—"

"Okay, I get it. I promise I'll take more breaks."

Will gave her a long deadpan look. Mira met his gaze, determined not to be the first to look away.

"I don't believe you. Okay, in every city you're doing one fun thing. With me."

Yeah, there was no way that was happening, and the reason why was probably still lurking out there in the lobby.

"I'm not sure—"

He held up a finger. "Think of it this way. If I'm hanging out with you, I'm less likely to be getting up to trouble elsewhere, right?"

She thought briefly about the kind of trouble Will had been prone to—hot girls by the score. If letting him drag her through a bunch of tourist traps in foreign countries would keep him clear of that kind of trouble, maybe it was worth it.

"Okay," she conceded. "If I have time. If *you* have time." She was pretty sure he'd get so busy he'd never even remember their conversation. In fact, she was counting on it.

He chuckled. "I'm holding you to that. And believe me, Mira, I have time for you."

Melbourne,
Australia

Mira glanced down at the name lit up on her phone screen and groaned.

"Hi, Penelope!" she answered with enthusiasm she didn't feel, as she approached the Lennox mobile office. Pen was still several weeks out from having the baby and going absolutely stir-crazy in bed, so Mira got one of these phone calls nearly every day. Some days, like today, they were an interruption she didn't want or need.

Penelope skipped the niceties and launched straight into a monologue of concerns. "Now the thing you must be aware of in Melbourne is that it's a street track, and that can lead to a whole host of new issues—"

Mira hummed her acknowledgment at various points in Pen's rapid-fire stream of directions, wedging her phone under her chin so she could retrieve her notepad from between the stacks of folders she was carrying. There was no place to spread out and work here. When they were back in Europe, they'd have their custom-built portable Lennox offices, masterpieces of modular design and overnight construction. But it was too far to transport them to Australia, so they were stuck with the pop-up facilities the venue provided. At least the weather was nice.

After Bahrain, she thought maybe—just maybe—she was getting the hang of things. Setup was a sort of organized chaos, but the Lennox team was seasoned, and it pretty much went off without a problem. The jump to Melbourne, the second race of the season, was proving to be a different beast altogether.

First, there had been the car adjustments. Aerodynamics wanted to rework a body part, Mechanics wanted to overhaul the fuel injector . . . between the two, everyone had worked around the clock to get it done in time to load into the containers being flown to Melbourne.

Second, Melbourne involved flying all the personnel and equipment to the literal far side of the world. Even though there were people to handle all of it, emergencies arose and she was the one expected to solve them. Keeping track of it all had been a mammoth undertaking.

"Now the next thing," Penelope continued, not having paused once. "I'm still getting calendar reminders and I've noticed we're almost to the deadline for signing off on the contract with Hintabi for next year's brake assembly. Paul *has* gone over the contract, hasn't he?"

Mira suppressed a groan. "Legal sent it to him last week for notes but he hasn't sent it back yet."

"Then you have to get it from him! Remember—"

"Yes, I know. Every issue big and small! I'm on it, Penelope! I'll take care of it right now. Get some rest!"

She ended the call before Penelope could add a dozen more things to her to-do list, and hurried to track down her father and get the contract signed off on.

Inside the office, the air buzzed with the low-key chatter of half a dozen engineers and strategists discussing the day's qualifying results. Her father was on the far side of the room, standing in front of a bank of monitors. She tapped him on the shoulder. "Sorry to interrupt, Dad, but have you had a chance to go over Hintabi's contract?"

"Ah, right. You need that from me, don't you? Can we—"

Just then the door banged open and Harry hurried in, with Will right on his heels.

"We've a problem, Paul. The front brake duct on Will's car is done."

"How the hell did that happen?"

"Fucking track debris," Will snapped. He was fresh off the track from qualifying, still in his race suit, his hair damp from sweat. He'd never tracked her down after the race in Bahrain to go do "one fun thing." Demands from the media had consumed his time, which was exactly what she'd expected. And considering the twinge of disappointment she'd felt, it was probably a good thing that he was now too busy for her. Safer that way.

"Street tracks," Harry growled. "Absolute menace."

So that's what Pen meant about street tracks. She might be relentless, but she was rarely wrong.

"Can we repair it on site?" Paul asked.

Harry shook his head. "No. Shredded. It'll need replacing."

Several of the engineers who'd been monitoring the race from their desks rose to join the conversation.

Paul groaned. "We don't have a spare here, do we?"

"Didn't get it finished in time to make the Melbourne pack out," David interjected. "It had a flaw. Had to scrap it and start over."

Harry rubbed his palm over his stubbly jaw. "I can work up some sort of replacement here but—"

"I've already run quali," Will said. "I'm in parc fermé. If we swap out for something different, I'll get hit with a penalty."

This was bad. Once a car starts qualifying, no substitutions of parts were allowed before the race the next day. Any replacements needed to match the specs of the original exactly, or the car would be penalized and forced to start from the pit lane.

"Where's the spare now?"

"Still back at the factory," David said.

"It's over twenty hours from Heathrow to Melbourne," Paul mused. "We'd never get it here in time for tomorrow."

"Fuck," Will groaned, turning away to pace the confines of the small mobile office. "I finally have a car I can drive and I'll be starting from the goddamned back of the grid. This cannot be happening."

Mira's heart started beating rapidly, and her mind raced. This could kill Will's season—Lennox's season—before it even started.

Will's race in Bahrain had been fine; he finished tenth. Not an embarrassment but nowhere near what he was capable of. In a car designed for someone else though, there were limits to what he could accomplish. This was the race that was supposed to change everything. But not if they had to switch out parts while in parc fermé.

Mira stared at her notepad, trying to see a solution to an impossible problem. There were only two matches to the brake duct in Will's car—the one in Matteo's, which was no help, or the backup back at the Lennox factory in England. It was no use. There was no way she could get it here in time.

Except . . .

"Wait!" Every pair of eyes in the room turned to stare at her. "Ohmygod, ohmygod! It's not at the factory. It's in Singapore!"

Paul scowled. "What? Are you sure?"

Mira nodded as she flipped through one of her folders. "I thought I saw it on the manifest for the advance shipment to Singapore . . . Ha! Here!" She ripped the manifest free and handed it to her father.

She'd been cc'd on an email from one of the guys back at Lennox to the shipping department, explaining they'd just finished the spare brake duct, but since they'd missed the last shipment to Melbourne, they'd put it in the Singapore advance container instead.

Paul, Harry, David, and Will hunched over the manifest. "There it is," Paul muttered. "How long is the flight from Singapore?"

"Seven and a half hours," she supplied. "Give or take."

"Can we courier it in?" David asked.

Paul glanced at his watch. "It would take too long to get someone out there."

"We could put one of our boys in Singapore on a plane with it," Harry suggested. "It's not that big. It'll fit in a carry-on."

Paul shook his head. "The guys in Singapore don't have Australian visas—"

Finally the millions of individual bits of information came together in Mira's head all at once. "Ollie's there! Or he nearly is. He already has one."

Harry scowled. "Oliver Hayes? He's got a visa for Australia?"

Frantically, she flipped through yet more papers until she found the one she was looking for. "Yes, don't you remember? You originally wanted him on the Australian team, but his sister was getting married and he couldn't leave until yesterday. So you bumped him from Melbourne and had him go with the advance to Singapore instead." Stabbing her fingertip on her travel cheat sheet, she traced Ollie's name. "There. He lands in Singapore in forty-five minutes. He's got the Australian visa already. If we get him on a plane to Melbourne in the next—" She glanced at the time on her phone. "Hour and a half, he should be here by morning."

"If he flies through customs, maybe . . ." Paul said.

Another random piece of information swam to the surface. "The governor-general of Australia is coming to the race tomorrow. We got him VIP passes."

"Who is it now? Is it still Charles Stapleton?"

"Yes, that's him. Do you know him? Would he help?"

Paul nodded. "I do, and yes, he might. Mira, get on the phone with the travel office. Have them book a charter flight for Ollie. Then set up a helicopter taxi from the airport to the track. Talk to Francois Bernard with Track Logistics if you need clearance for the heli. I want Ollie off that plane and at the track tomorrow morning before he's got time to take a breath."

"Done."

Paul turned away to consult with Harry, leaving her alone with Will, who was watching her. "I could kiss you right now," he said, low enough to reach just her ears.

It was just a saying, but she could tell from his face, from the flare of heat in his eyes, that he really meant it. If they weren't surrounded by people, she half-suspected he'd have just grabbed her and done it.

Ignoring the way that mental image made her feel, she let out a shaky laugh, still buzzing with adrenaline. "I've done my part. Now you get out there and do yours."

"Tomorrow, when I'm on that podium, it's going to be for you. And you're celebrating with me."

There was the cocky Will she knew and loved. "Well, then, you better get on that podium."

"See you after the race, Mira." The smile he gave her was criminal.

She watched him go, then turned her attention back to the crisis at hand, scrolling through her phone looking for Jo's number, the head of Lennox travel back in England.

"Harry," her father was saying. "Call the track in Singapore and have one of the guys unpack that brake duct and get it out to Ollie at the airport. I'll track down Sanderson and see what he can do to get us through customs quickly."

He walked toward the door, but paused when he reached it and looked back at her. She had already dialed Jo and was waiting for her to get out of bed and pick up.

"Mira," her father said, smiling with a warm light in his eyes she hadn't seen in years. "Well done, sweetheart." She was still basking in the glow of his praise when Jo's groggy voice on the other end of the line muttered hello.

14

"**O**kay, three long burnouts to your grid spot." Tae's voice crackled in Will's ear as he rounded the last corner in his warm-up lap. "And as always, ramp up rather than coast."

"Copy that," Will replied as he performed the obligatory maneuver, then settled into his grid spot, waiting for the start of the race. Engines snarled all around him, and sweat prickled on the back of his neck. It was a hot day in Melbourne.

Ollie Hayes had stumbled out of a helitaxi at the track just an hour ago. The crew had the part installed and the car sorted with just thirty minutes to spare. Not exactly the kind of anxiety he needed before he climbed behind the wheel, but it had all worked out, thanks to Mira. Not only was she persistently occupying a corner of his mind, but now she'd saved his ass, too. He'd have to make good on his promise and take her out properly in Melbourne . . . if she'd let him.

He'd been running on pure adrenaline since yesterday, but now, as he awaited the rest of the field to assemble behind him, calm settled over him. This was the moment when everything would come together. He could feel it in his bones.

Everybody always assumed that the nerves were the worst when he sat in the car, engine revving, waiting for the lights to go out and the race to start. But not for him. All his anxiety and self-doubt . . . that stuff plagued him off the track. Once he got behind the wheel, about to race, that's when all that noise in his head stopped and everything seemed so clear. He was in the right place, doing the thing he'd been put on earth to do.

As the lights went on one by one, he checked his revs, breathing slow and steady. The last light blinked on and he pulled the clutch and raised the revs. And then the lights went out—*go time*—and he let it rip. The car flew forward up the straight, pinning him to his seat with enormous force.

Tae launched into a rapid-fire assessment of every car's position on the track. Part of Will's brain tracked that, envisioning the cars moving behind him, while the rest of his brain focused on what was ahead.

Once the race started, it was like time slowed down and he didn't. It was almost as if he could see moments into the future, envisioning gaps between cars before they appeared, sensing who was about to miss their braking point, who would misjudge the apex of the turn. On the track, he found his superpower.

René Denis, the reigning world champion, was making a massive run up the inside, trying to catch him. As the grip came on, Will pinned him against the grass border, shutting him down, then he banged up the gears, smooth on the throttle, no wheelspin that might give away his carefully won pole position, and easily put a car's width between him and René by the entry to the first turn. This was Will's favorite part, the first few laps when the engineers and strategists let you maximize the car and race flat out. Soon they'd reign him in to play a strategic game of managing fuel load and tires for the rest of the race. But right now it was pure racing, just him and the car seeing what they could do.

René was still closer than he would like, but he got to work wrestling tenths of a second out of his opponent, one precise maneuver at a time. By the end of the first lap René was still cooling his heels behind him and Will was still holding first place.

Tae spoke into his ear. "I'm going to need you to manage your brake temps a bit, Will. Can you add some lift and coast into Turn Thirteen?"

Will cursed under his breath. If he was nursing his brake temps, it might give René room to gain on him. "You're killing me, Tae," he replied.

"Actually just trying to keep you alive," Tae replied.

Will went to work doing what he could to save the brakes while not losing too much time to René.

"Box, box, box!" Tae barked a few minutes later.

He flew into the box and landed dead on the marks, the jacks perfectly synced, and the Lennox pit crew leapt in to replace his tires.

One second, two seconds, three seconds.

Omar should be giving him the thumbs-up to go by now.

"What's happening?" he barked into his headset.

"Rear right wheel jammed coming off," Tae said. "Almost there."

"Fuck!"

All those precious tenths he should be gaining on René started flowing in the opposite direction, cutting into his hard-fought lead.

At last they dropped the car, Omar gave him the all-clear signal, and Will rocketed out of the pits with the engine pegged on the limiter. If he drove flat out, and if nothing else went wrong, he could still hold René off.

Then Tae put an end to that. "Still marginal on the brakes, Will. You're going to need to manage to the end."

"The hell I am. I'm getting it back."

Tae sighed. "You can chase, but only as far as the brake temps allow. We're not burning up the brakes."

He chased hard, only backing off when Tae insisted to hold up, but as he screamed down the final straight, René was still out in front by an agonizing two seconds. Two seconds too many, in the end, as the checkered flag came down with René Denis in first and Will in second.

When he pulled to a stop on the track after his cooldown lap, the entire Lennox pit crew rushed to surround the car. Paul himself reached a hand down to help him out, grinning wider than Will had ever seen him. "Smashed it, Will. We'll get the brakes sorted and then there'll be no stopping you, mate."

"Glad to hear it because I don't intend on letting anybody ahead of me next time."

"That's what I like to hear!" Paul clapped him on the back.

Tae was next, giving him a fierce one-armed hug. "I am *really* going to enjoy being race engineer for the Formula One world champion."

Will held his hand out to shake. "I'm buying your drinks tonight."

Tae grasped his hand. "Deal. Now go get on that podium."

"La Marseillaise" began to play over the loudspeaker as Will's eyes swept the crowds below. René, to his left and on a *slightly* higher podium, waved at his pit crew in Allegri-red jumpsuits below. They all screamed and waved back, celebrating their first-place win. Will hoped they enjoyed it, because after today the only national anthem he wanted to hear on the podium was bloody "God Save the King."

It was annoying to know he could have taken first if not for the brakes, but honestly, second place felt pretty great. In his entire F1 career, he'd never made podium. To be standing up there just two races into the season was nothing short of a miracle. He could get used to this.

Will waved to the Lennox pit crew, clustered together below. They were all grinning, celebratory, sensing that they were now on a team that was in the running for the championship. Paul, standing off to the side with Tae and David, raised his hands and applauded Will. Paul had taken a huge chance on him, and it felt great to vindicate that choice.

Mira was down there, too, right behind her father. She put two fingers in her mouth and whistled up at him. God, she looked beautiful. A race official stepped up to shake his hand and give him the second-place trophy. He raised it high overhead in triumph, then he pointed from it to her. This was hers, just as much as it was his. She threw her head back and laughed, and that felt almost as good as finishing on the podium. Then René blasted him with a spray of champagne and he was lost in the chaos of his first Formula One podium finish. It would absolutely not be his last.

There wasn't much time to glory in his success after the race. Will had been launched straight into interviews, press conferences, corporate events, and finally, a cocktail party. At this point, his face hurt from maintaining his smile for so long.

He had just extricated himself from the wife of one of his corporate sponsors and was calculating how soon he could leave when two feminine hands covered his eyes from behind and a warm body pressed up against his back. His momentary hope that it was Mira fizzled when a throaty voice with a lilting Italian accent purred in his ear.

"Surprise."

When he turned, she slid her hands away from his face, leaving them to rest on his shoulders.

"Francesca. This *is* a surprise."

Francesca made her living as a spokesmodel for some sponsor or another, one of the ubiquitous hot women peppering Formula One races. He'd hooked up with Francesca once, back in his first season. He wasn't surprised to see her, but he was a little surprised that she'd sought him out. They'd crossed paths at a few races over the past three years, but Francesca had chosen not to remember him, not when there were more successful drivers to pursue. But here he was, back in F1, and here *she* was, suddenly very happy to see him again.

"You were fantastic today, Will," she said, running her fingertips down the lapel of his jacket.

"Thanks." Over her shoulder he scanned the room for Mira. He'd been hoping he'd run into her at the after-party and convince her to go do something fun. They'd made a deal. If he got on the podium, she'd celebrate with him, but now she was nowhere to be found.

"Will, I seem to have lost my drink someplace. Isn't that sad?" He pulled his attention back to Francesca. After all, she was putting on quite a show with the dramatic pout. She was undeniably gorgeous, with long dark hair and sexy dark eyes. Her tight red dress left little doubt that every inch of her still looked as delectable as he remembered.

"So sad," he agreed.

Waiters were everywhere. All he had to do was raise a finger and one swept in with a full tray of champagne flutes.

Francesca plucked one off and took a sip, eyes on him the whole time.

"Mmm, delicious," she moaned, licking her lips deliberately. Had she been this blatant last time? "Will, how have you been?"

"Fine. Brilliant, really."

Francesca ran a hand up the back of his neck and slid her fingers through his hair. "Yes, I'm sure you are. Shall we go someplace a bit quieter and find out?"

He blinked in surprise. So *this* was an option, if he wanted it. Although it was a little surprising that *Francesca* was throwing herself at him, an invitation like this was nothing new. In F1, "pussy was plentiful" as the guys back in Juniors used to say. Even after he'd fallen down the rankings, he'd still had plenty of options for female companionship whenever he'd wanted it.

Did he want it with Francesca tonight? He stared down at her, the gorgeous face, the inviting cleavage, the killer body. This would be very easy, and no doubt a lot of fun. An interest of a sort stirred in his gut.

But not with Francesca.

He knew what he wanted and whom he wanted it with, and it made him annoyed with himself. Was he really about to blow off some no-strings sex with a hot brunette who'd spend the evening making him feel like a hero, to go find Mira, the only girl in F1 who was explicitly off-limits? Yes. Yes, apparently he was. What the hell was he doing?

"Uh, Francesca, I'm afraid I can't."

"You can't?" She probably wasn't turned down very often.

He scanned the crowd over Francesca's shoulder, desperately searching for an escape. He spotted Violet. "I see someone from our PR department frantically waving me over. You know how it is. I'm sure someone wants a word."

In truth, Violet was chatting up a bartender, not paying Will the slightest bit of attention, but Francesca didn't have to know that.

"Why don't you take my number so you can call me later?"

"I've got it already." Will patted his cell in his jacket pocket. He absolutely did not have her number.

"So I'll see you later?"

She hadn't wanted to see him during his three demoted years, so he didn't feel all that bad for stringing her along now.

"Absolutely."

She leaned up to kiss him, but he didn't notice in time. He jerked back, but she still planted a peck on his lips. He didn't look back as he slipped away from her and disappeared into the crowd.

"Violet," he said, when he finally reached her. "You've got to save me. Make sure I look very busy for the next ten minutes."

She gave him a bored look. "Why?"

"I've got a particularly persistent spokesmodel on my tail."

"Well, I'm afraid you'll have to save yourself, mate. I'm about to shove off."

"Where are you going?"

"I'm taking Mira out to a club. We're celebrating."

Okay, so a deal apparently wasn't a deal. She'd already made plans with Violet. That left him feeling something unfamiliar. Forgotten. Huh. "You guys are celebrating the race?"

Violet rolled her eyes. "Celebrating her genius, you numpty. You'd have started from the back of the grid today with shit brake ducts if it wasn't for her."

"Right," he said, suitably chastised. "So you're going out dancing?"

"Yeah, she's making all kinds of noises about being too busy, but I'm not letting her wiggle out of it."

Wiggle? Jesus Christ, what was Violet trying to do to him.

"What club?" He absolutely hated how desperate he sounded.

"This place called The Slide. I hung out there a bit when my ex was touring Australia. Hey, if you're not busy banging your spokesmodel tonight, you're welcome to tag along."

Tagging along. He might be debasing himself, but he didn't say no. At least she'd be there.

"Yeah, sure, I'll come."

She eyed him with naked speculation. "Really?"

He pointed in Francesca's direction. "I'm desperate, Violet. And I need to thank Mira, right? How about I buy the drinks?"

"Well, then, you've got a date. Meet us in our lobby at eleven."

Mira was definitely going to bail on Violet. Clubbing sounded awful right now.

Besides, she was a hot mess. She hadn't stopped moving since yesterday's crisis. She'd woken up four times last night to check on the status of Ollie's flight, and she hadn't drawn a full breath until Will had driven his repaired car onto the grid. The anxiety had to have eaten at least two years off her life.

Just when she could finally enjoy her moment of glory, she'd walked into the cocktail party to find Will wrapped up in some tall, gorgeous dark-haired woman. She'd known this would happen eventually, and now it had.

Knowing it had been different than seeing it, though. And seeing that woman's hands in his hair, his hands on her hips . . . it was frustrating to admit, but it had felt like a punch to the gut. She *liked* him. She'd tried so hard not to, but she did. And she knew he liked her, too, in his way. But his life was about to become a whirlwind of press and parties and beautiful, available women. There was no way he was going to keep hanging around her just for some PG-rated teasing and flirting when there were tons of better offers out there. His promise to show her a good time in every city was about to become a distant memory.

She refused to attribute her bad mood to that, however. She was just tired after all the stress. *That's* why she'd turned right around and left the reception. She needed rest and maybe a good Netflix show to binge. Not because she couldn't bear to watch him leave with that woman. Of course not.

After she'd gotten back to the hotel, she'd peeled off her rumpled clothes and walked straight into the shower, turning it up as hot as she could stand it, and stayed under the spray until her fingers shriveled. And now she was staring at her reflection in the bathroom mirror in dismay. Her hair had dried naturally, which meant it had dried *curly*, a wild pile of messy blond curls, and there was no time to straighten it.

Plus she had nothing to wear. All she had were a bunch of conservative blouses and pants, with a few understated dresses for more formal functions. She didn't go to clubs. Like, ever.

Violet's knock came at her door and she groaned.

"Violet," she said as she swung it open. "Sorry, but I'm not—"

Violet threw up her hand. "Don't even try to tell me no. I knew you would."

Mira waved a hand helplessly at herself. "But I'm a mess—"

"It's a *bar*, Mira. Wear that. It's fine." Violet waved a hand at her and strode past her into her room, snatching her black boots off the floor. "And wear these. These are brilliant . . . I wish you wore my size so I could steal them. Put these on and let's go."

She glanced down at herself in faded jeans and a tank top. "Are you kidding? This is not a going-out outfit."

Violet gave her an exasperated look. "What do you wear when you go out in LA?"

"I don't."

"Well, that's just sad. Mira, I know you'll be shocked to hear this, but you're a *young person*. Going out, having fun . . . it's a bit expected, you know? And after today, you've earned a little celebrating!"

Fine, she'd go. One drink and then she'd plead exhaustion and catch a cab.

"My hair—" She started for the bathroom but Violet grabbed her arm and yanked her back.

"Is divine. Honestly, I don't know why you straighten it every day. Those curls are glorious."

Her relationship with her hair was complicated. First of all, it was her *mother's* hair, the tumble of platinum curls that had made Cherie Delain famous. But Mira's was a little less golden, a little less ringlet-y, just . . . less. Second, her hair was . . . well, it was the first compliment *he'd* ever paid her. He'd told her the riotous curls made her look untamable. And at the time, that sounded amazing. Ever since that had blown up in her face, she'd worn it straight and pulled back, as a reminder of what *not* to be. Tame was okay, actually.

Mira gave her reflection one despairing glance before Violet tugged her away. She managed to snatch her black jacket off the back of a chair before Violet shoved her out the door.

"You wouldn't have believed this website guy, Mira," Violet said as they waited for the elevator.

"That one from *Formula Fan*?"

Violet rolled her eyes. "Thought he was bloody Tom Hardy, trying to charm me into getting him an interview with Matteo. I swear, I get so tired of having to play nice with these wankers."

"So maybe you should—"

The elevator doors opened in front of them but it wasn't empty.

"Well, hello, ladies."

Mira didn't know him, but everything about him screamed driver. He was crazy good-looking, with jet-black hair and eyes and a killer body. He slouched against the railing with that innate physical confidence they all had.

Violet sighed, a sound of deep disdain. "Chase."

"Violet," he replied, grinning, his teeth flashing white against his tanned skin.

Violet hooked her arm into Mira's and steered her into the elevator, pointedly facing away from him.

Undaunted, he reached a hand between them toward Mira. "Chase Navarro."

Violet let out a disgusted snort and rolled her eyes.

Mira twisted awkwardly—since Violet wasn't releasing her arm—and shook his hand. "Miranda Wentworth."

"Paul Wentworth's kid, right?"

"She's also a kick-ass assistant, thank you very much!" Violet shouted.

Chase raised his hands in defense. "I'm sure she is. Congrats on the race today, by the way. Lennox looks great."

"Thank you. And you—?"

But she was cut off by the elevator doors opening on the second floor. Chase pushed off the wall of the elevator, brushing past them. "This is me. Miranda, nice to meet you. Violet . . ." He paused as he left the elevator, then smiled at her again. "Always a pleasure."

"You little—" But the elevator doors slid closed again, cutting her off.

"Who in the hell was that?"

"Nobody!" Violet snapped.

"Well, he's clearly somebody."

She sighed impatiently. "He's on Hansbach's Formula Two team. Can you *believe* that name? A driver named 'Chase'? As fake as the rest of him."

"How do you know him?"

"Oh, he's F2, so he's *always* at the parties. Last season I was doing my job, chatting up this journo, and the asshole sailed right in and stole her away so he could flirt with her. I mean, all the drivers sleep around, but Will's got *nothing* on that one. He's the worst."

Just then, the elevator doors dinged open in the lobby, and the first thing she saw was Will himself, as if Violet had summoned him.

"What is *he* doing here?"

The last time she'd seen Will, he'd been well on his way to getting laid with that hot brunette. Now he was pacing slowly around the lobby, alone, head down, hands in the pockets of his very nicely fitted jeans. His dark gray T-shirt should have been entirely unremarkable. But there was nothing unremarkable about the way it hugged those glorious shoulders and kept hugging down over his broad chest. Nobody should look that good in a T-shirt and jeans.

"Oh," Violet said with false innocence. "Did I forget to tell you? Will's coming along. You don't mind, do you?"

She wasn't sure if she minded. On one hand, she was feeling an embarrassing flood of relief that he wasn't off somewhere fucking the brains out of that gorgeous brunette. On the other hand, going out with him might mean she just had to watch him hook up with someone else, from a much closer vantage point. Violet's words about Chase Navarro were still hanging in the air.

All the drivers sleep around.

Will heard them and turned. When he spotted her, he froze, his eyes widening slightly. If she'd felt uneasy up in her room, now she felt downright uncomfortable. Her hair was a mess. She usually wore this tank when she was doing laundry—she was pretty sure her bra showed through it. Hurriedly she shrugged into her jacket.

"It's fine," she said.

Will was still staring at her as they approached him.

"What?" She tugged her jacket closed but she still felt wildly exposed.

"Your hair," he blurted.

"It's a mess."

"I like it. A lot."

She reached up to touch it self-consciously and then cursed herself. Who cared if Will liked her hair? Why was that supposed to matter?

His eyes dipped down her body briefly. "You look different. Good. Really good."

She rolled her eyes to cover her discomposure, and tucked her hair firmly behind her ears, where it refused to stay. "Are we going?"

"Absolutely," Violet said, heading toward the revolving doors and out into the night. "And Will's buying."

The bar was a rundown dive near the river, down an alley and a narrow flight of stairs. Mira could hear the band when they were still twenty feet from the door. People were scattered across the alley, smoking and laughing, a sea of faded band T-shirts, piercings, and tattoos. Of course Violet found this place halfway around the world. At least nobody would recognize Will. They didn't seem like they'd be into motor sports.

Will paid their cover charge and shouldered his way through the crowd to the bar, Violet and her slipping along in his wake. When he found a clear spot, he angled himself to allow them to get in next to him. Somehow Mira ended up wedged up against him, her shoulder pressed to his chest. Being this close to him felt shockingly intimate, with the warmth of his body pressed all along her left side, his face just inches away from hers.

The bartender was run off his feet, but somehow Violet commanded his attention with a single word. She ordered a shot of tequila, and Will asked for a beer.

"Club soda," she said when it was her turn.

Violet turned to her. "Really, Mira?"

"*Fine.* Vodka cranberry." Maybe a drink might help her stop feeling so self-conscious.

"Better," Violet said, beaming at her. "I mean, just look at this place. It's crawling with hot men. We're going to have so much fun tonight."

"I think I'll just listen to the band for now."

Violet shrugged, her attention already snagged by a lanky blond guy at the end of the bar. "Suit yourself. What about you, Will? Any girls catch your oh-so-experienced eye?"

Mira cast a quick glance at him and then looked back to her drink. Oh, god, was she going to have to listen to him decide whom he was going to go after and then watch as he did it? She took a long swig of her drink through the straw. This was a *terrible* idea.

He cleared his throat. "I'm just going to, um . . . listen to the band, too. For now."

Mira shot a glance at him, but he was looking down at his drink.

"Well, I'll leave you two to grow roots here. I'm off to suck the lips off that hot Aussie at the end of the bar."

With that, Violet downed her shot, turned away, and headed toward her quarry.

"Seriously?" Mira muttered. But within seconds of approaching him, the blond guy was smiling down at her, buying her another shot. Well, then. Violet was a woman who got what she wanted. Guess she and Will were on their own.

He leaned in to speak close to her ear. His words came on a warm wash of air across her neck. "I believe I owe you a thank-you."

When she turned to look at him, his face was just inches away. "You said your win was for me. So we're even, right?"

"Not even close. This is my first Formula One podium, and you made it happen. So thanks." He lifted his beer toward her and she clinked her glass against it.

"You're welcome." She was surprised he could hear her breathless reply.

He held eye contact a little too long before his gaze flickered down to her mouth. She rapidly looked back at the band, taking another deep swig of her drink.

"They're pretty good," she said, as if the band in the Australian dive were putting on the most fascinating live performance she'd ever witnessed.

"They are."

She took a few more sips of her drink. It was nearly gone already. The bartender must have used a lot of ice.

"Do you want another?" he asked, again, close enough to her ear that she felt his words as much as she heard them.

"Oh. Sure, I guess." It was hot in the bar, and the drink was cold. By the time she polished off her first, she could feel the vodka starting to do its job, chasing the tension out of her neck and spine. Shrugging out of her jacket, she threw it over the stool behind her. Will handed her another drink and she sipped it gratefully. He was still so close, his T-shirt brushing her bare arm, his hip bumping hers as he moved. Her whole body tingled with awareness of his. She kept her eyes on the band, even though she was barely processing what she was hearing.

The dance floor was between the bar and the stage, and it was packed with people bathed in blue light. Everybody looked like they were having so much fun. She remembered that feeling, fueled by music and dancing, like anything was possible, like anything could happen. Like anything *would* happen, if she just wanted it enough.

Violet was right. She was allowed to have a little fun, especially tonight. She'd kicked ass at work—saved the day, really. That deserved a little bit of celebrating, didn't it?

Before she knew it, she was moving along with the pulsating drumbeat. How long had it been since she'd danced? She abandoned her empty glass on the bar and moved to the dance floor so she could fully sink into it, the darkness, the heat, the music. Maybe it was the vodka but who cared? She felt flush with the day's triumph and the feeling of endless possibility. It'd been so long since she felt that. It felt *great*. Violet was right. She was young and tonight, she wanted to enjoy it.

Will could only stare. Mira might be drunk. Well, maybe not drunk but definitely a little buzzed. That was the only explanation. She was *dancing*. Mira. Out there in the crush of people on the dance floor, head thrown back, eyes closed, arms in the air, absolutely lost in the music. He couldn't look away if he tried, and he wasn't trying.

He *wanted* her, with an intensity that shocked him. The pulse of the music, the pulse of his blood, the pulse of his need had all mixed into one throbbing beat.

He imagined those bare arms wrapped around his shoulders, and those thighs wrapped around his hips. He imagined the lacy black bra barely covered up by that thin white tank and her breasts underneath it, and imagined his hands and mouth on them. And he imagined digging his fingers into that goddamned unbelievable hair as he kissed her, pushed her down, covered her body with his own. He'd never guessed that when she finally unleashed her hair from that ponytail, it would be this—a long, gorgeous tumble of messy blond curls that made her look as if she'd just climbed out of bed after a really good shag.

Before he knew what he was doing, he'd ditched his beer and followed her out into the crush of bodies. Immediately they were surrounded, pressed in on all sides, jostled up against each other.

She glanced back over her shoulder and when she registered it was him, she smiled and closed her eyes again, falling back into the music. Someone bumped into him from behind and he reached out for her, hands finding her hips, to steady himself. And when he'd gotten his balance back, he kept his hands on her, not grasping, just touching. She didn't shake him off. Every time the crowd swayed, so did she, up against him, into him, until his arms were nearly around her, her hair tickling his chin, her scent drifting up every time he inhaled. When he lowered his head, resting his temple against hers, he felt her slow, easy surrender, her body going boneless against his. There was the invitation he'd been hoping for.

The song kept spiraling, the heavy beat growing louder as they swayed to it together. He gave her the gentlest nudge to spin her around. She was facing him now, just inches between them. Her face was bathed in blue light, her hair a glowing halo around her. Her lashes fluttered upward until those big eyes were looking into his, glittering under the lights.

Everything that happened next felt inevitable, like he was just a comet orbiting her, drawn inexorably in by her gravity. His hands came up, cradling her face, so small compared to the span of his fingers. As his head lowered, her eyes slid closed again. He paused, just the length of a breath, savoring the moment, and then he pressed his mouth to hers. It felt like there was nowhere else on earth he was supposed to be. Right here, right now, in the light and the music, kissing this girl. Nothing had felt this right since the first time he'd gotten behind the wheel to drive. He could feel it happening, like something locking into place in his heart. He was falling for this girl like he'd fallen for racing: hard, fast, and irrevocably.

When he opened his mouth over hers, she let him in, and he sank into the perfection of her lips, her tongue. Every fantasy he'd entertained about her paled in comparison to the reality of her. Kissing someone had never felt so good, so intense. Maybe it was because he'd wanted her for what felt like forever.

Her hands danced up his arms, and then slid over his shoulders, finding their way into his hair. The scrape of nails against his scalp sent shock waves of pleasure down his spine. He slid a hand down her back, molding her body to his, finding her hip, pulling her even closer, until it seemed like he could feel her heart thumping against his chest in time with the music. Hips to hips, her tongue sliding against his, he felt himself grow hard. Even through the relentless pounding of the music, her ragged breath mingled with his own heartbeat and echoed in his ears.

His hand slid back into her gorgeous hair and fisted it, so soft around his fingers, just like he'd imagined. Mira moaned into his mouth, a soft, low sound of surrender that made him nearly lose his mind.

When they finally broke apart, her hands were still gripping his shoulders and his arms were still wrapped around her, their foreheads touching.

Reaching up to cradle her face in his palm, he rubbed his thumb across her cheekbone. "I'll get us a cab, okay?" They needed to be out of this hot, crowded bar.

He ducked his head to the side, kissing her cheek, the side of her neck, the edge of her ear. "I want you so much," he whispered into her ear. "Come home with me."

When he lifted his head, her eyes were closed, brows furrowed. Then her fingers released their grip on his shoulders.

Gently, she pushed back. A sliver of air slipped between them. "No . . . I . . ."

"Mira . . ."

She pushed against him harder and he released her. "I can't. I'm sorry. I shouldn't have . . ."

When she opened her eyes and looked up at him, she looked on the verge of tears. His desire curdled into guilt. Was she drunker than he thought? Had he just taken advantage of her when she was too impaired to stop him?

"Hey, what's wrong? Talk to me." He reached for her, taking her gently by the shoulders, attempting to draw her back to him.

As she swatted his hands away, the tears spilled over. "I need to go to the restroom."

She shoved away from him and pushed her way through the crowd, leaving him standing alone in the middle of the dance floor feeling like a massive arse.

Mira slammed the bathroom door and fell back against it, breathing hard. Her entire body was still vibrating. Her face was wet with tears, and her throat ached with a sob she swallowed down.

No, no, no, no, no.

Why did she do something so *stupid?*

She couldn't even blame it on Will, even though he'd initiated it. Yes, she'd been drinking, but she wasn't drunk, unless being drunk on music and a moment counted. Swept up in everything she'd been feeling out there on the dance floor, she'd turned to face him and she *knew.* His intention was clear the minute she looked up into his eyes. She'd known what was coming and she'd stood still and let it happen. Welcomed it. Because she wanted it, too.

And when she'd gotten it . . .

I want you so much.

She closed her eyes and let out a helpless little moan. God, she wanted him, too. The aftershocks of that kiss were still firing through her body. She could still feel his fingertips on the back of her neck, his hand in her hair . . . she could still taste his mouth on hers. Her nipples were tight, and between her legs, she ached with need, remembering his whispered words.

What was *wrong* with her? Didn't she ever learn? They were barely into the season and she was already making out with some guy in a bar. And not just any guy—*Will*. Will, who raced for her *father's* team. Will, whom she was beginning to think of as a legitimate friend. Will, the only guy—possibly in the world—who could ruin everything she was working toward. It was like she was determined to find some way to sabotage herself.

She ripped some paper towels from the holder on the wall and dried her face. Well, the difference was, last time she was sixteen and dumb. Now she was twenty-three and much smarter. Smart enough to step back and regroup instead of charging blindly forward into disaster. No matter how he made her feel, what happened out there could not happen again.

When she unlocked the bathroom door, Will was waiting outside, leaning against the wall, arms crossed over his chest. "Are you okay?"

"Look, I'm really sorry," she said. "I never should have done that. It was wrong of me."

He pushed off the wall, taking a step toward her. The smile he gave her made her heart twist up in her chest. "I'm pretty sure I did it."

He reached out a hand toward her, but she backed away, shaking her head, on the edge of panic. "I shouldn't have let you. I can't. It's—"

His smile melted away. "Why?"

"This can't happen. You and me."

He was silent for a moment, a silence so heavy it felt as if the weight of it might crush her. He was staring at her—she could feel his eyes on her—but she couldn't bear to look him in the eye.

"So you just want to forget this?" he finally said.

"I think that would be best."

He let out a scoff of humorless laughter, but he didn't argue. "Okay, yeah. It never happened."

"I like you, Will."

"What?"

Now she made herself raise her face and look at him. He was scowling, trying to puzzle out what she meant.

"You're my friend and I really like you."

"Friend," he echoed.

"That's all I can be."

More silence. His face was impossible to read as he turned that over. Finally, he gave a small nod and let out a tired exhale. "Right. Friends."

"I think I should go."

He nodded tightly. "I'll get us a car."

"No, you don't have to—"

"Mira, I'm not letting you go back to the hotel alone at this hour."

"I won't go alone. I'll find Violet."

"Then I'll take you both back."

"You don't have to go—"

"I'm not staying here without you."

Lacking the strength to argue with him, she slipped past him and went to look for Violet. She found her at the bar, chatting with a guy—not the one from earlier.

"Violet, sorry to interrupt, but I need to go."

Violet spun to face her, eyes dancing between Mira and Will, and whatever she saw made her bite back the questions she so obviously wanted to ask. Instead, she just nodded. "Sure. Let's go."

AS THE UBER wound through the dark Melbourne streets back toward their hotels, Will's mind was back there on the dance floor, pressed up against Mira, wildly turned on and ready to do everything he'd been fantasizing about since he'd met her.

But now she was on the other side of the cab, curled into a little comma of misery, staring out the window blankly, not saying a word. He'd told her he'd follow her lead and forget what had happened. But that was a lie, because there was no way he was ever going to forget what she felt like, what she tasted like. Even now, as he sat in tense silence in the back of a dark cab, just thinking about that kiss had his blood heating and his dick impossibly hard.

It seemed pretty fucking clear that she was every bit as attracted to him as he was to her, but for whatever reason, she was refusing to indulge it. His spine itched with frustration and thwarted desire, but there wasn't a damned thing he could do about it. She'd cried. He'd kissed her and she'd *cried*. Remembering that cooled his lust a fraction. A very small fraction.

The car pulled up in front of his hotel and he leapt out the door.

"I put in your hotel as the second stop," he said. "So you should be set."

"Thanks," Violet said automatically.

Before he closed the door, he hesitated, glancing over at Mira, who was pointedly turned away from him, looking out the window. Violet looked from him, to her, back to him again, and shrugged.

Fine. He wasn't getting answers from her tonight. He might never get them, because that was her prerogative. She'd told him no. So now he just needed to get over it and move on. As if it were that simple.

"Text me when you get back to your hotel," he finally said.

Mira didn't reply, so Violet jumped in after a beat. "Sure thing. Thanks for the drinks."

He ran a hand through his hair, still humming with frustration. "Any time."

He stood outside for a bit, watching the car disappear down the street, before heading into the lobby.

Almost immediately, he spotted Rikkard, one of Lennox's reserve drivers, on his way into the bar off the lobby. "Hey, look who it is! Mr. Motherfucking Second Place!"

"Hey, Rikkard."

Rikkard was from Finland, twenty years old, and just starting out his career. He showed a lot of promise as a driver. Actually, Rikkard reminded him a lot of himself at that age: raw talent in need of experience, and a tendency to party hard. Right now, he was quite obviously and significantly drunk.

"Will, come with me." Rikkard slung an arm around his shoulder. "There's a bar full of women in there desperate to congratulate you."

"I'm not sure I'm up for it," he said, stalling.

Rikkard stumbled to a stop and reared around to face him. "Will." He clapped his hands on either side of Will's neck. "You made the podium! Your second race back! What the fuck do you mean you're not up for it? It is your *duty* to get in there and party! Drink some champagne, fuck some women. Come *on*. This is the best part of racing!"

Maybe it wasn't the *best* part of racing, but Rikkard wasn't wrong. He finished on the podium. He should be celebrating.

So things with Mira had just blown up in his face. That didn't mean he had to go crawling off to his room to feel sorry for himself.

The sound of music and laughter drifted out into the lobby as he considered. Just then, a figure materialized out of the dimly lit bar. A shapely figure in a tight red dress.

"Hello again, Will."

"Hello, Francesca."

18

The Uber deposited Mira and Violet in front of their hotel a few minutes after they dropped Will off.

"Thanks for coming home early with me," Mira said as they pushed through the revolving doors. "I appreciate it."

"It seemed like you needed it," Violet said evenly.

"I did." Mira's hands were still shaking. Every time she closed her eyes, she pictured his face as he looked into her eyes on the dance floor, and she heard the urgent rasp of his voice in her ear as he begged her to come home with him.

Violet let out a gusty exhale. "Mira, I'm crap at this, but if you want to talk—"

"No, that's okay. I'm fine, I just—"

"Mira?"

That was the one voice she didn't want to hear. Not tonight. Slowly, she turned around to face her father. He had just come into the hotel, Natalia on his arm. There had been a party thrown by a team sponsor, she dimly remembered. She probably should have gone with him. Doing her job, sticking with her father all night . . . that's where she should have been. Because look what had happened when she didn't.

When she said nothing, Violet jumped in. "Hi, Paul. You're just getting back, too?"

Paul's eyes roved over the two of them. Mira wanted to die. Why couldn't the polished marble under her feet crack wide open and swallow her whole? What a wreck she was—her wild hair, her eye makeup smudged with tears, her kiss-swollen lips, all of it.

"Looks like our evening wasn't quite the adventure yours was."

Violet laughed; Mira didn't. She heard the judgment in those words. This was exactly what he'd been afraid of when she asked to come on board—exactly what he was afraid she'd do. And here she was, proving all his fears correct. He didn't even know about Will. He might never speak to her again if he knew what she'd done with him tonight.

"I dragged poor Mira out to a club with me to hear a band. She was a good sport about it, though."

"Doesn't seem quite your thing these days, Miranda." His frown deepened.

Her face flamed and she shivered in misery as she made herself meet his eyes. "The music was good," she murmured. "But yeah, it wasn't really my scene."

The silence was so brittle, even Violet seemed too intimidated to break it. Was it just yesterday when she'd saved the race and he'd looked at her with eyes full of pride and told her she'd done a good job? He wasn't looking at her that way now.

"Well, I'm exhausted," Natalia said, ever the diplomat. "We're going to head upstairs and get some sleep."

"Goodnight," Mira said, as they passed her.

Paul paused. "I'll see you on the plane tomorrow, Miranda? I was hoping to catch up on some of our paperwork during the flight."

"Of course. Anything you need." She'd haul her laptop and every document and folder she possessed onto that flight tomorrow. Forget catching up on sleep. She would work every minute they were in the air.

"Goodnight, Miranda."

In silence, she and Violet watched Paul and Natalia walk away. When the elevator doors closed behind them, Violet rounded on her. "What the hell was that about?"

"Nothing."

"Nothing? I felt like your dad caught us sneaking in after curfew. Was he *mad* at you for going out?"

"Not mad. Disappointed. Which is so much worse. I shouldn't have gone."

She started toward the elevator, but Violet caught her arm. "Mira, why on earth would he be upset because you went out and had a little fun? You're an adult."

They got in the elevator. "He's got a good reason. That's all I can say," she said when Violet looked like she wanted to protest. When the elevator stopped, Violet put a hand against the door to hold it as Mira stepped out.

"Hey, this is not the same as before. You're not the girl from those headlines anymore." The look in Violet's eyes told Mira all she needed to know. Of course Violet had dug up whatever dirt was still out there.

"I—" she began but the words wouldn't form.

"Mira, chill. I've got your back. Go get some sleep." A moment later, Violet released the door and it slid closed.

The polished brass door threw Mira's reflection back in her face, another silent accusation. Hair a riotous mess, face pale, eyes red and watery. She certainly looked like the Mira from a lifetime ago, whom she thought she'd left behind for good.

Tomorrow she'd start fresh and banish that girl to history once and for all.

Singapore

Two days after that night in Melbourne, a photo showed up online of Will and the dark-haired girl Mira had seen him with at the party. Except they were in the lobby of his hotel, clearly *after* they'd dropped him off.

She'd been stunned breathless, but if she needed yet another reminder that the kiss had been a mistake, there it was. Yes, he'd kissed her. Yes, he'd asked her to go home with him. But he'd clearly found a quick replacement when she'd told him no.

The close call strengthened her resolution to steer clear of him whenever possible. It turned out to be quite easy to accomplish. With everything she had on her plate as the team moved on to Singapore, she didn't see him once. Maybe he was avoiding her, too. Despite his assurance that he considered her a friend, surely that aborted kiss and her subsequent freak-out had put an end to it. He'd obviously moved on. Time for her to do the same.

So it shocked her on the team's first full day in Singapore to get a text from Will an hour after the team press conference had ended.

His text was terse and urgent.

Meet me in the hotel lobby. I need help.

What could he possibly need her help with? If there was a problem with his suite, the hotel management would bend over backward to fix it. With the load-in and setup of the Lennox garage at the track still underway, it was a terrible time for her to be absent. But like it or not, Will was part of her job, and if he said he needed help, she had to go help him.

The cool air of the white marble lobby was a relief after the relentless humidity outside. She swiped the perspiration from her forehead as she scanned the room for him. Will was slouched in a leather armchair, scrolling on his phone. At the same moment she saw him, he looked up and spotted her. He smiled broadly. She'd done nothing but work since that night in Melbourne, determined to purge the moment from her memory through sheer exhaustion, but one flash of that devastating grin laid waste to all that.

She didn't return his smile, instead schooling her face into impassivity. She also attempted to avert her eyes as he unfolded his gorgeous body from his chair and advanced across the lobby toward her. She was a hot, sweaty mess after the walk from the track and there he was looking like he'd just stepped out of a Calvin Klein underwear ad. Except with more clothes. Women—and one or two men—stopped what they were doing to watch him, a god among mortals. He seemed oblivious to their reactions.

"What is it?" she asked when he was close enough. "What's wrong?"

"I need T-shirts," he said, his expression somber.

"What?"

"I need new T-shirts, so I'm going shopping and you're coming with me."

Closing her eyes, she shook her head in confusion. "You pulled me out of the garage setup to help you buy *T-shirts*? Are you serious?"

He waved a hand dismissively. "Those guys have set up the Lennox garage a million times before. They're fine."

"But what if something goes wrong? What if there's a question? What if—"

"They can text you. Like I did."

"Except that would be an *actual* emergency, not a T-shirt shortage!"

"My situation is definitely an emergency," Will said gravely. "Besides, I told you I was going to make sure you had fun on the road."

"Don't you have someone else you can call for this?" she finally asked in exasperation. When he just looked confused, she elaborated. "That girl? In Melbourne? There were pictures of you with her online."

He grinned, wide and shameless. "Keeping tabs on me, Mira?"

"Violet showed me." That was a lie, but he didn't have to know that.

He shrugged. "That was just Francesca. I think she's hooking up with Rikkard. Whatever. So—"

"You didn't sleep with her?"

The grin returned. "No, Mira. I didn't sleep with her."

Her face flamed with embarrassment and she looked down at her feet, unable to bear his undoubtedly smug expression. "I mean, it's not like it's any of my business—"

"I didn't."

"Okay."

"So . . . T-shirts? And then a fun surprise."

She was still discombobulated. He didn't sleep with her. Not that it mattered. But still, some tiny part of her was crowing in delight, despite her best efforts. If she was smart, she'd tell him to go buy his own stupid T-shirts and leave her alone. Spending time socially with him had already proved to be dangerous. There was plenty of other work to do back at the track, even if Will was right and the garage setup didn't strictly require her oversight. She should definitely turn around and leave.

But, that unfortunate kiss aside, she *liked* being his friend, and she was currently fighting a mighty wave of relief that he hadn't hooked up with someone else that night.

Giving a weary sigh, she acquiesced. "You owe me for this one."

He grinned, and she fought not to smile in return. She even put up a good show of complaining as he dragged her out of the hotel lobby.

"YOU PROMISED ME a fun surprise. So where is it?"

"Patience, Mira. And didn't I buy you a Starbucks?"

"That wasn't fun. That was a matter of survival." She sucked down the last of her iced latte, ignoring Will's smug smile. Thank God Starbucks was global. You could find them nearly everywhere, even at a mall in Singapore.

"Do you always consume caffeine with such enthusiasm?"

"Mmm . . . yes, always." Caffeine was her favorite food, ahead of cheese and ice cream. It was *that* kind of love.

"I'm not surprised. That explains a lot about you."

"So where are we going now?"

"Patience, I said."

"Give me a hint."

"You're displaying the opposite of patience right now."

"I don't like surprises."

"Also not surprising."

"Will—"

"There." He stopped walking and pointed straight ahead.

"A Ferris wheel?"

"That's not a Ferris wheel; it's an observation wheel. The Singapore Flyer: Asia's largest observation wheel! You can see panoramic views of the entire city from air-conditioned observation compartments."

"You sound like you're quoting a website."

"I am," he conceded. "I saw someone post about the best Singapore tourist attractions and this was at the top of the list."

"You're serious."

"A promise is a promise. Let's go."

When the ticket agent realized they were there with the Formula One race, they were immediately handed VIP passes and got an entire observation car to themselves, even though it could have easily fit twenty people.

"Do you do this in every city?" she asked as their car began its ascent.

"Buy T-shirts? No, I told you, this was an emergency."

She laughed. "No, not shopping. This. Touristy stuff."

"Nah. I spend most of time in my hotel suite and the gym."

"And here you were giving me a hard time for never getting out."

"See, getting out benefits me, too. Stop being so selfish, Mira."

"Okay, okay." She watched the view as they slowly rose over the harbor. "I admit, this isn't so bad."

He bumped his shoulder into hers. "No, it's not."

When had he gotten so close? They were sitting side by side on the bench in the middle of the compartment, his thigh so close to hers she could feel the warmth of his body. His hand was grasping the edge of the bench right next to hers, the outsides of their fingers so close she could swear sparks arced across the tiny gap.

What was it about him? She'd spent the past week avoiding him, reminding herself of all the reasons he was dangerous, and she'd nearly done it. Now, after an hour in his company, just sitting next to him was turning her into a bundle of raw nerves, her willpower forgotten, left down there on the ground as they rose into the air. Being alone in the compartment was a terrible idea. There was no one—no babbling tourists or screaming kids—to act as a buffer.

Taking a deep breath, she shot to her feet, leaving him on the bench in the center of the compartment, then moved to the rail along the glass wall. The sun was beginning to set. Beyond the skyline, the harbor stretched into the distance, lit up gold and orange.

"The view really is pretty," she said with forced brightness. "You can see for miles from up here."

Next she'd be making bland remarks about the weather, or asking him how his flight had been. But she had to say something to diffuse this aching want that was threatening to swallow her whole, and she couldn't, for the life of her, think of anything more sensible.

Behind her, she heard him get up and walk toward her. "Yes, it is."

Friends, friends, friends. She repeated the litany in her head to remind herself of what this was. They'd had fun today. Even buying his silly, overpriced T-shirts had been enjoyable. They couldn't screw it up with anything more.

"Oh hey, look, you can see the track from here." She pointed down at the twisting shape of the Marina Bay Street Circuit below them, roped off and cleared of traffic in preparation for tomorrow's practices.

"Looks so easy from up here," he said, leaning on the rail beside her.

"You just drive that, sixty-one times, really fast. Honestly, Will, I don't know why you guys get paid so much. Anybody could do it."

Will chuckled, close enough that their shoulders touched again. Did he know? He must realize that every time he touched her, her whole body flooded with heat. Even though their compartment was air-conditioned, it felt like the warm, humid Singapore air was pressing in on her. Her chest felt flushed, and the back of her neck felt damp.

Swallowing hard, she scanned the Singapore skyline, looking for something . . . anything . . . to focus on. "What's that island out there?" she asked, painfully aware of the hint of desperation in her voice.

He shrugged with that enviable physical grace of his. He looked cool and unbothered. "That's Sentosa Island. Have you never been? I figured your dad would have taken you."

"He never had time for stuff like that." *Yes, good. Let's talk about my dad.* That'll shut down this ridiculous flush of hormones.

"You'd have liked Sentosa Island as a kid. It's full of theme parks and stuff."

"You've been out there?"

He cleared his throat. "Um, yeah. My first year on the circuit. But not for the theme parks."

She chuckled. "Got it. If there was a bar involved, I can imagine the rest."

"Then you know more than me, because I blacked out for most of it. It was on a beach. There were some girls. After that, it's a blur. The hangover was brutal. And I had to race the next day."

"Wow."

"Yeah, I was an idiot."

They were silent for a minute, watching the city grow smaller beneath them. The sun sank lower in the sky, and lights had started to come on across the city. Below them, they reflected in rainbow colors on the waters of Marina Bay.

"Mira?"

She knew. The minute she heard him say her name in that particular low rumble, she knew what would come next. When she turned to look at him, his eyes were fixed on hers. Her heart was pounding so hard she was sure he could hear it, slamming against her ribs. Then he leaned in to kiss her. Except the kiss never came. He stopped, just a few inches away from her mouth. The setting sun brought out a riot of amber highlights in his dark hair that she'd never noticed before, and his blue eyes darkened dramatically. She blinked, unable to pull back or even breathe.

"Are we still not kissing?" he murmured.

His question rippled across her mouth, a seductive warm current of breath. Her lips tingled as if his were already on them. She knew exactly how he'd feel, how he'd taste. It would be good—*great*—because she'd kissed him before, and now she knew how he kissed, and that was a hard thing to forget. Fingers curling into the metal railing, she fought the impulse to lean into him.

"Yes," she whispered when she could gather her wits enough to force the word out. Wait . . . "I mean, no. No, we're not."

His gaze dropped to her mouth and he held there, still just inches away. Then he tipped his head to the side and let out a sigh, one that also washed across her mouth, a hot, tantalizing promise of what she could have if she just leaned forward the tiniest amount. Her muscles tensed and she felt herself doing it, like he was a magnet and she was helplessly drawn to him.

"That's too bad," he said.

She felt his fingers brush against her hip, across to her lower back. "What are you doing?" The words came out as a whisper.

"Not kissing you." He flattened his hand, his palm pressing against her lower back. Her thighs clenched and she stopped breathing, imagining the heat of his palm everywhere else, smoothing over every inch of her skin. Maybe if he just touched her enough she could stop *thinking* so much.

His lips curved into a wicked smile, and his hand slid lower, over the curve of her ass and down to the back of her thigh. She inhaled and it came back out in a slow, shuddering breath. His eyes darkened and his fingers tightened, fisting the back of her skirt. She'd worn a skirt today because it was so hot and humid, but now she felt half-naked, like any second he could slide his hand under the hem and up between her thighs.

Oh, god, she wanted that. She wanted him to press her back against the railing and lift her skirt. She wanted to slide her own hands up under that stupid overpriced, soft-as-sin T-shirt of his and feel the heat of his skin.

"This is . . ."

His eyes dropped to her mouth. "Still not a kiss. Right?" His eyes shot back up to hers. "Unless you want it to be?"

Yes, please, just kiss me so I can stop fighting with myself.

But she didn't say that. She didn't say anything at all, unable to push him away or give herself permission to give in. He watched her face for another moment, as if he could see the war she was waging inside. Then he sighed, and his hand dropped away.

Will leaned against the railing, his expression unreadable.

"You tell me when, Mira," he said, his voice rough.

She was shaking as she turned back to the railing, biting her lip to keep herself from doing just that.

When they came down, the night was still young and Will was hungry to keep Mira near him. They were still too close to the track, where she might suddenly decide she was needed for work, so he kept talking, distracting her, as he steered her over the bay through the Helix Bridge, the twisting steel aglow with blue and purple lights, curving over their heads. From there, a path took them along the edge of the marina, the lights of the city glittering on the water as it grew dark.

As the sun set, the temperature finally cooled a bit, although the night air was still tropical. A breeze rippled across the water, blowing Mira's hair across her face, and the scent of mandarin and clove shampoo drifted over to him.

"So the last time you were in Singapore . . ." she began, then trailed off.

He glanced over at her. "Yeah?"

"You got so drunk, you don't remember it? You'd just been signed to a Formula One team," she said in disbelief. "I don't get it."

"Ah, yeah," he said, shrugging in discomfort. He'd been such an idiot back then, playing fast and loose with the chance of a lifetime. That was a mistake he only intended to make once. "My head was not in a great place."

When she just kept watching him in silence, he sighed. She wasn't letting him off that easy.

"So you know my family is . . . well, they're . . ."

"Rich?"

He sputtered a laugh. "Well, yes, they're that, too. But I just meant they're . . . uptight. They don't approve of me."

Her brow furrowed in a way he was rapidly finding adorable. "But, why? There are maybe thirty people on earth who can do what you do."

"Careful, Mira, you're starting to sound impressed."

She chuckled, nudging him with her shoulder. He nudged back. Whether she was aware of it or not, she wasn't shying away from touching him like before. That had to count as progress. He could still feel the shape of her thigh under his hand. Now it was seared into his brain, and he wanted more.

The path emptied out into a plaza, so they kept walking, skirting the marina, and getting farther and farther away from the track, the hotel, and all the other reminders of the real world.

"Come on," she said. "Tell me what happened."

"Well, to start, unlike you, I was rubbish at school. It was all so bloody boring. The only thing I was really good at, the only thing I *really* wanted to do, was racing. And that was fine when I was just racing karts as a kid. But I was supposed to leave all that behind when I grew up. Get serious, go to uni, go to work in the family firm."

"I'm guessing that wasn't part of your plan?"

He scoffed. "I didn't even try for uni. I'm the first person in my family since the Norman Conquest without a university degree."

"I'm pretty sure they hadn't invented college yet."

He chuckled. "Maybe not, but let me tell you, as soon as they built unis, the Hawleys sent their spawn. My family owns a bank. Did you know that?"

"I heard something about it. Like Citibank?"

"Not exactly. There's only one branch of Hawley and Sons, near Temple Bar, and it doesn't take new clients."

"So who banks there?"

He scoffed. "The same dusty English families that have been banking there since time immemorial. Hawley and Sons is about *tradition*. Everything done just as it would have been in the time of George the fucking Third."

"And then you came along."

"And then I came along. I swear, I can't even breathe in that place. It smells like a tomb." Just thinking about the mahogany and velvet interior of Hawley and Sons made him feel like his skin was too small for him. If he'd had to spend his whole life in that place it would have driven him mad.

"Yeah, I can't picture you in a place like that at all."

"Neither could I, and thankfully I had options. When I landed a spot in Hansbach's young drivers program, the parents were willing to give me a year or so to get it out of my system. I mean, most drivers don't make it. They figured I'd wash out with the masses and get on with real life."

"But you didn't."

"Nope. I got signed to Hansbach's Formula One team instead." He paused for a moment, remembering when he'd gone home to tell them about the contract, stupidly thinking they'd be happy. It was only the biggest news of his life, the best thing that had *ever* happened to him. Dumb kid that he'd been, he thought it would prove to them that he was doing the right thing, that he was in the right place. It hadn't even occurred to him that they wouldn't see it as good news.

Inhaling deeply, he flashed her a forced smile. "They were, to put it mildly, not happy. Huge bloody row. Lots of horrible things said. You get the idea."

"And they still haven't come around?"

"I have no idea. I didn't speak to them again for years. Only started again recently and as little as I can manage."

She reached out, laying a hand on his arm. "I'm so sorry."

He glanced down in surprise at her small hand on his forearm. For so long people had been judging him on all the bad things he'd done, he wasn't used to someone feeling sorry for him.

"Look, before you start feeling too much sympathy for me, let's be clear. Nobody's to blame for the shit I did that year except me. But . . . yeah, I was mad. If I couldn't be good, then I'd be really, *really* bad, you know? And now? Fuck it. They know where to find me, if they care, which they don't."

"That's sad, Will."

"Hey, what did I just say? No pitying me. I'm fine."

"If you say so."

He threw his hands up in exasperation. "I am!"

"Will—"

"Are you hungry?" he asked abruptly, stopping in the middle of the sidewalk and turning to face her. "I'm starving."

"Well . . ." She paused considering. "Yeah, I am, actually. Do you think there's anything open around here?"

They'd wandered into the business district, surrounded by glass skyscrapers, all empty this long after the workday had ended.

"Wait . . ." He pulled out his phone and searched the map. His memory was fuzzy, probably because he'd been drunk the last time he was here, but he remembered someplace amazing and he thought it was close by. "Aha. I was right. This way."

Another few blocks and they were there.

"What is this place?"

"It's a night market. Basically a market for street food vendors."

"Street food?" Mira asked dubiously. "Like meat on a stick?"

"Yeah, but the *best* meat on a stick. Come on."

They followed the smell of grilling meat to a bunch of satay stands ringing the outside of the pavilion. He placed an order at the one that had the most people clustered in front of it and passed her a skewer.

"God, that's amazing," she moaned after taking a bite of charred chicken.

"See? Meat on a stick can be good."

"*So* good."

His eyes snagged on her mouth as she licked sauce from her thumb. *Don't think about her lips*, he lectured himself. *And absolutely do not think about her tongue.*

Inside, the stalls sold everything from Japanese udon to Indian curries to Malay fried rice.

"What do you want?"

"I don't know. There are so many things, and it all smells so good." Just then someone passed them balancing a plastic tray with a huge steaming bowl of soup. The scent trailing behind him was unreal.

"That one," they said in unison.

The man behind the counter, burly and dressed in a rumpled white chef's smock with the sleeves rolled up to reveal thick forearms roped with muscles, jerked his chin at them. "Soup?"

Will pointed at the guy who'd passed them. "Two of those."

"You got it, boss."

The chef went to work, dumping noodles into two bowls, then vegetables and a handful of greens, before ladling steaming broth over everything. With a pair of tongs, he scooped various things out of an assortment of bins spread in front of him—a fat white fish fillet, a cluster of prawns, some octopus.

At his side, Mira sucked in a breath and grabbed at his arm. "None of that."

"None of what?"

She closed her eyes and shuddered. "That. With the suckers. *Nope.*"

"The octopus? Are you allergic?"

"Phobic," she spit out through clenched teeth.

"You have a phobia of octopuses? Octopi? Whatever?"

Her eyes were still squeezed shut. "Tentacles."

"You have a phobia of *tentacles?*" He started to laugh, but when he saw the look on her face, he stifled it. He looked back to the chef and shrugged. "No octopus?"

The chef sighed deeply and shook his head. "Your loss."

It was crowded, but they wound their way through the forest of small tables nearby to an empty one. Will began poking through the assortment of condiments on the table.

"What's that?" Mira asked.

"No idea."

"Is it spicy? I love spicy."

"Looks spicy." He passed the bottle to her and she sprinkled some on her finger to taste. He kept his eyes on his soup so he wouldn't stare at her sucking on her finger *again.*

"So a tentacle phobia? Really?"

"Just the . . ." She waved her fingers. "And their little . . ." She made a sucking sound. "Just . . . nope."

"Wow, something that intimidates Miranda Wentworth."

She looked up from spooning hot chili paste into her bowl. "If you laugh at me, I will strangle you."

He bit his lips to hold back his laugh and shook his head. "I am absolutely, definitely not going to laugh at you."

"Oh, and I'm sure you don't have any embarrassing little personal quirks?"

"Not a one." He grinned, nudging her foot with his under the table. "You know I'm perfect."

"Very funny. Everybody's got something. Now you know my big embarrassing hang-up. You have to tell me one of yours."

"I don't have any phobias."

"Fine. Something else. Something that embarrasses you."

Leaning back in his tiny chair, he looked up at the ceiling fans high overhead, their lazy spinning barely stirring the humid air. "There's nothing, really."

Across the table, she narrowed her eyes at him. "You're lying. I can tell."

He huffed, then closed his eyes. He couldn't believe he was about to tell someone about this. That he was about to tell *Mira* about this.

"I have delicate inner ears."

She blinked. "What?"

He waved a hand beside his head. "My inner ear canals. They're sensitive to everything."

"Seriously? Your inner ears?"

"See? That's why I didn't want to tell you. I'm a Formula One driver, nerves of steel and all that shit. I'm not supposed to have fragile ear canals."

"I promise, I'm not laughing at your ears." She was totally laughing at him; she was just fighting to hold it back. "So what happens with your ears?"

"They react to everything, especially my diet. Salt, alcohol. It makes me prone to dizziness the next day. That's why I was such a mess my first season with Hansbach. The drinking was bad enough on its own, but the next day, my ears were a disaster. Every time I went into a tight turn, I'd get dizzy."

"Delicate inner ears," Mira mused, fishing a prawn out of her soup with chopsticks and pointing it at him. "See, I knew there was more to you than meets the eye."

"If you tell anyone, I'll have to kill you."

She looked up and met his eyes, a smile playing at the corner of her mouth. "I won't breathe a word. After all, you know one of my secrets, too."

He stared back at her until the air between them grew thick with tension. "Tell me another one," he murmured, nearly a whisper in the midst of a hundred conversations surrounding them.

Her throat moved as she swallowed and dropped her eyes. "Maybe we should just eat."

21

"**D**o you know where you're going?" Mira asked. They'd been talking while walking, not really paying attention to where they were, and now nothing around them looked familiar. She couldn't even see the Singapore Flyer anymore and that thing was huge.

Will held up his phone in front of them. "No, but Google does. The hotel is over that way."

Mira scowled, glancing up and down the sidewalk. "Are you sure? Because this is a temple, Will. Like, an actual temple. I don't remember a temple near our hotel."

While Will looked at the map on his phone she marveled at the long, low, ornate building. It was dark, but through the gate, she could make out a courtyard surrounded with painted columns and bushes full of pink flowers. The rest of the street was lined with two- and three-story buildings, with restaurants and shops on the ground floors and brightly colored shuttered windows above. It buzzed with energy as people had dinner or enjoyed the balmy night, and here in the middle of it all was this beautiful temple.

"I had no idea Singapore was so great. Even if we're lost in it."

"We're not lost. Just trust me," he said. "I mean, trust my phone. This way."

"That's not a street, that's an alley."

"Where's your sense of adventure, Mira?"

The alley spilled into another street, which was really just a slightly wider alley. On one side were the backsides of all the restaurants behind them. On the other was just . . . a wall. If she was sensible, she'd head back out to the main street, order an Uber, and go straight back to the hotel. But for reasons she couldn't explain to herself, she kept following him. A stairway appeared on the right, cut into the wall.

He stepped back and waved her in front of him. "This way."

"Are you sure?"

"Yes. Sort of."

She shot him a dubious look as she started up the wood steps. The staircase turned once and then abruptly opened out into a small park a story above the street below.

Her breath left her in a rush when she saw it. "Oh."

The park was tiny, just a space carved out of a hillside, shaped by the irregular intersection of a few streets, but it was lushly landscaped, with winding paths disappearing around explosions of greenery, and wooden benches every few feet. She could hear the city traffic nearby, but filtered through the low canopy of tree branches, it felt very far away. Little bulbs were strung through the trees, providing the only light, and it was *magical*.

"It's beautiful."

Mira was suddenly aware that for all the traveling she'd done with her father in years past, she hadn't actually seen much of the world. Airports, hotels, and racetracks. That had been her experience of most countries.

"This is fun," she said abruptly.

Will turned to look at her. "What is?"

She shrugged, suddenly feeling embarrassed, like she'd said too much. "Just . . . this. You were right. I never saw any of the places I visited. Not the Ferris wheels, or the markets, or the temples, or the parks . . ."

He rubbed a hand over the back of his neck, giving her a smile she'd almost describe as bashful, if it was coming from anyone else but Will. "I'm having fun, too. For the first time in ages."

"So Singapore is like, the first real city for both of us."

"I guess it is."

"Well, now you're back in Formula One, so you'll have all those parties and stuff. I'm sure that's fun?"

He shrugged, looking up at the trees overhead. "I guess. What about you? You like the Formula One glamour?"

"It's not really my thing, you know?" She hopped up on one of the benches, walking along the edge like a tightrope. The warm night air rustled through the trees overhead and the string lights shuddered, making the shadows dance around them. "I guess I'm just too uptight."

He scoffed. "No, you're not."

She stopped in surprise and swiveled to face him. "How do you know? You barely know me."

He stopped too, turning to face her. Up here on the bench, she was a little taller than him. The shadows of leaves danced across his face, those cheekbones, the sharp angle of his jaw. The breeze ruffled through his dark hair, black as night in this light. She sighed internally. He was *so* so pretty. She could stare at his beautiful face for the rest of her life.

Slowly, he reached up, snagging a curl blowing across her face and tucking it behind her ear, and her chest fluttered in response. "Come on, now. That's hardly true anymore. I know you. We're friends, right?"

She sucked in a breath and held it. His fingers lingered, tracing the edge of her ear, then he ran a fingertip down the side of her neck. Her skin felt like it burst into flames in the wake. Whatever this was, it felt like a whole lot more than "friends."

It was a hunger, a yearning, that she was sure he felt, too. Suddenly, they felt very alone, and real life felt very far away, like the world had stopped turning and had paused in its orbit, just waiting for him to kiss her. Or for her to kiss him. Like the next tick of the clock, the next beat of her heart, depended on their lips meeting.

The moment of silence dragged out like it had on the Ferris wheel—him staring up at her, her staring down at him. He didn't move to close the gap this time either.

His hand came back up to her neck, then he slowly ran his fingers through her hair.

"I like it like this," he murmured.

Her eyelids fluttered down, meeting his gaze. "I know you do."

"Did you leave it down for me?"

"Maybe. A little," she conceded on a whisper, finally admitting it to herself. She'd declared defeat after Melbourne, unable to summon the will to straighten it every day. It was about saving time, she'd insisted to herself. It had nothing to do with Will's face when he looked at her like this.

"Are you *sure* we're not kissing? Because I really want to kiss you right now."

She wanted it more than she wanted to draw her next breath. She let out an unsteady sigh. "No, I'm not sure, and that's the problem."

Please, she begged silently. *Choose it for me so I don't have to.*

He reached for her hip with his free hand, then lazily dragged it up her side, nudging her arm up until her hand was resting on his shoulder. Her fingers flexed, digging in. His other hand ran through her hair again before coming to rest on the side of her face. His thumb traced the bottom edge of her lip and she leaned in to him, eyes half-closed. "Maybe you should try it again," he said softly. "Just to be sure."

The dark and the trees and the dancing lights were making her feel lightheaded. It was hard to remember her own name, never mind why she shouldn't be giving in to the impulse to kiss him. So she stopped fighting it, and suddenly gravity seemed to do the rest, the strength of her desire pulling her body inexorably into his.

She let her eyes slide closed, quieting the last reminders of the real world, and a second later, her lips were on his. In the days since that kiss in Melbourne, she'd almost convinced herself it hadn't been as magical, as electric, as she'd thought.

She was wrong. This was, hands down, one of the best kisses of her life. Those lips felt as good as they looked, and when his tongue traced her bottom lip, she opened to it, letting it sweep in and stroke her own. The breathy moan that escaped her throat sounded loud in the quiet of the tiny park.

Will's hand tightened on her hip, and her fingers slid up to grip the back of his neck. She wanted to climb off the bench and wrap herself around him, feel him wrap himself around her.

His fingers slipped under the edge of her shirt, and his palm settled against her bare back.

When his teeth nipped gently at her bottom lip, she groaned, pressing closer to him. His hand slid down to the back of her thigh once more, urging her forward. And so she leaned in to him, letting him pull her body against his and lift her clean off her feet.

Slowly he lowered her to the ground. Her body slid down the length of his, his mouth never leaving hers. As her chest slid along his and her thighs pressed against his, a moan escaped her and disappeared into his mouth.

His kiss turned hungry, his teeth dragging along her sensitive bottom lip. His hands were on her hips, then sliding up to her waist, just under the hem of her shirt again, hot against her bare skin. It was all too much . . . too much heat and need and wanting. She felt like nothing but exposed nerves, and every place he touched her flared to life. All she could do was hang on to him, arms wrapped around his hard shoulders to steady herself.

"You are just . . ." he muttered as his lips left hers for an instant. But she didn't get to hear what she was as he turned his head and kissed her again, from a different angle, licking at her lips, at her tongue.

His hand was on her rib cage, his palm like a brand on her skin. Then he was cradling her breast and she arched up under him. It was so good, but not enough. She wanted more. Her nipples were so hard they ached, and when his thumb scraped across one over the thin lace of her bra, it made her feel near to exploding. A persistent ache pulsed between her thighs. His hard body pressed to hers wasn't enough to ease it. Only one thing would.

He shifted his weight, sliding one of his thighs between hers, and suddenly he was pressed right against where she needed him most. She gasped as he broke from her mouth, kissing across her cheek and down the side of her neck. She gasped again, her breathing ragged as his thumb eased down the edge of her bra and slid across her bare nipple.

God yes, that's what she wanted. His hands on her body. Everywhere.

"Oh . . ." she sighed into the warm night air. His thigh pressed into her and she shuddered.

"Mira . . ." he moaned into her shoulder.

Somewhere far away, something buzzed. It stopped then started again. At first it seemed like one thread of the distant city noises, but gradually it pierced her awareness. Not the city. Her phone, somewhere from the muffled depths of her bag.

Will's fingers dove into her hair, holding her face close to his. "Ignore it." He kissed her again and she almost—almost— gave in, but now that her phone had reminded her of the real world, it came crashing back in like a tidal wave. Work. Will. This thing they weren't supposed to be doing.

"I can't." She leaned back, untangling herself from him.

She reached for her bag, but his hand closed over hers. "Mira . . ."

She pulled her hand from under his. "This is too complicated. I can't do this with you."

"Why not?"

"Because I can't do this to him. Not again."

"Do this to who?"

"My dad!" she shouted. "Okay? I can't do this to my dad again."

Will blinked in confusion. "What does he have to do with anything?"

"Everything."

He ran a hand through his hair in frustration. "Look, I know it's tricky, you working for your dad and me a driver for the team, but—"

She shook her head forcefully, the last of the day's magic vanishing. "No, it's not tricky. It's impossible. This is impossible."

"Mira, we're both adults here. So your dad might disapprove? Fuck that."

"You don't understand."

"So explain it to me!" His shout sounded loud in the quiet of the park.

She said nothing, because she couldn't explain it, not without telling him everything.

"I'm getting a car back," she murmured, swiping to unlock her phone. It lit up with missed messages and calls. Her stomach plunged. Harry, Omar, Ian, Violet, Dad . . . "Fuck."

"What?"

"Something's happened at the track and I wasn't there because I was here, with you, the one place I am not supposed to be."

She turned to run, but he caught her by the arm.

"Mira, stop. I'm sure it's fine—"

She jerked her arm free. "It's not fine! This is what happens when . . ." She stopped and swallowed hard. "I don't think we should hang out anymore."

He blinked. "What? Now you can't be my friend, either?"

That forced a scoff of humorless laughter free from her throat, thinking of the last few intoxicating minutes . . . his mouth on hers, his hands on her body, his leg pressed between her thighs. "Come on, Will. This isn't exactly a friendship."

"No," he snapped. "It's a little more than friendship, if you'd quit lying to yourself about it."

"Because of course, it's all about you getting laid."

He snapped back like she'd slapped him. That was a low blow and she knew it. But she was panicking, and she just needed him to stop—stop pursuing her, stop tempting her—because she'd very nearly given in to him just now, and that was the one thing she couldn't do.

"Sure," he finally said, throwing his hands in the air. "Because that's who I am, right, Mira? You're no better than all those bloody reporters. You made up your mind about me before you ever knew me."

The sting of that lodged deep. But he was right—she had judged him before she ever really knew him. She realized she was wrong now, but it didn't matter. Let him believe that if it put an end to this.

"This is really for the best, Will. You don't want to get involved with me anyway. Trust me."

She couldn't handle looking him in the eye right now, so she didn't. Turning away before he could see her eyes glass over with tears, she ran the rest of the way across the park, out to the nearby street, where she could call a car, get back to work, and leave fantasies behind her, where they belonged.

Barcelona,
Spain

As Mira made her way across the blacktop of the paddock, it almost felt like the soles of her shoes were melting into it. Spain was in the middle of an unprecedented heat wave. The sun beat down relentlessly on the asphalt, and the breeze, as hot as a gust from an open oven, had her credentials dancing at the end of the lanyard around her neck. Her hair stuck to the back of her neck like a hot, wet towel.

At least here they had the comfort of their custom mobile facilities that traveled with them to the European races, and she personally thought Lennox's were the best on the circuit. Lennox's impressive two-story glossy-blue structure had the garage below, offices above, and a race command center off to the side. Despite its size, the whole thing came apart like LEGO bricks, to be trucked to the next race. Their hospitality center was even larger, with a glass-fronted dining room and a roof deck.

She slipped into the race command center as quietly as possible, exhaling as the cool air hit her. Even though she'd come here to find him, her stomach twisted with anxiety when she spotted her father puzzling over a snarl of data on one of the monitors. It had been three weeks since that disaster in Singapore and she still felt like she was trying to make up for her fuckup.

During the garage load-in in Singapore, one of the massive equipment carts had come loose from its rolling dolly, pinning one of the guys from the pit crew against a wall. In the end, Ben hadn't been too badly injured, but he'd had to go to the hospital for X-rays and stitches. It was chaos and no one knew how to reach his wife back in England. That's when Miranda's absence had been noticed. She should have been there, pulling up Ben's emergency contact info and calling his wife herself. Instead, she'd been off in some park, kissing Will, and forgetting every single other thing, while half a dozen people were trying to track her down, including her dad.

She'd felt sick with mortification. And she'd seen it, that doubt in her father's eyes again. Seeing it was bad enough. It was worse to know he was right to doubt. She'd fucked up. Again.

She'd spent the rest of Singapore and all of Shanghai leaving the track just long enough to sleep, determined to put herself back on course. What happened with Will was a mistake. The accident with Ben had proved that.

Finally, she forced herself to join her father. "Hey, Dad."

His eyes flicked briefly to her and then back to the bank of monitors. Things had felt like they were getting better, like maybe their relationship was getting back to where it had been before. But since that night in Singapore, he'd been brusque and all business with her. It killed her a little bit every time.

"What are you looking at?" she asked.

"Trying to solve Will's issue of the clutch temperature at the start."

"It spikes when he's idling for that long, right?"

"Exactly. I need Harry to come look at these temperatures with me and he's not answering on headset."

"I can go find him," she offered.

"I can ask Omar to send him over—"

"No, let me go," she insisted, and hurried away before he could protest again. If she just kept her head down and kept working, she'd erase Singapore.

When she reached the garage, both cars were surrounded by mechanics, but Harry was not with them. "Omar, have you seen Harry? Paul needs him."

"Getting lunch," Omar said without looking up.

Out in the paddock, the sun was at its apex, and the strip of asphalt lined with team facilities was crowded with people. She was passing the Deloux team headquarters when she spotted *him*. During the past few weeks on the road, she'd managed to duck out of the way whenever he popped up, so while she'd seen him several times, he'd never seen her. Until today.

He was coming out of the Deloux team headquarters and paused at the top of a short set of metal steps. At that very moment, all the people around her suddenly evaporated, one cluster of guys peeling off to the left and another group of people stopping to duck into the Hansbach offices. Suddenly she was all alone in the middle of the blacktop, too far away from anything she could hide behind for cover.

His eyes scanned the crowd, passed her by, and then jerked back. Her stomach bottomed out and she froze. No matter how adept she'd become at avoiding him, especially since the hotel lobby in Bahrain, she'd known this would happen eventually. She'd practiced it in her mind, and nearly convinced herself that she'd be able to put up a good front.

But practicing it in her mind turned out to be useless when he was standing twenty feet away and looking directly at her.

If he came over, if he spoke to her, she wasn't sure how she'd handle it. Sweat beaded on her forehead, even though her skin felt clammy. Her heart was pounding so hard she could almost hear it.

Then the corner of his mouth twitched, almost a smirk, if he'd cared enough to make it one, and he looked away, already dismissing her from his notice. He jogged down the steps and disappeared into the crowd.

She couldn't see him anymore, but she still couldn't make herself move. Her lungs refused to fill with air, sucking the blood from every other part of her body until her hands and feet began to tingle. The constantly shifting sea of people was slowly whited out by the bright sunlight until she could hardly see anything at all.

"Mira?"

The familiar voice echoed through the roar of her pulse.

"Hey, what's wrong?"

She blinked and his face swam into focus in front of her. It was Will, ducking down to look at her. She'd managed to avoid him since Singapore and now he was there in front of her, exactly when she didn't want him to be.

"I . . ." But her lungs were still trapped in a vacuum. Panic flooded in hot on the heels of everything else she'd been feeling. She dragged in one thin, wheezing breath, which only made her feel more lightheaded. The intense sun and sweltering heat pressed in on her from all sides like a suffocating blanket.

"Mira, you're about to pass out."

He was right. Her head felt disconnected from her body and everything had gone white, like an overexposed photo.

"Here, sit down." He nudged her backward, stumbling, until her calves hit a set of fold-out steps leading up to someone's portable office. She sank down on the hot metal. "Head between your knees," Will directed, a gentle hand on the back of her head.

With her face in the darkness of her lap, things began to clear. His fingers gently swept her hair to the side and she sighed in relief as air hit the back of her neck. The horrible, pounding, racing heartbeat slowed and quieted. Her vision came back. Feeling returned to her hands and feet. When the swell of nausea had subsided, she raised her head. Will was crouched in front of her, worry filling his face.

"Will you be okay while I go for help?"

She reached out to grab his arm before he could rise. "I don't need help."

He brushed a lock of hair off her face, clammy with sweat. "You're sick."

"Not sick. It was a panic attack. Just give me a minute. I'll be okay."

"A panic attack?"

"I've had one before." A handful of times. It had been years. Mortification made her cheeks flame, and she closed her eyes against it. Jesus, one look from that asshole and she reacted like that?

"Let me go get your dad."

"No!" Her eyes flew open and she grabbed for him again. The last thing she needed was for her dad to get dragged back into this. Especially not now, when she was still trying to dig herself back out of a hole. "I'm really okay. I just need a second for my head to clear."

Will shifted his weight to the balls of his feet and examined her skeptically. "What caused it?"

She shook her head. "Nothing."

"Come on, Mira. That was not nothing. Tell me what's going on."

"Just a ghost from my past. He caught me by surprise."

His eyes narrowed as he pieced it together. "The guy? He's *here*?" He swiveled around to look, but thankfully, there was no one for him to see. He was long gone.

"I guess I wasn't as ready to deal with it as I thought."

"Who is it?" His voice sounded tight, angry.

Her voice was still shaky, but she forced a small smile. "No way am I telling you, Hawley."

He blew out a frustrated breath. "Are you sure you don't want me to get your dad?"

"Absolutely sure. I have to find Harry and—"

"Bullshit. You're going back to the Lennox offices and you're going to get something to drink and you're going to sit down in the air con."

"God, you're bossy."

He put the back of his hand on her forehead and examined her face again, as though a panic attack might've caused a spontaneous concussion. "Right now I am. There's no way you're heading back into that crowd when you nearly passed out a minute ago. Come on, I'll walk you back."

Gently, she brushed his hand away from her face. "Why are you being so nice to me?"

"Why wouldn't I be nice to you?" His eyes were as blue as the heat-baked sky behind him as he scowled at her. His thin blue Lennox polo shirt pulled taut across his shoulders and biceps. A few dark strands of his hair stuck to his forehead, and she clenched her hands against the impulse to brush them away.

"Because I yelled at you the last time I saw you. I'm sorry."

He dropped his eyes to the tarmac and caught his lower lip in his teeth. "You were defending your boundaries. Don't ever apologize for that."

She sighed. "Will—"

Abruptly, he lifted his head and she was looking straight into those eyes, fringed by black lashes. She blinked, unable to look away. "Look, Mira," he said, brushing his fingertips along the side of her hand. "I like you. That's no secret. And I can't seem to stay away from you. I want you. I guess that's no secret, either. I know you have your reasons to stay away from me, and I will respect them. But you should know that's how I feel."

Oh.

She could like him. She could like him so very much. But the last fifteen minutes had reminded her why she shouldn't. *Couldn't.*

"Thank you." Those words felt entirely insufficient, but they were all she had to offer.

"I mean it."

"Where are you coming from?" She was desperate to change the subject before her heart said something her brain didn't approve of.

"I had a press event with Velocity. Heading over to suit up now." Velocity was one of his sponsors, a huge sportswear company. Will had done an ad for them a year ago—a stark black-and-white photo featuring him in a pair of loose-fitting Velocity basketball shorts and nothing else—that had become a minor viral internet sensation even before the buzz of this season had started. She *might* have it secretly bookmarked in her browser. "Lucky for you, I saw you just before you went down."

"Lucky for me." Her voice was far too weak, far too wistful for her liking. "You'd better go. Dad will want you there early."

"Not without you." Will stood and reached a hand down to her. "Come on. You need to get out of this sun."

She took his hand, trying her best to ignore the warmth, the tingles, the desire to grab hold and not let go. He pulled her to her feet and she released him as soon as she was steady.

"You sure you're okay?"

Taking a deep breath, she lifted her chin, determined to sweep that pesky ghost of her past back into the dark, dusty corners of her memories where he belonged. And to keep this flesh and blood temptation from her present at a safe distance where *he* belonged. "Yes. I'm just fine."

23

Suzuka,
Japan

Will felt like his body was a live wire. As his success grew, so did his nerves. Controlling the car was immensely complicated, requiring constant analysis of data and tiny adjustments, all while processing race stats and instructions from Tae through the headset and reacting accordingly. And now that podium finishes were within his grasp, the stakes were that much higher. A difficult drive now had so much more riding on it.

Thanks to the finishes he'd been pulling, the Lennox team ranking was the highest it had been in years. Today's race was number six, not quite a third of the season. A win today might finally shift the narrative away from the "troubled bad boy seeking redemption" to an acknowledgment of his talent.

Which was why, as he suited up for the Japanese Grand Prix, the last thing he should have been thinking about was Mira. But ever since he'd caught her in the middle of that freak-out in Barcelona, he'd been unable to stop turning it over in his mind. The drawback of having a driver's pathological focus was an inability to let things go.

So the guy from her past was on the circuit. Did he know him? He kept flipping through the hundreds of people traveling the circuit, wondering who it could be, but the possibilities were endless. If she'd wanted him to know, she'd have told him, right? It was why he'd never snooped through her socials to figure it out for himself. He hated it when people thought they knew everything about him from the few photos of him online. Mira deserved her privacy. Which meant he should leave it alone and move on.

She wasn't even his business, anyway. She'd drawn a line in the sand and firmly pushed him back to the other side of it, which rankled, but really, what was he hoping for instead?

Yeah, he was attracted to her . . . an attraction bordering on obsession, if he was being honest. Yes, she was fun to talk to and hang out with. But what would happen if they slept together? She was his boss's daughter, so some casual sex, while enjoyable, would be seriously awkward the next day, and every day after that. And if she wanted more than casual? Was he really ready to declare himself someone's boyfriend? *Mira's* boyfriend? That was a little terrifying, especially if it didn't work out. The team, the race season, his entire career might suffer if things went south.

Not that it mattered what he wanted or didn't want. Since that day in Barcelona, she'd gone back to keeping her distance from him. He'd caught no more than a glimpse of her in Japan. Which was fine, because he was supposed to be focused on other things. Like driving.

As he climbed into the car, a horde of track workers buzzing around him, he resolved to leave all the unproductive, distracting thoughts of Mira back in the paddock where they belonged. There was too much to accomplish out on the track.

"Okay, Will," Tae said into his earpiece. "You've got a pole position. No need to blow it all at the outset. Drive steady and you'll have no problem with this field."

Will begged to differ. Maybe he didn't *need* to drive the ride of his life to win today, but that wouldn't keep him from doing it. He would leave nothing on the starting line, nothing in the tank, nothing on the tires.

"Tae, how many races have we done together?"

"Yeah, yeah. Just nod your head and say yes so the engineers stop crawling up my ass."

"Yes, sir. I'll do just what you said, sir."

Tae laughed uproariously as Will fired the engine and made his way out onto the track.

As he took his place on the pole, the other cars assembling on the grid behind him, he settled into the zone. The whine of the engine felt like part of his bloodstream, keeping him alive breath to breath. Time slowed as the lights went on, one by one, till all five were lit. They filled his vision as he brought the engine up to the proper revs, held it steady, and prepared to launch.

As the lights went out, he dumped the clutch and the engine's wail hit the stratosphere. The g-force pinned him to the back of his seat as he rocketed into the first turn complex. Sensing other drivers nipping at his heels, he danced the car through the turn then got early on the throttle exiting Turn Two. Running wide to the edge of the track, he shut the door on everyone crawling up his ass. Nobody was getting around him today. Seeing a gradually widening gap behind him, he smiled to himself as he sliced through the esses. Perfect start. The rest of the field would be hard-pressed to catch him now.

An hour later, the last pit stop approached, and he was almost ten seconds ahead of the three drivers closest to him. An easy win was nearly in his grasp.

"Box, box, box," Tae said in his ear, calling him in for a pit stop.

Thanks to Harry's ruthless drilling, this pit stop was perfect, and then he was back out on the track, screaming into the straight. Tae fed him a steady stream of stats, letting him know exactly how the rest of the race looked out on the track. Everything was going according to plan.

"I've got it, then," he said into the headset.

"Not so fast. McKnight's still up there."

"But we were ahead on strategy."

"They haven't boxed yet. Currently he's in first."

"But he has to pit."

"We think they're trying to do a two stop and make those tires last. He's pitted twice to everybody else's three. They've outlasted everyone so far."

Brody McKnight had been around forever—Formula One for a while, Indy Car, Le Mans, reserve driver for a few teams—he'd been all over. It was kind of surprising he'd landed a Formula One drive again this season, at his age. He'd never been in serious contention for the world championship, and had only found himself on the podium a handful of times, and the odds were against him seeing one again. If he'd skipped his final pit stop, he must have had a remarkably good day and seen a podium finish in his grasp. That meant running the end of the race on worn-out tires, one of which could blow at any second. It was a hell of a long shot, but it's not like Brody was going to get on the damned podium any other way.

Fine, Brody wanted to drive cautious, save his tires, and spare a pit stop? Let's see how he managed that with Will Hawley crawling up his ass. He laid on the throttle, letting the whine of the engine and the scream of fresh tires stoke his adrenaline.

Around another turn and into the chicane and then Brody's car was there ahead of him.

"I'm overtaking," Will informed Tae.

"Bury him, Will." But that wasn't Tae responding; that was *Paul.* Why had Paul taken over from his race engineer?

It didn't matter, because he wasted no time following his orders. He shrank down, until he was one with the car, until he didn't have hands and feet and a heartbeat, but four wheels and a powerful engine. The world fell away until there was only Brody's car ahead of him, to be overtaken and dominated.

But every time he saw an opening and dove for the gap, Brody shifted his line, cutting off his avenue. At first it was just subtle, Brody lining himself up to take the best apex in the turn. Annoying, but predictable. But then he was moving across the track on the straights, something that would lose him time, but keep Will from passing.

"Goddammit!" he shouted into his mic. "The fucker is blocking me!"

"Yes, he is," Paul said. "Try to stay right in this curve."

Will stayed outside, and just as a path opened up in front of him, Brody slid over to block him.

"Fucking bastard!" While he was stuck back here, forced to drive at Brody's pace, his rivals were rapidly gaining time on him, obliterating the time gap he'd fought so hard to create at the outset of the race. "I have the speed but I can't get around him. He won't let me."

"He's asking for a penalty," Paul snapped, his voice icy with rage. "And I'll make sure he gets one if he doesn't back down." Their conversation was being broadcast straight to Race Radio for everyone to hear, so Will knew what Paul was doing. He was laying down the not-so-subtle threat of a formal complaint if

Brody kept up his bullshit. But a complaint was only that, and it didn't help Will now, when Brody kept weaving into Will's path with every move he made.

"He's in violation."

"Tae's talking to Race Control right now," Paul said, his voice lethal. "He's handling it on our end. Just look for an opening on yours and decimate that bastard."

There was more going on than this single incident in this one race. Paul sounded like he was out for blood. This was personal. Well, that suited Will just fine, because now it was personal for both of them. He'd destroy that asshole—for Paul and himself.

When Brody swung to the outside to line up to take the apex of the next turn, Will hung back, giving him space to do it. And when Brody was all the way to the outside of the turn, Will cut right and stayed on the throttle, taking the turn hard and to the inside. It was tight, but he clung to the roadway as he ripped past Brody with only inches to spare, into the next turn.

Being on the inside of the first turn shunted him straight into the next turn, this time to the outside, and he headed straight toward the ideal point, where he could carry the most momentum. All he had to do was hit the apex and accelerate out of it. Except when he turned his wheels to the left, ready to lay on the accelerator, Brody was there. He'd chucked a dive bomb up Will's inside that he had no chance of pulling off.

"What the fuck is he doing?"

Brody had no chance of overtaking him on this turn. He was there just to fuck with him. When Will felt a shudder rip through his car, he knew Brody had succeeded in doing just that.

"Contact!" he shouted into the radio. "He's clipped my tire." The back of the car shimmied horrifically. The onboard computer relayed the bad news. Tire pressure was dropping rapidly, and his speed with it.

"You're almost to the pits," Paul shouted. "Come in!"

"Goddammit. That's a fourth pit."

"Brody's front wing is wrecked. He's coming in, too. The boys are ready for you. Come in."

Another goddamned pit stop. It would take a phenomenal bit of driving to make up for it. And fucking Brody McKnight. Yes, he was pitting, too, but only his third to Will's fourth. They'd come out of this pit stop neck and neck. Except Brody had come in fast, on solid—if old—tires. Will had limped in on a flat. In overall race time, which is all that mattered, Will was behind and slipping farther back with every second.

He waited, pulse racing, heart pounding, as the pit crew changed out his tires. It took less than three seconds but it felt like three hours. Paul had left his customary position in front of the monitors and was standing in the pit lane, right behind the crew. His face was a mask of fury. He spoke, his voice crackling into Will's headset. "I want you to get out there and rip him to pieces, Will. No mercy."

"Don't worry, Paul," he said through gritted teeth. "It's done." Will let loose with everything he and the car had, ready to visit retribution on Brody and anyone else who stood between them.

With ten laps to go, four drivers had taken time out of him during that pit stop. But Will had fresh tires, the softest, fastest tires. Within three laps, he'd fought back the time from three of them. But so had Brody, now on fresh tires, too. Relentlessly, he pushed the car, watching the engine rev to the red line.

Up ahead, Brody passed the last car of the front-runners, reclaiming the lead of the race. Will was a quarter of a lap behind him, the time he'd lost with that punctured tire.

Finally, almost in slow motion, he passed the last car between him and Brody, clawing himself back to second place. Around one more turn, he could finally see the back of Brody's car again.

Brody whipped into the next turn and Will momentarily lost sight of him. As he screamed into the double apex, trailing Brody, Will gave himself over to the car, trusting that it could handle what he was asking of it. He'd never gone into this turn at such speed before. The car shuddered. He could feel the rear end coming loose, the car threatening to spin off the track at any moment. Hands gripping the wheel, a quick twitch of opposite lock, playing throttle and brake pedal, slip angle, and turn radius against each other, he guided the car through the turn by sheer force of will and a soul-deep trust in the physics. When he powered out of the turn, Brody was right there, a mere three car lengths ahead.

Will buried the throttle. The engine screamed in response. Two car lengths. One. Paul was screaming in his ear. He was on Brody's gearbox as he exited the last turn, whipping the wheel to the right, lining himself up to pass Brody.

The checkered flag flickered in his peripheral vision, and Brody made it under, half a car length ahead of him.

When the pit crew helped him up out of the car minutes later, he ripped his balaclava off, ready to let loose with his fury, but he was stunned into silence when he heard Paul unleashing a torrent of rage like he'd never heard from him before. Everyone was there, the pit crew, the mechanics, Tae, Harry, and the team strategist. They stood in a wary, silent semicircle with Paul as its explosive center.

"I will have his goddamned license!" Paul shouted, pacing the confines of the Lennox paddock. "He hit Will on purpose! You saw it, Tae!"

"I did." Tae nodded in solemn agreement.

"I want him to get a penalty. He starts from the back of the goddamned grid at the next five races!"

Will had the uneasy feeling that he was caught in the middle of something much bigger than a bullshit piece of strategy in a single race. Paul's anger was old, but still red-hot. This wasn't about the race, or the way Will had been fucked with—this was about Brody.

Harry cautiously laid a hand on Paul's shoulder, probably the only person who could have done so in the moment. "We're talking to Race Control, Paul. We'll handle it."

"What was that about?" Will ventured. "What's his problem with me?"

Harry seemed to leach some of Paul's fury away. He closed his eyes, and dragged in a deep steadying breath. When he spoke again, he was marginally calmer, closer to the tightly controlled man Will had come to know.

"That wasn't about you, Will. It was about me," Paul said. "And I will make sure the bastard pays for it, one way or another. He's going to be penalized. I don't care how high I have to go to see it done."

Will knew how hard it would be to get the accusations to stick. It would be up to Race Control to issue a ruling, and everybody would see what they wanted to see. It was anyone's guess how the damned thing would be decided.

"And if not, we'll get him in the next one." Harry looked to Will for confirmation.

"Hell, yes, I will. I will ruin that asshole," Will said.

Paul met his gaze, his rage still sparking in his eyes. "Yes, you will, because before this season is over, you're going to be the goddamned world champion, whether Brody McKnight likes it or not."

Paul turned on his heel and stormed away, taking Harry and most of the pit crew with him. As the crowd thinned, Will spotted Mira hanging back near the monitors, the first time he'd seen her since that day in Barcelona. Something in his chest gave a twist—some weird thrill of excitement. Abruptly, the rage he'd been nearly choking on moments ago ebbed, and all the noise in his head went quiet.

Then he registered the look on her face. Her eyebrows were knit together and she was biting her lip as she watched her father storm away toward FIA headquarters. He handed his lid and gloves to Beata. "Can you take these?"

"Sure thing. Good job out there."

"Thanks, B."

The few people left in the pit were clustered in twos and threes, staring after Paul's receding figure and whispering about what had just happened. Will was the one who'd just run the race, but nobody's attention was on him.

He crossed to Mira. "What's wrong?"

She looked up at him, eyes full of misery. "I'm really sorry, Will."

"What for? Because that washed-up asshole decided to fuck with me? Whatever. I'm fine."

"He could have killed you."

He scoffed. "Brody will have to work a lot harder to do that."

"But—"

"Look, whatever happens, everybody's gonna know how Brody got that podium spot today. And it's probably the last win of his shitty career, right? Brody's never come close to winning a world championship and this is sure as fuck not going to be his year."

"I can't believe you're so calm about this."

Honestly, he was a little surprised himself. He'd been breathing fire when he came off the track, but now that he was next to her, talking with her for the first time in over two weeks, he just couldn't find it in himself to be mad. That was new and different for him. No woman had ever managed to take his mind off the track. And that probably meant that where Mira was concerned, he was in deep trouble.

"I can handle Brody and anybody else who comes at me." He finally managed to get her to crack a smile.

"I know you can," she said quietly.

Now that he had her, he didn't want to let her disappear again. "Hey, let's—"

"I have to go catch Dad," she said abruptly, stepping away from him.

He sighed. "Right. See you in Austin?"

She nodded. "Austin."

Then she was gone, hurrying through the paddock in the direction her father had gone. He stood watching as long as he could see the bright flash of her hair in the crowd. Yeah, he was definitely falling into the deep end with her.

Austin,
Texas

"The press got some good shots of you with the head of Marchand Timepieces, which is brilliant." Violet had her arm hooked through Will's and was steering him through the crowd at the post-race reception for the Circuit of the Americas. "And your agent invited the PR associate who's in charge of your new line at Velocity. His name is Ryan and he's a *complete* wanker, but we've both got to be nice to him, so I'll bring him over when he arrives. If I drink enough before then, maybe he won't seem like such an asshole."

Will stopped in his tracks and forced Violet to look at him. "Violet, I've been chatting people up for hours. Can I take a break?"

"Darling boy, do you think David Beckham or Michael Jordan never had to stand around making idiotic small talk with a lot of corporate lunkheads? It's part of how the game gets played, and you have just leveled up in that game."

Violet always spoke to him like he was a child, even though he suspected he might be older than her. Didn't matter—she was right. During the gap between Suzuka and Austin, he'd flown to New York to meet with Velocity. They were already his biggest sponsor and now that his season was going so well, they wanted to roll out an entire line under his name. Trainers, track pants, the works. He was about to become high profile in a global way. The accompanying PR circus was pretty odious, but the money would be worth it, and not just for him. Formula One was staggeringly expensive. It was part of his job to do whatever he could to offset some of that expense. Velocity's money would go a long way toward that.

Ahead of them, he caught a glimpse of Mira heading in their direction. Her hair was pinned up, but some curls had escaped, brushing her face and shoulders. As she ducked between guests, he saw what she was wearing and his mouth went dry. It was a simple black dress—just a slip of silky fabric—but it hugged and hinted at every curve underneath. He suspected there was no bra under there, which sent a powerful throb of desire rippling through his body. *Fuck.* He wanted to slide those skinny little straps off her shoulders and watch that fabric slither down her body and puddle at her feet. By the time she reached them, he'd almost gotten that vivid fantasy under control.

"Violet, Simone's got that press guy from *NASCAR Nation* pinned against the bar, talking his ear off. You might want to lend a hand."

"The day a NASCAR publication runs a feature on Formula One will be the day hell freezes over. She's wasting her breath. Besides, I'm on Will Duty."

"I don't need a babysitter, Violet."

"When it comes to your PR commitments, I beg to differ."

Mira shot him a sympathetic look. It was all he could do to keep his eyes on her face, not on her bare shoulders, or the shadow between her breasts at the edge of her dress, or the hint of her nipples under the silk. That dress should be illegal.

"Hey," he said to her, "we've been to three cities without a single adventure. I bet you didn't even have sushi in Japan.

"I did!"

"The takeout I brought to you at your desk doesn't count," Violet interjected.

"Come on. Let's get out of here. Adventure time."

"Not a chance, Will," Violet said. "You've got asses to kiss and I mean to make sure you do it."

He sighed, his eyes skimming over the sea of older men in conservative suits and their surgically enhanced, expensively highlighted wives. Across the room, he spotted a familiar face, but it took him a moment to place her.

"Hey, isn't that the woman from those jeans ads back in the nineties?"

Violet and Mira turned to look and spoke in unison.

"Oh, that's Paul's ex-wife," Violet said, at the same time Mira cried out, "Mom!"

"She's your *mother?*"

"You didn't know Paul was married to Cherie Delain?" Violet said.

Mira stood on tiptoes, waving over the crowd to catch her mother's attention.

"No, I missed that bit of info."

Cherie Delain had been huge back in the nineties. The iconic series of jeans ads she did were before his time, but they lingered on in pop culture to this day, and so did Cherie. The woman weaving through the crowd was definitely older, but no less stunning, and that famous head of platinum blond curls was recognizable anywhere. Mira was half her size, with a more delicate face, and her blond hair was darker, but now that he knew, he could see the resemblance.

Cherie Delain was smiling widely, arms outstretched when she reached them.

"Baby girl!" She swept Mira into her arms and hugged her tight.

Mira returned the hug and then pulled back to look at her. "Why didn't you tell me you were coming?"

Maybe because he knew her father so well, it had never occurred to Will to wonder much about Mira's mother, or her life back in LA. Her mother was a *supermodel*, which made him see that whole growing-up-in-LA thing from a new perspective. No wonder the glamour of Formula One didn't seem to faze her.

"My darling daughter's finally back stateside," Cherie said, beaming down at her. "Of course I want to see you. And I told your dad to keep it a secret so I could surprise you."

Mira was obviously very happy to see her. They seemed really close, which was a bit of a foreign concept for him. He couldn't imagine ever being happy to see his parents.

"It's a very nice surprise. How long are you staying?"

"Just tonight. I have a vendor showcase starting Tuesday."

"But you missed the race!"

Cherie laughed and rolled her eyes. "You share *that* obsession with your dad, not me." She cast a quick glance at him and Violet. "I don't want to interrupt if you're working."

"No, it's okay. This is Violet, my friend from PR. And this is Will Hawley, one of the Lennox drivers."

Cherie shook Violet's hand. "I feel I know you already, Violet, since Mira's told me so much about you. Glad to finally meet you in person." Then she turned to Will. "Nice to meet you, too, Will."

Oh, so Mira told her mother all about *Violet* but hadn't even mentioned him? Mira had a real knack for cutting him down to size.

She turned back to Mira. "Can you get away for dinner?"

Mira shook her head. "Sorry, I need to stay with Dad."

"I'm sure he'll understand," Violet urged her. "Go have fun with your mum."

"But I have to work—"

Her mother cut her off. "Then let's invite your father and Natalia, too."

Will got the impression that Paul wouldn't dare say no to Cherie.

"Okay!" Mira said, her smile brightening.

"Great! Would your friends like to come, too?" Cherie asked, nodding at both Violet and himself.

"Mom," Mira murmured. "I'm sure Will's too busy to come have dinner with us."

"If dinner means I can stop talking about endorsements, then lead the way."

Violet grabbed for his arm. "But the guy from Velocity—"

"Come on, Violet," he groaned. "Haven't I done enough?"

"Okay, fine," she said with a huff. "I didn't want to talk to the asshole either."

Cherie clapped her hands together. "Great, it's settled! Let's go find your dad and clear out of here."

"**Y**ou look great, baby girl. You haven't worn your hair like this in years." Her mother reached across the back of their cab to tuck a curl behind her ear.

"Mom." Mira brushed her hand away. Soon she was going to lick her thumb and wipe a smudge off her face.

"I'm just saying. It's so pretty on you."

"It was too much work to straighten it every day." And the way Will's eyes lingered on it whenever he was near her didn't hurt either.

"And this dress. New, right?"

Mira squirmed under her mother's scrutiny. Of course she'd notice every little change. The dress *was* new, and not her usual style. She'd seen it in the window of a fancy shop in Barcelona and it stopped her in her tracks. It was so soft and sexy, so . . . everything she wasn't. The slippery silk, the tiny straps, all the bare skin . . . it made her feel confident in a way she hadn't in years. Not confident about spreadsheets and customs paperwork. Confident as in . . . hot. She hadn't felt hot in so long. She hadn't *wanted* to feel hot. Before she knew it, she'd bought the dress.

"I like Violet," her mother said.

"She's great. I'm so glad she's out on the circuit with us. It's nice to have a friend here."

"And—was it Will?—he seems nice, too."

"He is."

"And hot."

Mira made a face. "Mom . . ."

Cherie held up her hands. "Just making an observation. Besides, he's only got eyes for you and that dress. He couldn't stop staring."

Her heart gave an unwelcome lurch, and her cheeks warmed. "You're deluded, Mom."

Thankfully, Cherie was already flitting off to the next subject, as usual. "How's the job going?"

"Good. I had no idea how hard it would be. But I think I'm finally getting the hang of it."

"And your dad? How has it been working with him?"

She could have tossed off a breezy "fine," but her mother would see right through that. She knew how thorny the past seven years had been for them. At least she finally felt like she'd gotten that Singapore disaster behind her. Whenever he needed her, she was right there, ready with every answer, and it felt like they were regaining their equilibrium. "It's getting better. I know he didn't want me back—"

"You don't know that—"

"I'm right though. I think it was Natalia who finally went to bat for me." The subtle shift of her mother's eyes away from her own made her suspect maybe she had both Natalia *and* her mother to thank for the intercession. "But that's okay. I'm determined to prove to him that he can count on me, and I think he's starting to."

Cherie laid a hand on her knee and squeezed. "You know your dad loves you, right, baby? Job or no job."

She swallowed back an uncomfortable tightness in her throat. "That's not enough. I want him to respect me, too."

"I'm sure he does."

"If he doesn't, then he will. Look, we're here."

EVEN AT 9 P.M. the Texas air was muggy and hot as they waited outside the restaurant. Will tugged at the collar of his dress shirt, while at his side, Violet fanned herself with her hand.

"I found this place the last time we came through Austin," Natalia said. "The food is delightful, and it's a bit more off the beaten path."

"Natalia knows every good restaurant in every city on the racing circuit," Paul said, smiling at her. "And she can get a table with a single phone call. I don't know how she does it."

"I just hope it's got air con," Violet groaned.

Just then a car pulled into the circular drive behind them, and Mira got out with her mother. Every time he looked at Mira in that dress, his mind went to truly filthy places where it was best not to linger, especially as he was about to sit down to dinner with both her parents.

"Cherie! You look lovely." Natalia and Cherie embraced and kissed cheeks. "How's the business going?"

There was clearly no bad blood between them, which was not surprising for Natalia. She was a class act, and Mira's mom seemed the same.

Mira tugged on Violet's sleeve. "Come on. Mom will talk about work all night if you let her, and it's hot. Let's wait inside."

"Please. I'm desperate."

Will followed them in, but almost plowed into Violet, who'd run into Mira when she stopped short just inside.

"Mira," Violet groused. "What the fuck?"

But Mira was still frozen in place, staring at the dining room in front of her. Will scanned the room to see what had taken her so by surprise, and when he spotted that asshole Brody, he cursed out loud.

"Goddammit, what is *that* fucker doing here?"

Brody was sitting at a table twenty feet away, telling a story to his rapt audience, that irritating Aussie accent of his carrying through the room. He had an arm around some pretty young thing staring up at him with an adoring expression.

"Fuck," Violet muttered. "Hey, Mira—"

"What the hell is that bastard doing here?" Cherie snapped behind him, and Will looked back at her in confusion. Yeah, Brody was a wanker, but why would Cherie Delain hate him, too? Why did it suddenly seem like there was a lot more going on here than the stunt Brody had pulled in Japan?

Mira spun around to face them and the look on her face stopped him cold. She was ghostly pale, and her green eyes were wide with terror.

"Mom, please . . . let's just go."

"Has he been on the circuit the whole time?" Cherie demanded, looking from Mira to Paul.

"There's no avoiding him, Cherie," Paul said through clenched teeth. "Believe me, I've tried."

"Mira, honey, you can't stay out here with that creep hanging around."

And just like that, the penny dropped. Will's eyes shot to Brody, still carrying on at his table, oblivious to the drama by the door. It was *him*. It was Brody. The guy from Mira's past. The love story that wasn't a love story. But . . .

"Mom, I can handle this. I've *been* handling it. I'm fine." Mira's voice was high and tight, and right now she looked anything but fine.

He mentally scrambled to piece it together. Brody McKnight and *Mira*? But it had been years since she was on the circuit. She'd just been a kid. And Brody was . . . absolutely not a kid.

"How *dare* that bastard sit there so smug?" Cherie snapped. "Maybe I'll just go have a chat with him."

"No! Mom, don't. Leave it alone." Mira snagged Cherie's arm, holding her back, and at the moment, it looked like Cherie Delain needed restraining, because the look on her face was murderous.

"Cherie," Paul interjected. "He's a driver for a competing team. We've already had one run-in with him this season. If we have another, it could put the team in jeopardy. You *know* what that could cost us."

Paul's eyes shot to Mira, and if Will had any doubt left, Paul's expression would have confirmed it. He looked like he was just as ready to murder Brody as Cherie was. And as the truth settled in, Will was ready to do some unaliving, too. *How dare he? How fucking dare he?*

"Well, *I* don't work for this team," Cherie said, and before Mira or Paul could stop her, she sailed through the restaurant toward Brody.

Paul exhaled loudly. Mira groaned and turned away.

"Excuse me," Cherie said, towering over Brody's table like a vengeful blond Valkyrie. "Mr. McKnight, I just want you to know, one day karma will come for you, and when it does, I'm going to be celebrating." The whole table stared at her in confusion. Brody opened his mouth to reply, but Cherie bull-dozed over him. "Enjoy your dinner."

Then she was marching back through the restaurant, and Will was surprised there was anything left of Brody. That look could burn a man to ashes.

"I've lost my appetite," Cherie muttered on her way back out of the entrance.

Mira watched her mother leave, then glanced over at Paul. Natalia was whispering urgently to him, probably trying to keep him from creating an even bigger scene. Then Mira's eyes flickered to Will's and his heart sank. She looked so miserable. Scared and sad and ashamed and . . . Jesus. He needed to get away, too, or he'd be the one ripping Brody apart with his bare hands.

"Excuse us," Paul muttered before he left.

Natalia threw a small, tight smile at Mira before hurrying after him.

"I better go make sure Mom is okay," Mira murmured. "I'm so sorry, everyone."

"Mira . . ." Will reached for her, but she was already out the door. He watched her go, feeling like his chest was in a vise. Next to him, Violet cleared her throat. "Guess I'll call us an Uber."

It took the rest of the cab ride to calm her mother down, but eventually—after promising to meet her for breakfast—Mira managed to shove Cherie out of the cab in front of her hotel.

She didn't blame her mother for what happened. As carefree and sweet as she could be, she turned into a mama bear when her baby was hurt, and Brody McKnight had certainly done his fair share of hurting.

When Mira finally got back to her hotel room, she left the room mostly dark, flicking on just one bedside lamp. She'd just stepped out of her shoes and unpinned her hair when someone rapped softly at her door. She groaned. Probably Natalia rushing in to make sure she was okay. She swung it open, ready to reassure her and politely shove her back out, but the words died on her tongue. Will was standing on the other side. He'd lost his suit jacket from earlier. His hair was an artful wreck, as if he'd spent half an hour raking his fingers through it, and a dusting of dark stubble had started to shadow his jaw.

As she stared at him, he raised the bottle of scotch he held.

"Figured you could use a drink."

Wordlessly, she swiped it out of his hand and turned around to retrieve two tumblers off the minibar. She sloshed a couple of inches into both glasses and handed one to Will after he'd come inside and closed the door. She tossed back a hefty sip and winced.

"Ugh, that's awful."

"*That* is a three-hundred-quid bottle of scotch."

"Hmm." She passed him her half-empty glass. "Maybe I'll just leave this to you." She turned toward the window overlooking the lights of downtown Austin.

"So . . . the guy you told me about . . . the love story that wasn't a love story . . . it was Brody McKnight, right?"

"I think that's pretty clear."

"Brody's been around forever, though. He's got to be—"

"He's thirty-seven now. He was thirty when we . . . when I knew him."

"How old did you say you were?"

"I didn't." She swallowed thickly, keeping her eyes on the glittering nighttime landscape of Austin down below. "But I'd just turned sixteen." Behind her, she heard him draw in a sharp breath. She might have been keeping Will at arm's length, but it still hurt to think of him judging her the way everyone else had. "Look, I know how bad it sounds. I was young, stupid, feeling rebellious . . . it was a lot of things."

"Hey, look at me." His voice was soft, a comforting vibration skittering down her spine. When she turned to face him, he was standing just a foot behind her. He reached out and touched the side of her face, fingertips skimming down her cheek before he pulled back.

"It might have been a lot of things, Mira, but one thing it *wasn't* was your fault. You were just a kid."

"I appreciate that, Will. More than you can imagine. But it's not that simple."

"How did it . . ." He stopped, turned, and sat on the edge of the bed. Patting the spot next to him, he said, "Sit. Start at the beginning."

The usual knee-jerk denials were right there on the tip of her tongue, but there was no point in keeping it buried anymore. At least, not with Will.

She dropped down on the bed next to him. He leaned in to her, pressing his shoulder to hers, and passed her his glass of scotch. When she sipped it this time, it wasn't so bad.

"Dad and I weren't very close when I was little. It's a long commute from London to LA, and I didn't get to see him often. I idolized him anyway, though, and I loved racing because of him. When I was ten, I begged him and my mom to let me spend my summer vacation with him on the circuit. That summer was a dream come true. I got to spend all day at the track, and I finally felt like I had a dad. After that, I spent every summer with him. We were really close during those years."

"Huh."

She glanced over at him. "What?"

"It's just . . . half the time you seem like you're walking on eggshells around him. I get it. He's intimidating. But I would have thought it would be different for you."

"It was. Once. I'm getting to that. The year I turned sixteen was rough. Mom had met this guy she was serious about. Mom's an icon for a lot of people. It can get weird. So she's always been very cautious about dating. This one was the first to get past her defenses. That Christmas, they got engaged. I hated him."

"Why?"

She lifted one shoulder. "Bad vibes? I was right, by the way. Mom ditched him six months later. But that's not the point. Because Mom had been so careful about letting men into her life, it had always been just her and me. And then suddenly there was this guy there all the time . . . I just . . . I wanted my mom back and I couldn't have her. I was happier than usual to leave it all behind and go travel with Dad for the summer. Except on my first night there, he introduced me to *Natalia.* This is stupid, but I felt really *betrayed.* First by Mom, and then by Dad, who'd really just started being a dad to me a few years before. It was like I lost him again."

"You love Natalia, though. I've seen you with her."

"I do now. But at first? I just wanted her gone. So anyway, there I was, prowling race tracks in various foreign countries, angry at everything and looking for a distraction."

"And you found Brody."

"He found me, actually. I'd snuck out with this girl from Logistics to go dancing in this club in Barcelona. I wasn't looking for trouble. I just wanted to dance."

For a second, she was blindsided by the memory of that night in Melbourne, dancing with Will. That had been the first time she'd gone dancing since Barcelona. Funny, it had ended in a kiss, too. But she was coming to realize that magic moment with Will on the dance floor in Melbourne was light years away from what had happened with Brody. Because it wasn't about the dancing and the kiss. It was about the man.

Taking a deep breath, she pushed forward. "Anyway, he came over to me, bought me a drink, told me he'd seen me around the track. He talked to me like another adult. He flattered me. He told me I was beautiful . . . sexy. It was nice, being treated like a grown-up."

"So far nothing you've told me sounds the least bit your fault."

"Getting to that. I might have felt like I was being so grown-up, but I still had sense enough to keep it a secret. Dad would freak. Even setting aside the age difference, Brody drove for a rival team."

"Ouch."

She flinched. "I know. It was so shitty."

"Hey, no, that's not what I meant. I meant for you, being put in that horrible position by someone who knew better."

"I knew better, too. I lied to everyone, all for him. And the lying wasn't even the worst of it." Swallowing hard, she braced herself for the next sordid tidbit. "He was engaged."

She half-expected Will to turn on her at this point. God knows, she'd beaten herself up over it enough. But he held tightly to her hand and he didn't seem to be making a move to flee, so she soldiered on. "In my meager defense, he told me he wanted to end it with her, but she was really unstable. It was Lulu Heatherington. You know her?"

"The actress? Yeah, I've heard of her."

"He said she was this emotional basket case and he wanted out, but he was afraid it would push her over the edge and she'd kill herself. I bought the whole story. I actually felt sorry for her. And I thought he was *such* a great guy, trying to do the right thing by Lulu, even when he didn't love her anymore. I was such an idiot."

"You weren't an idiot. He was a fucking liar."

The venom in his voice surprised her and she twisted to look at him. "But he was engaged. And I just blew that off."

Will closed his eyes and blew out a frustrated breath. "Mira, that had nothing to do with you."

"But—"

"No, he was the adult with the commitment. You were the kid. And he *lied* to you. None of this was your fault."

She'd been so afraid of him learning the truth, afraid he'd think the worst of her. She should have known better.

"So what happened? Did your dad catch you with him?"

"That would have been far too easy. Some paparazzo caught us making out in a bar. Brody's a bottom-feeder in Formula One, but he's a pretty big deal in Australia. By the next morning, it was all over all the internet. Have you ever walked through a room knowing every single person was talking about you?"

Will cocked an eyebrow. "Well, actually—"

She let out a burst of shaky laughter. Only Will could make her laugh at a time like this. She shoved his shoulder with her own. "Of course *you* have, but not like that. Like . . . like they all know something terrible about you, and you have no idea what it is."

She would never forget that feeling. It was like the worst anxiety dream she'd ever had, except she couldn't wake up from it. Everywhere she looked as she walked across the paddock that morning, people were staring, pointing, whispering . . . about *her*. Then she'd heard his name, "Brody," murmured in her wake and she *knew*.

One internet search on her phone was all it took to bring the whole house of lies crashing down on her head. The picture was bad enough, but they'd also found out who she was. Lennox team principal Paul Wentworth's teenage daughter. She'd fought back nausea as she'd read what they were saying about her.

Desperate racing groupie.

Trackside Lolita.

Home-wrecking teen.

And those were just the articles themselves. The comments were her first peek at the true ugliness hiding in people's hearts.

Fucking whore.

Stupid slut.

I hope she dies.

"Mira? What happened?"

Will's voice startled her back to the present. She'd seen only a fraction of what was said about her, but it was enough to stay with her until this day. Even now, with seven years between that moment and this one, she felt the cold horror and shame creeping over her skin like it was yesterday.

"I ran straight to Brody's hotel room. He knew already, of course. His publicist had called him first thing that morning. He'd been manning the crisis for hours at that point."

"And the asshole didn't think to give you a heads-up?"

"I wasn't his main concern anymore, as I was about to find out. I said it was too bad it had come out this way, but maybe it was for the best. Once people could see how in love we were, they'd stop saying such horrible things about me." .

Will exhaled, his hand tightening on hers. "I'm afraid to ask what he said."

Letting out a humorless huff, she shook her head. "He smiled this patronizing little smile and said girls always blew things out of proportion. Then he told me I needed to move on, because he was marrying Lulu, and it would be really *awkward* for him if I made a big stink about our little fling."

"I hope you told him to go fuck himself."

She sighed wistfully. "That would have been nice. You have no idea how many hours I've spent imagining the epic 'fuck you' speech I should have given him. I used to practice it in the shower, and in my car when I was stuck in traffic."

"Yeah, those things never come to you when you want them to, do they?"

"Especially not when the man you loved with all your heart just ripped it out of your chest and fed it into a paper shredder. When he got tired of my hysterics, he handed me a wad of euros and told me to go buy something pretty to cheer myself up. Then he told me to go back to my room and clean up because I was embarrassing myself. Then he kicked me out."

"Christ." Will downed the rest of his scotch in one gulp.

"That's when I had my first panic attack, in a bathroom stall in his hotel lobby. We were in Budapest, and I walked around the city all night, crying. I wanted to walk until I couldn't think or remember what had just happened. It doesn't work that way, of course, so eventually I had to go back to the hotel. I hadn't counted on the press lying in wait for me."

"Shit. Mira . . ." He stroked a hand down her hair.

"It's okay," she said quickly, squeezing his other hand. "That's when Natalia showed up. She got me inside, up to my room, just the two of us. I thought for sure she'd start screaming at me, telling me how stupid I'd been."

"I'm guessing she didn't do that?"

"Nope. She took one look at me and held her arms out. That's all. I cried forever and she just held me. Natalia is the best. And she stayed right next to me while I told my dad everything. He knew already, of course. It was all over the media. God, the press . . . the things they said about me . . ."

"Nobody said anything about goddamned Brody seducing a kid?"

"Brody's good. Or at least his PR people are. He got it out there that it was all me pursuing him, seducing him."

"You think *he* talked to the media?"

"I can't prove it, but after the photo hit, I'm pretty sure he got out in front of it right away to make sure he looked like the victim. No matter what that made me look like."

"That fucking asshole. I knew he was a shit, but I had no idea . . . I get it now. How angry Paul was in Japan after that shit with Brody."

She looked up at him. "I'm sorry you got in the middle of that."

Will smiled at her as he reached out and tucked a strand of hair behind her ear. "Don't worry about me. I can handle Brody. I'm guessing Paul and Brody had it out, though?"

"Dad went after Brody the next day, confronted him in the paddock, got in his face, shouting and screaming. Took a swing at him. He threatened to end his career, kill him with his bare hands . . ."

"Sounds about right," Will muttered harshly. "Good for Paul. If I'd have been here, I would have held him down while Paul did it. I mean, Mira . . . you were a kid. Couldn't Brody have been arrested?"

"Believe me, my mother was screaming for his head. But all the . . . all our *encounters* . . . had taken place in a million different countries. It was legal in most places. Brody had it coming, but Dad was a team principal, threatening a rival team's driver. Threatening to *kill* him. Brody's team filed a complaint with the FIA. They didn't care about me and Brody, since it was technically legal. They only cared about what happened after, between Dad and Brody. In the end, they penalized Dad and Lennox for the fight. Dad was suspended from racing for a year. The *team principal.* Suspended from the sport."

"I knew Paul was out of the sport for a while, but I didn't know why."

"It took him another year after that to convince the Lennox board of directors to give him back the team. They weren't going to at first. And during that time, a ton of the personnel

Dad had spent years recruiting left for other teams. Lennox won the constructor's championship the year before all this happened. By the time Dad was back, Lennox was ranked twelfth on the grid. All because of me."

"No," Will snapped, eyes blazing with fury. "Because of Brody fucking McKnight. He's the bad guy here."

"But I'm the liar who dragged everyone I love into my mess. I almost ruined Dad's career. I almost ruined this team."

"That's bullshit. Brody's the one who should have paid. It might have been legal, but that doesn't make it okay. He was a grown adult. Didn't people give him shit for it?"

"Brody might be a wretched human being and only a mediocre driver, but he's brilliant at crafting his narrative, I have to give him that. A month later, he married Lulu. All these gorgeous pictures of their fairy-tale wedding on Lake Como were splashed across the media. He was a handsome racing star. She was a beautiful actress. I was just some kid from LA, desperate for attention. He told everybody I'd been throwing myself at the drivers all season and he just had a 'moment of weakness.' Lulu called me a 'sad, disturbed girl' and she hoped my parents would keep better control of me in the future."

"What a bitch."

"Hey, she probably just believed his lies. They're divorced now, so I'm guessing she saw through him eventually."

She rubbed a hand across the back of her neck, emotionally wrung out and exhausted.

Will scooted back on the bed until he was leaning against the headboard, then patted the spot next to him. "Come here."

She crawled up the bed and dropped down next to him, leaning against his shoulder. Like he could sense how tired she was, Will lifted an arm and wrapped it around her shoulders. She let herself snuggle against his chest. He smelled good and felt even better, so warm and strong under her cheek.

"What did you do afterward?" he murmured, his voice a low, soothing rumble through his chest.

"I couldn't stay on the circuit. I wanted to, but . . ." Abruptly her throat closed up with emotion. Every word from her last conversation with her father, before she left for LA, was still burned in her mind. He'd been so angry, so frustrated, so disappointed in her. And the suspension hadn't even been handed down yet. She couldn't imagine what he'd have said if she'd been there for that. But she wasn't. By the time he was kicked out of the sport he lived and breathed, she was back home in LA, not to return for seven long years.

"Everybody agreed it would be best if I went back to LA. People were saying horrible things about me, and I kept having these panic attacks. So my mom came over and took me home. The next year was rough. I just fell apart. I wish I hadn't let him win." She hated admitting how weak she'd been, how she'd shattered like glass under the pressure.

He pressed his lips to her hair. She grabbed a fistful of his shirt, letting herself be wrapped up in his steady, safe embrace. After a few moments, he nudged her head back until he could look her in the eye. "Mira, he didn't win. You're back here, aren't you?"

"I guess. It got better. Eventually. I finished high school, got accepted to college, and tried my best to just get on with it. I never came back here, though." She blinked against the burning in her eyes. "That was probably the hardest part."

"I'm surprised you wanted to come back at all after that."

"I *begged* to come back. I love racing too much to let him keep taking it from me. And my dad . . . I ruined that. I had to come back and try to fix it."

"Why do you think you ruined things with your dad?"

"Come on, Will. I cost him a year with the team."

"He can't possibly blame you—"

"He does. He said that it had been a mistake. Having me here with him."

"I'm sure he didn't mean it."

"Yes, he did. That's why I had to fight so hard to convince him to give me this chance."

"Ah. I see."

She lifted her head enough to see his face. "See what?"

"That's why you work so hard. You think you've got something to prove."

"I *do.* I'm never making a mistake like that again."

"I'm guessing that's also why you hated me so much when we first met. You thought I was like him."

She laughed, nudging her shoulder into his ribs. "I didn't *hate* you. But you definitely threw up a couple of red flags."

He tightened his arm around her shoulders, drawing her closer into his side. "I hope you know by now that I'd never do something so shitty to someone."

She laid her head down on his chest again. "I know that, Will. You're—"

You're perfect. That's what she wanted to say. But it seemed like too much, especially now when she'd been crying all over him for an hour.

So she pressed her cheek against his chest instead, and whispered. "You're one of the good ones."

Her eyes felt hot and swollen with tears. She blinked against them, sighing with contentment as his chest steadily rose and fell under her cheek. He felt warm, and safe, and . . .

Will turned his head and his cheek brushed against something warm and soft. He opened his eyes. Mira's hair. Mira's dim hotel room, Mira's head on his chest, Mira's small body breathing slowly and steadily next to him as she slept, Mira's leg draped across his.

He rarely slept—actually *slept*—with another person, and he sure as hell didn't cuddle. If he went to bed with someone, he usually got her out of there shortly after the fun stuff had concluded. Not that he'd done that in a while. It had been ages, now that he thought about it. *Not since . . .*

Mira sighed in her sleep. Not since this had started. Whatever *this* was.

He reached down and eased his phone from his pocket, checking the time before he set it on the bedside table. Two thirty. This felt . . . nice. He wanted to close his eyes and sink back to sleep, pressed up against her warm body. But would she freak out when she woke up in the morning and discovered they'd spent the night sleeping together?

Just then, she shifted. Her hand contracted, gripping his waist, sending a zing of awareness through his body, as he imagined her doing that intentionally when she was wide-awake. Then she lifted her head and peered up at him through a tangle of blond curls.

She looked rumpled and adorable and hot as hell.

"Hey," he murmured.

"Hey," she whispered back.

He was half expecting her to scramble off the bed, to start babbling excuses, then chase him out of her room. She didn't. She just looked back at him, with something he couldn't quite define in her expression.

Raising his hand, he brushed her hair out of her face, tracing the shape of her cheek as he did. "Want me to go?"

Her big green eyes stayed fixed on his for another long moment as she considered. Something changed in her eyes. All that misery from earlier had faded away in her sleep, to be replaced by . . . something that looked like hunger. Slowly she shook her head. "No, I don't want you to go."

Then she pushed herself up on her elbow, leaned in, and kissed him.

He froze for a beat, overwhelmed by her sleep-softened mouth on his, and the press of her breasts under the thin layer of her dress against his chest. Then her lips moved, a sweet sensual caress of his, and everything in him woke up, suddenly, painfully alert. His hand, which had been hanging uncertainly in the air, found its way into her hair and he kissed her back.

But just before they'd fallen asleep, she'd said he was one of the good ones. And a good one should not make a move on his friend when she was emotionally wrecked.

"Mira," he whispered against her mouth. "Are you sure?"

She lifted her head enough to look him in the eye. "I'm tired of denying myself something I want so much," she said, before pressing her lips to his once again.

When she kissed him this time, he didn't stop her or hold back in any way. He took her face in his hands and returned the kiss, letting himself indulge in the heat of her mouth. When she tipped her head to catch a breath, he rolled over, pushing her onto her back, and he kept kissing, dropping one on each dimple, and more along her jaw and down her neck, reveling in her startled gasp and the way her fingers fisted into his hair. God, he'd wanted her like this for so long. His pulse was pounding with need, but he didn't want to rush it. Not now, when he had her at last.

His fingers found the thin silky strap of her dress and he toyed with it, tugging it tight against her shoulder and then releasing, as he drew his tongue through the shallow hollow at the base of her throat.

Mira moaned, a soft sound of sensual delight, and then she dropped her shoulder, sending the strap of her dress slithering down her arm. Such a small gesture, but his cock pulsed in response, at the sight of her bare shoulder, and at the promise of more.

Pushing himself up on one elbow, he reached for the other strap. He met her gaze briefly, checking in that she was okay to go further. Her lashes lowered as her teeth caught her kiss-swollen bottom lip and she nodded. Slowly, he slipped the other strap over her shoulder, and kept dragging, watching as the silky black fabric slid down her chest, caught briefly on her hardened nipples, and then down her rib cage. He stopped when it was nothing but a pool of fabric around her waist.

He'd been right earlier. No bra. Fuck.

He let out a strangled sound, somewhere between an exhale and a grunt, as he gazed down at her breasts, pale, perfectly shaped, rosy-tipped.

"Mira . . ."

Smiling, she took his hand in hers and raised it, settling it over one breast. The gentle weight felt perfect in his palm. He squeezed, then rolled her nipple between his fingers, and she let out another soft moan of pleasure, arching her head back, with her eyes closed. He was so hard he felt like he might die.

Dipping his head, he replaced his fingers with his mouth. For endless minutes, he lingered there, despite the desperate straining of his cock. The silence of the hotel room broken only by the rustle of their clothes and her occasional sighs of pleasure. He didn't stop, even when she was writhing underneath him.

"Will." His name came out as a breathy exhale. "Please," she murmured, clutching at his shoulders.

"With pleasure," he murmured. He reached down with his left hand, at first just resting it on her knee. Slowly, he rubbed his thumb back and forth across the soft skin of the inside of her knee. Her legs fell open, the muscles in her thighs relaxing. Drawing his palm up the top of her thigh, he pushed her dress up as he dragged his head up from her chest to kiss her mouth again.

Her kisses were frantic with her desire, as were her hands, running through his hair, down over his shoulders, gripping him anywhere she could reach.

When his fingers touched her knickers, she jerked under him. He stopped there, stroking over the fabric softly, listening to her increasingly desperate breathing. Her thighs fell open, allowing him to sweep aside the fabric and touch her, the slick, wet heat of her. This time it was his turn to moan. He wanted to thrust himself inside her until he exploded, but he also wanted this to last forever. As long as possible. All night.

He explored her, rubbing the length, dipping inside and back out, and then finally, up to the sensitive heart of her.

Her hands stilled, clutching his biceps as he set up a steady, stroking pace. Against his mouth, she gasped as he drew her closer to the edge. Her thighs clamped around his hand, but he didn't stop. She broke their kiss, her head falling back. She arched up, strung taut, ready to fly. Her thighs trembled around his hand and she gasped for air, every tiny pant ending in a whimper as he drove her closer to the edge. Finally he tipped her into her release, drawing it out until she went slack underneath him again.

"YOU'RE BEAUTIFUL when you do that," Will whispered in her ear, and Mira weakly raised her hand to run her fingers through his thick, silky hair. Her body was still humming, little aftershocks of pleasure zipping along her limbs, and he was still kissing her, down her neck, her shoulder, her cheek.

"I want to fuck you, Mira," he murmured against her skin. "Can I?"

His words were like a match tossed onto kindling, and her body went up in flames. She wanted him so badly.

"Yes."

She hooked her hand behind his neck, pulling herself up to kiss him hard. He pressed her back down onto the bed, rolling over onto her. She moaned into his mouth, finally—finally—feeling the weight of him pinning her to the bed.

His kiss was hard and hungry, his tongue sliding along hers, his teeth nipping at her lips. He shifted his weight and his knee slid between hers until his thigh was pressed right against her sex. She was still so sensitive that she felt like she could just press herself against him and come again, but that wasn't what she wanted this time. She'd finally quit this war she'd been fighting with herself. She was letting herself have him and she wanted every single inch of him tonight.

She worked a hand between their bodies, so she could unbutton his shirt, but she couldn't manage it. Rearing off her, he brushed her hands away, and took care of the buttons. She'd seen his bare chest before. She'd seen most of him bare at one point or another. But never like this, in this dimly lit room, tangled in bed together, with his hungry eyes roving over her body as he imagined what he was about to do to her. She shivered with the delicious anticipation of it.

When he'd gotten his shirt open, he shrugged out of it and tossed it to the floor. She watched the gold light play across the ripples of his muscles as he moved, and her mouth literally began to water. She wanted to explore every dip and ridge on his body, first with her hands and then with her mouth.

He dropped back on the bed, on his back, silently inviting her to explore. She reached out her hand and laid her palm on his chest, right on his breastbone, spreading her fingers over his warm skin. A smile curled his lips as she made her way across, and when she brushed his nipple, the muscles of his abdomen clenched. So she bent over him and took a swipe at him with her tongue, too.

He hissed, his hand coming up to cradle the back of her hair. "Mira . . ."

She broke off and sat up, shimmying her rumpled dress back up her body and off over her head. He watched her, one hand fisted in the bedspread and the other tracing over her shoulder, along the side of her breast, and down to her hip. His finger caught in the band of her thong. "This, too," he murmured.

She smiled at him as she slid it down her legs and flung it to the floor. Then she threw her leg over him and sat up astride his thighs. The landscape of muscles across his abdomen contracted as he sat up, his arms coming up to encircle her.

Now that she'd finally given herself permission to enjoy him, she meant to do it thoroughly, running her hands over his shoulders and down to his biceps.

"God, you're gorgeous," she whispered.

He reached up to cradle her face in his palms, nudging her chin until she was looking into his shadowed eyes. "So are you."

His fingers slid back into her hair, fisting and bringing her face to his. He kissed her, slow and thorough, and so long, until she was twisting in his arms, desperate to get closer to him, to feel his bare skin on hers. She scooted forward, until her breasts were pressed to his chest, reveling in the friction against her hard, aching nipples. She could feel his cock pressing right against her sex. Will groaned, bringing one arm down to band around her hips and haul her closer still.

Her hips seemed to lift on their own, undulating against him, and he groaned again, his own hips lifting under her. She gasped as a shaft of pleasure jolted through her body. He was taking her apart so easily and he was still half dressed.

She pushed back just enough to get her hands between him, going to work on his belt buckle, then on the zipper of his pants. Will leaned his weight back on one hand, watching her work.

"Touch me," he whispered.

She kept her eyes on his face as she slid her hand down inside the fly of his pants, her palm sliding down his rigid shaft in his boxer briefs. His lips were parted, glistening and damp from her kisses, and his lashes cast shadows on his cheekbones. She curled her fingers around him and squeezed. His brows furrowed and his mouth fell open as he gasped. "Mira . . ."

Every time he said her name in that pleasure-strangled groan, her nipples tightened.

"Lie back," she said, releasing him and pushing gently on his shoulders. He obeyed and she went to work tugging his pants down his hips, but he reached out to grab her wrist.

"Wait."

She brushed a hand across bulge of his cock about to spring free. "Really? Wait?"

He offered her a pained smile and ran his hand up her arm to her shoulder. "Just a second."

Releasing her, he fished his wallet out of his back pocket and retrieved a condom.

Her stomach clenched pleasantly with nerves and anticipation. This was really happening. Now that they were finally here, she was desperate for it, desperate to feel that hardness sliding into her, to know at last what he felt like.

"Such a Boy Scout," she murmured.

"You should always be prepared."

She scooted back off his legs. "Just put it on."

He moved with an athlete's enviable efficiency, kicking off his shoes, then his trousers and boxer briefs. When his cock finally sprang free, she had to bite back a noise. She'd imagined it—she could finally admit to herself that she'd imagined it quite a bit—but the reality was infinitely better. The sight of him wrapping a hand around it while he rolled the condom on was going to be playing on repeat in her imagination for quite some time. Every moment of this night would be impressed on her memories for the rest of her life.

When he was ready, she started to lie back, but he stopped her, pulling her back up and urging her onto his lap again.

"No, like this. You're in control of this. Anything you want."

She looked down at him, naked and finally hers, and felt momentarily overwhelmed. "I want you to kiss me again," she whispered.

He reared up, catching her face in his hands again and kissing her, long and deep. She lost her head when he kissed her, so overwhelmed by the taste and sensation of him that she didn't have room for anything else. All she could think of was getting more of him. Her hand slid down the ridges of his abdomen until she found his cock, wrapping around him to nudge him into place, and he groaned into her mouth. Slowly, she slid down over him. He broke away from her mouth on a gasp.

"God. Oh, god. Mira."

He was so hard, and so big. Her body stretched around him with a toe-curling perfection, sending shivers of sensation up her spine. Her fingers curled into his hard shoulders as she slowly pushed herself farther down on him.

Suddenly his hands grasped her hips and he thrust up once, seating himself fully inside her and forcing a gasp out of her.

"Okay?"

"Yes," she sighed, leaning forward until her forehead was pressed against his. "Oh, yes." She felt utterly filled, surrounded, and consumed by him. Good. It was so good. For a moment, they both held still, breathing hard.

"Whatever you want, Mira," he whispered, brushing an open-mouthed kiss across her lips. "However you want it."

He pulsed inside her and she groaned, grinding herself against him.

"God, yes," he muttered. He braced his arm across the back of her hips, helping her rock against him. Her head fell forward onto his shoulder, her aching nipples brushing against his chest with every thrust. She wrapped her arms around his shoulders, reveling in the feel of his hard body pushing against hers. Her hand came up to fist in the back of his hair as the pressure began deep in her core. So close, but not quite.

"I need you to touch me," she murmured into his shoulder.

He lay back on the bed and gripped her thighs, helping her move against him. She gasped as he picked up the pace. He was so strong, his abdominal muscles clenching and hips pistoning up with every thrust.

"More," she moaned.

He lifted a hand to her breast, squeezing, then rolling her nipple between his fingers. So good, but still not exactly where she needed him. She took his hand and slid it down her body. From there, his fingers unerringly found the right spot. Pleasure rippled out, intensifying with every second.

"Oh . . . Will." His name came out in a gasp.

"You're close, aren't you?"

She just whimpered in reply, too overwhelmed by the sensation to speak. Then it burst upon her like glass shattering all around her, a cascade of glittering sensation, rippling down over her. Her hands gripped his biceps as she rode it out, as the pleasure flooded out through her limbs.

As it ebbed away, she lifted her head to smile down at him. He raised a hand to cup her cheek, his thumb brushing across her bottom lip. The look on his face, the tenderness in his eyes, sent floods of a different kind of feeling through her. Her heart ached, so full of emotion, she couldn't speak.

She leaned down to kiss him, feeling him still rock hard inside of her. "I want to make you feel good now," she whispered against his mouth.

"You've already made me feel so good, Mira."

She flexed her hips and he groaned. "Better, then."

"Oh, sweetheart," he sighed. Then he wrapped his arm around her back and levered his body up, neatly flipping her onto her back. The pressure of his body, of feeling pinned to the bed by him, was perfection. She ran her hands up his arms, the ridges of muscles flexing as he held himself over her, then gripped his shoulders. His body felt impossibly hard and strong.

When he finally moved his hips, she moaned. "Yes," she whispered. "Just like this."

He was beautiful like this, so desperate and undone as he chased down pleasure. She wanted to press it all into her consciousness so she couldn't lose it. The gold light on his skin, the sheen of his sweaty forehead, the dark knit of his eyebrows, the bunch and release of his muscles as he thrust into her. He squeezed his eyes shut and bared his teeth, a flash of white in the dim light. Then he went rigid and he stilled, a groan ripping out of his chest, ragged and uninhibited. Every muscle in his body locked tight as he rode it out, and finally he gasped in release.

Collapsing down on her, he buried his face in her hair. His hand came up to her face, cradling her cheek as he rubbed his thumb across her cheekbone. She ran her fingers through the hair at the nape of his neck and he moaned in approval.

"Please tell me you're not going to kick me out and make me go back to my room," he muttered into the pillow beside her head. Her body jostled deliciously against his as she laughed. She couldn't get enough of him. As spent as she felt, she wanted to do it all over again.

"I'm not going to kick you out." She drew a hand down his neck and across his shoulders, and pulled him in close. "I want you to stay," she said, this time quieter. She wanted him like this for as long as she could have him, however long that might be.

He lifted his head enough to look at her. "I want to stay." He leaned in and kissed her, gently and slow.

"Give me ten minutes," he said when he pulled back. "And we can do that again. If you want to."

She tightened her arms around him. "Oh, yes, I definitely want to."

28

Mira's phone alarm went off at its usual six thirty. She woke in a groggy blur, groping blindly for the nightstand, every muscle protesting. After tapping to silence it, she dropped her head back on the pillow. Her arms felt weak and the insides of her thighs ached. Will's naked body, hard and unbelievably warm, was pressed up against her back, one arm slung across her waist, his face against her shoulder.

Blinking the sleep out of her eyes, she watched the light glow through a crack in the drapes, reliving the night before. First came that long, painful trip down memory lane, but then after . . .

They'd crossed a major line last night, one she'd tried so hard to avoid, and there was no going back now. As unwise as it still might be, though, she just couldn't bring herself to regret it.

Maybe last night was nothing extraordinary for him, but she couldn't say the same. It had *never* been that good. Not even close. Everything felt tender, glorious, and brand new, and she was absolutely determined to enjoy it.

"Why are you awake at this ungodly hour?" he rumbled behind her. His breath was hot against her shoulder as his hand swept up her naked side. God, how did he do that? Just a few words and a touch and she was already aching for him.

She did her best to keep her voice steady, so he wouldn't know how desperate he made her. "I always get up at six thirty."

"But there's no race today."

"I get up early anyway. I'm most productive in the morning."

"Of course you are," he muttered, then he pressed a sleepy kiss to the back of her shoulder, making her bury her face in the pillow to hide her grin.

"Well, I suppose I don't have to get up *right* this second."

"No, you don't." His arm tightened around her waist, pulling her in against him until his cock, hard and ready, pressed into her lower back.

"No, I don't," she sighed, relaxing into his arms. Oh, god, there was no way she was getting up now. With his free hand, he brushed the hair away from the back of her neck so he could drop a trail of kisses down it. She arched back, pressing her ass against him.

His hand slid up her rib cage and cupped her breast and she sighed. When he rolled her hardened nipple with his fingers, the sigh transformed into a moan. "Maybe you don't need to go anywhere at all today," he said, shifting his weight so that his cock slipped between her thighs. She was already so wet for him.

"But we'll have to get up eventually."

"Let's think about that tomorrow."

But tomorrow was going to come. And they'd have to decide what happened when they got out of this bed. A wave of insecurity made her throat constrict. If he wanted to just slip out of her hotel room and go on with business as usual after today, it was really going to hurt.

"Um . . . do you need to . . . I mean, do you want to . . . do you have to be somewhere?"

Will paused. Then he took her shoulder and turned her in his arms until she was on her back and looking up into his face. His hair was adorably wrecked, his eyes were squinty, and he had a sheet crease up one side of his face. She'd never seen anything hotter.

"Is that your way of asking me if I'm about to do a runner and pretend this never happened?"

That was probably exactly what they should do, but her stomach gave a sickening lurch at the idea. Right or wrong, that was *not* what she wanted.

"Um . . ."

"Because I'm not," he said. Then his expression grew cautious. "Unless you want me to? Is this not . . ."

The surge of relief would have brought her to her knees, had she been standing. "No. I mean, yes. I mean—" She let out an exasperated breath. "I don't want to forget this happened. Unless you do."

A slow, devastating grin spread across his face, and she knew she was in so much trouble with him. "I don't."

"So we're . . ."

He ducked his head to start kissing his way down her neck as he slid his knee between her legs. "We're whatever we want to call it." His hand came back to her breast, kneading and pinching. She was about to lose her mind entirely, to pull him over on top of her and forget the rest of the world existed. Except the rest of the world *did* exist and it was complicated.

She'd spent the whole of last night relating the disastrous fallout of her last major relationship, and now here she was in bed with the one guy who could drag the whole sordid story back into the light.

"I don't want you to take this the wrong way—"

He lifted his head to look at her. "This almost never ends well."

"No, it's just—you saw what happened at the restaurant last night. With my parents. And Brody."

"Yeah?"

"This? Me and you?"

Understanding dawned in his eyes and his expression cooled slightly. "You want to keep it a secret."

"That sounds so terrible."

Something flickered across his face and the muscle near his jaw clenched. "It's true, though, isn't it?"

"Will, it's not you."

He exhaled and started to roll off her. She grabbed at his arms to stop him. "Listen. You heard all about the last driver I was involved with. And you're not just any driver. You drive for my dad's team—"

"Got it. I'm just another bastard that can't be trusted."

"I didn't *say* that. I trust you. I do. But you weren't here, so you don't know what it was like for me. What people said about me. I just can't—"

He hesitated. "Yeah, sorry. I wasn't thinking. I get why you'd be worried about what people would say."

"Worried doesn't begin to cover it." Just the thought of it set off a low-grade panic in her chest.

He nodded tightly. "Understood. I'll keep it quiet."

Those were the right words, but she didn't like the way he said them, like she'd offended him in some way.

"I promise, it's better for you, too. The last thing you need at this point in the season is that kind of heat."

"I can handle heat, Mira. I've done it before."

"I know you can. But the only thing people should be talking about right now is your driving. Anything else is a distraction."

He looked at her from under his furrowed brows for another beat before nodding tightly. "You're right. Sorry I was a dick about it."

"You weren't. And I'm sorry I come with all this bullshit."

He was still propped on one elbow, leaning over her, looking down the length of her body as he considered. Then he reached out and slowly dragged a fingertip up her thigh. By the time he got to her hip, every inch of her was on fire.

"Right now, I'm thinking the bullshit is worth it."

"Is it?" She was practically panting already.

"Spending a whole day in bed with you? Yeah, worth it." His teasing was a relief. She'd been so afraid she'd scared him off before anything had even started, like he'd get up and storm out of the room and everything they'd shared until now would be burned up in his wake. But he was still here. And he still wanted her, even with all the bullshit. She was so relieved she could cry.

"Spending a whole day in bed with you sounds like heaven but it can't be this morning. I'm meeting my mom for breakfast. I'd ask you to come, but—"

"Yeah, that wouldn't be suspicious at *all*, rolling into breakfast together, you looking freshly—"

She slapped a hand over his mouth. "Stop right there."

He chuckled and kissed her palm. "I'm teasing. I saw her last night, too. She's terrifying. I'm not about to draw her fire in my direction."

"Wise man."

He slid his knee between hers, until his thigh pressed against her sex. Her breath caught. "Surely you're not meeting your mother at this hour."

He rocked into her and her eyes slid closed.

"She runs her own business," she mumbled, trying desperately to hang on to her thoughts. But it was so hard when his mouth was doing that to her breasts. "She's an early riser, too. And I need a shower."

His hand slid between her thighs. "A shower? Happy to join you. In a minute."

"A minute?"

"Many minutes. When we're done."

"Okay. I guess I can be a little late."

"Yes, you can."

Budapest,
Hungary

"If I don't get something to eat, I'm going to pass out," Violet groaned as they hurried into the hospitality center. The morning had been grueling for both of them, but they'd finally stolen five minutes to grab lunch before the afternoon's race.

Mira surveyed the picked-over remains of the lunch service and sighed with disappointment. "Looks like all that's left is the vegetable curry and it's getting crusty."

"I don't care." Violet seized a plate and heaped a spoonful of congealed curry onto it. "I just need to eat. So what are you doing for the break?"

Mira dumped a pile of lukewarm curry on her plate. "Back to Essex with my dad, I guess." The midseason break was just around the corner, after the race at Silverstone. FIA rules dictated that no one could work, so it was a forced vacation of sorts.

"You should come to Thailand with me," Violet said as they found seats at a table.

"Why are you going to Thailand?"

Violet smirked. "I'm renting a bungalow on the beach; drinks are cheap as fuck, and hot boys will teach you to wind-surf. *That's* why I'm going to Thailand. Seriously, you should come."

"I don't know . . ."

"C'mon, Mira, you need a vacation more than anyone I know." Violet paused, eyeing her. "And you desperately need to get laid."

"Um."

Violet hiked her eyebrows. "Unless you've been getting some and you're holding out on me?"

Her scoff of laughter sounded completely unbelievable to her own ears, but Violet just shrugged. "Suit yourself."

The pathetic truth was, she was hesitating because she didn't know what Will was doing for the break. Would she see him at all? Would he even *want* to see her? Maybe he'd made plans he hadn't shared with her. Maybe he was going to see someone else. He hadn't said a word about seeing her over the break. They hadn't exactly declared themselves exclusive, or declared themselves anything other than a secret.

She'd just wanted a little time to figure things out. But in the few weeks they'd been doing this, she didn't feel like she'd figured out anything at all. Their nights together had been amazing. She wouldn't give them up for the world. But was that all they were? Hookups? Were they even "dating" when they didn't go on "dates," or even out together in public?

Ugh, when had she started to care so much? Annoyed with herself, she dug back into her cold curry.

"Mira, do you have a minute?" Her father appeared behind them, laying a hand on her shoulder. This was, of course, the other part of the problem. She couldn't imagine her father's face if she should ever tell him.

She jumped to her feet. "Sure, Dad, what do you need?"

"It's a bit of an unpleasant task, to be honest."

"Those are my specialty."

"There's a young lady working for Rally Fuel who is apparently an old friend of Will's." He coughed and raised an eyebrow, which explained exactly what sort of old friend she was. Dread knotted in Mira's chest, but she schooled her face into disinterestedness. "One of the pit crew heard her saying she was heading over to his motor home to say hello. I'd rather he not have that sort of . . . erm, *distraction* just before his race, if you know what I mean."

"So you want me to go accidentally interrupt them?" Her voice sounded remarkably steady, considering the pit in her stomach.

"Exactly. Can you come up with an excuse?"

"I'll think of something."

"Thank you, Mira."

"No problem."

The track was buzzing with race day energy, but Mira ignored it all as she made her way to Will's motor home. Stupid motor homes. It was a coveted Lennox perk—they traveled personal motor homes for the drivers to every European race. But right now all that meant to her was that Will had a private place at the track where no one could see what he got up to.

What was she about to walk in on? Maybe it *was* just an old friend saying hi. But she suspected Will didn't have that kind of old friends from his past.

At the base of the stairs, she paused, staring at his door, straining for any sound, any suspicious thumps or banging or moaning. There was nothing, but that didn't mean anything. He had a couch in there.

Furious, she shook herself out of her stupor. She was being crazy. This was *Will*. He'd never treat her that way. Right?

Stomping up the shallow steps, she rapped briskly on the door.

"Come in," he called from inside, no flustered stumbling, no hesitation.

Taking a deep breath, she opened the door and stepped inside. Will was leaning casually against the bar. The girl—woman—sat in one of the armchairs, sipping a beer. They were both laughing about something.

"Mira," Will said, giving her a heart-stopping smile as she came in. "This is Roza. I knew her back in my first season. We were just catching up."

Mira cast a quick, appraising glance at Roza. She was beautiful, tall and built, with long dark hair and blue eyes. She smiled at Mira, open and welcoming, and raised a hand to wave. "Hi."

"Roza, this is Miranda. She's the principal's assistant."

"I'm sorry to interrupt," Mira said, feeling foolish because it was clear she hadn't interrupted anything. And now she felt doubly foolish, because in her haste to get over here and bust in on Will's suspected tryst, she hadn't come up with a good reason for her interruption. "Paul needs to see you. Ah . . . emergency team meeting." Internally, she winced. Emergency team meeting? That was the best she could come up with?

Will's lips twitched as he suppressed a smile. "Oh. Emergency team meeting. Sounds very important."

"It is. I'm sorry."

"Oh, no, it's okay." Roza stood, unfolding her long legs. Her smooth voice carried a hint of a Hungarian accent. "I need to go. I just wanted to say hi and wish you luck before the race."

Will smiled at her. "Nice to see you again, Roza. And congratulations."

"Thanks!" She gave him a brilliant smile as she swept her hair back over her shoulder. It was then that Mira noticed the flash of a very large diamond ring on her hand. Roza leaned in to give him a peck on the cheek, then smiled again at Mira and headed to the door.

"Sziasztok!" she said brightly to both of them and then she was gone.

In the silence following her departure, Mira kept her eyes on the door, too embarrassed to face Will.

"Emergency team meeting?" he finally asked.

"Oh, shut up."

He burst into laughter, nearly doubling over from it. "Seriously? Emergency team meeting?"

"I know, jeez," she said, heat rushing to her cheeks. "My dad sent me over here to interrupt you and your guest, and I was so distracted by the fact that you had a gorgeous woman in your motor home that I forgot to come up with a decent excuse for interrupting you."

Will sobered. "I wouldn't do that to you."

Relief rushed through her. Of course he wouldn't. "I didn't know . . . I mean, we've never talked about that—"

He reached for her hand, rubbing his thumb across her knuckles. "I wouldn't," he said again.

She smiled weakly at him. "I know that now."

He shifted in discomfort, and ran his hand over the back of his neck. "Okay, in the interest of *full* disclosure, Roza and I did have a very short thing. Ages ago. But she came by to tell me she's engaged to Andres Basilio. He's an old friend from my junior driving days."

"Yeah, I noticed the ring."

"So what did Paul think he was sending you over here to interrupt?"

Mira smirked. "He was just worried your guest might 'distract' you before the race." She air-quoted the word.

Will's smile returned, broad and predatory. Those dark blue eyes flashed. He shoved off the bar and advanced on her. "Then he shouldn't have sent *you* over. Because now I'm *definitely* distracted."

WILL BACKED MIRA UP until she was pressed to the door. Reaching for her hips, he dipped his head to the side, kissing down the side of her neck.

It honestly had not occurred to him what having Roza in his motor home would look like to her until Mira stumbled in so flustered and on edge. The idea that she might have been jealous, possessive even, was doing something to him, making him feel his own kind of possessive. God knew he felt jealous every time he saw her goofing around with Omar, chatting with Ian, joking with Dom. She didn't notice how they all looked at her, but *he* did. She was free to talk to anybody she wanted; he just wished they all knew she was with him when she did.

"Mmm, I love distractions like this." He slid his hands under her shirt and up over her rib cage to cup her breasts. His dick sprang immediately to attention, and he pressed himself against her hip seeking some friction and relief.

"Me, too," she whispered.

He nipped at the corner of her jaw, then soothed the spot with his tongue.

"Dad's really going to be mad if I'm the one distracting you before a race."

"Then please don't tell him," he said into the hollow between her breasts. Suddenly he was desperate for release, desperate to sink himself inside her.

She ran her fingers through his hair in that way he loved. He closed his mouth over her nipple, tonguing her through her bra, and she sighed, her head falling back and making a soft thump against the door.

"Seriously, though, Will." She tugged gently on his hair. "There isn't time. You have to go race."

He groaned and pressed his head into her chest. "I know. I hate it, but I know." As much as he wanted to strip her bare, pull her to the floor, and fuck her hard, it was going to have to wait. Someone was going to be along any minute to call him to the track.

Her fingers stroked through his hair again. "Well . . ."

He straightened up to look at her. "Yeah?"

She stared up at him for a moment, biting her lip, contemplating something. Whatever it was, he was game, as long as it involved her and his dick.

Suddenly she reached for him, spinning him around until he was the one pressed up against the door. "You have to be quiet," she said. "And quick."

"What . . . ?"

Then she dropped to her knees in front of him.

Oh.

Oh. She was going to . . . His dick grew impossibly harder and sweat broke out across his forehead just imagining it.

"Mira . . ."

But he couldn't remember what he was going to say as she started working the fly of his race suit open. It was so tight, and there were his fucking Nomex long underwear to get through, too. She'd never manage to get him out. He reached down, brushing her fingers out of the way. Reaching through the layers, he grasped his swollen dick, and freed himself.

Then she pushed his hand out of the way and closed her fingers around him.

He looked down at her. Blond curls, bare shoulders, parted lips, and the head of his cock right there in front of her. Fucking hell. "I can't believe you're going to—"

"Shhh," she admonished. "Remember, quiet and quick."

Then she slid him into her mouth. He immediately let out a loud guttural groan. She pulled off and glared up at him.

"Okay, okay," he panted. "Quiet. Just please don't stop." *Please don't ever stop.*

"And quick."

He let out a strangled laugh. "That won't be a problem." He was so close to exploding already. This was going to take no time at all.

When she took him back into her mouth, he hissed through his teeth and pressed his fists to the door, grinding his teeth to hold back the groan building in his chest. Her mouth was soft and wet and warm and he was so hard, pulsing against her tongue with every stroke.

"So good," he whispered. Tentatively he reached for her head, his fingers tangling in her curls. "Can I . . . ?"

She hummed her assent, the sound vibrating right through him, amping up the pleasure. He wanted to grip her hair and thrust, but he held back, gently guiding her up and down his shaft, desperately trying to hold still. But as the pressure built in his gut, he couldn't hold back anymore. His hips began moving in time with her strokes, and his fingers tightened in her hair of their own accord.

"I'm close . . ." he warned her, panting.

She answered by taking him deep and sucking hard. That was all it took. His orgasm exploded through him, pleasure racing through him, leaving him spent and shaking.

He tipped his head back against the door, dragging air into his lungs, dimly aware of her tucking him back in and closing up his drive suit.

"Goddamn," he muttered when she finally rose to her feet.

She put a hand behind his neck and pushed herself up on tiptoe until she could whisper in his ear. "Now go win me that race and return the favor tonight."

His mind immediately went to work, imagining all the shit he wanted to do to her when he finally had her back in his bed. He caught her around the waist and hauled her up against him. "I will *wreck* you tonight," he promised her.

Silverstone,
England

"Will, we need to go over your itinerary for the break," Violet said as she strode along at his side. The Lennox paddock was packed, and that was probably mostly because of him. Reporters, sponsors, wealthy fans, and patrons . . . the interest in Lennox was at a fever pitch as he racked up the wins. While it was gratifying, theirs wasn't the attention he wanted right now.

Violet was still talking. "I know you've got a lot of time booked with Velocity, but there are other sponsors asking for time as well, so it would be helpful to know what your other plans are."

He stopped and faced her. "What other plans?"

Violet shrugged. "Just wondering. If you'd . . . made plans. With anyone."

Will scowled and looked back at his mobile. Plans? Right now he'd be happy if he could just get Mira to answer his text. They saw each other plenty of times during the day but always as coworkers, never as . . . whatever they were to each other. At this rate, he'd be sneaking into her hotel room after midnight. Again.

"No plans," he snapped.

"So I can book the other sponsors?"

Will let out an annoyed huff. "Sure. Yes, book away."

"Okay, great. Now, about your parents. Shall we clear out the VIP lounge, or do you want to have them to your motor home?"

"My parents?"

"They're coming today." Violet glanced at her phone. "In ten minutes, actually."

Will stopped walking, dropping his head back and groaning. "That's today?"

"You said—"

"I'm sure I did. I just forgot."

"It's race day. It's *Silverstone*."

"I *know*." How could he forget? The Formula One circuit was on British soil, racing at Silverstone, which was like the home field for Lennox. His sister had told him she was dragging their parents here. It had just slipped his mind. Maybe on purpose.

"Oh, look, here comes Mira," Violet chirped. "She's sure to make you less grumpy."

Will's eyes snapped up and there she was, picking her way through the crowds, ever-present notepad clutched in her hands, her credentials swinging between her breasts. A few nights ago, when he'd stripped her clothes off, he'd left those credentials on and wrapped her lanyard around his fist as he'd—

"Hey," she said when she reached them.

It took a herculean effort to school his face into disinterestedness. All he wanted to do was smile at her and say something to make her laugh, or maybe back her against the nearest motor home and kiss her senseless. But Violet's voice was too bright and singsong to be believed. She could sense that something had changed between them, despite their best attempts to give nothing away.

"What's up?" he asked, looking not at her, but at a spot over her right shoulder.

"The guy from Rally Fuel was hoping to get a word with Simone, but she's tied up in the press pen. Do you have a minute for him, Violet?"

"Sure. If you can wrangle Will's parents for me."

Mira looked at him in surprise. "Your parents are coming today?"

He shrugged. "I forgot."

"Okay, I'm going to go steer the Rally guy toward hospitality. Mira, here are the passes to the VIP lounge for Will's family. I'll send a photographer around to his motor home later to get some family shots."

"No photographers," Will said quickly. "My mother . . . she doesn't like being part of this racing stuff."

"Why not?" Mira asked.

"She's okay with being in the press for one of her charity events, but sport isn't her thing."

Mira's tone turned sharp. "Not even when her son is on track to win the world championship? Not even when he's about to sign the most lucrative sponsorship deal in the sport's history?"

Her offense on his behalf was sweet. And now he wanted to touch her again, but not with Violet here and photographers everywhere. He probably shouldn't even be spending this long talking to her. "Not even then."

Mira's eyes went soft. "I'm sorry, Will."

Violet's interested gaze was ping-ponging back and forth between them. Will cleared his throat and glanced away.

Violet gave a disappointed sigh. They weren't fooling her at all. "Okay, have a good drive today, Will."

"Thanks, Vi."

He and Mira stood side by side in silence, watching her go.

"Hi," he finally murmured, giving her the smallest smile he could manage.

"Hi." She kept her own face blank, but her lips were twitching, her dimples appearing and disappearing. He wanted to reach out and trace one, or take her hand, or touch her hair, but that was all off-limits. There were eyes everywhere and it always seemed like every move he made was being noted by someone with a camera. The ubiquitous press—the *other* reason they were still hiding this thing. After Brody, Mira's involvement with another driver would send them all into overdrive. And with him? The Once and Future King of the Party Boys? They'd never let it go.

"So your parents are coming."

"My whole family, actually. The entire executive suite of Hawley and Sons Bank."

Mira blinked. "You have brothers and sisters?"

Had he really never mentioned Jem and Ed to her? Maybe if they spent time together outside of bed, it might have come up. "One of each. Jemima and Edward."

"And they both work for the bank?"

"Everybody but me. Understand now? This trip was my sister's idea. Jem's been trying to patch things up between me and my parents. I think it's hopeless."

Just then, a familiar voice cut through the din of the crowd. "There he is! Will!"

He scanned the crowd and spotted his sister standing on tiptoe, waving an arm over her head to signal to him. His mother, right beside her, was whispering something to her rather forcefully, probably another admonition that drawing attention to herself was unseemly. Jem was, as always, flatly ignoring her.

Philomena Hawley, in a pink suit and a pearl necklace, looked completely out of place on the racetrack. His father was no better. Only Edward Geoffrey Arthur Hawley III would show up at a Formula One race in a Savile Row gray flannel suit. At least Ed had left the suit and tie at home today. And Jem looked like another species entirely in her bright floral dress.

He waved to Jem. "You're about to meet them all," he muttered to Mira. "God help you."

When they reached him, he leaned in to kiss his mother's smooth, powdered cheek, careful to not actually touch her. She hated that. "Mum, Dad."

"Hi, Will." Jem swung an arm around his shoulders and planted a noisy kiss on his cheek.

He hugged his sister tightly. "You look great, Jem."

"William, you're looking well," his father said. The words were friendly enough, but the tone wasn't, and neither was his disapproving perusal of Will's blue race suit, covered in sponsor logos. He reached out for a perfunctory handshake, as second nature to him as breathing. His father's handshakes were so regulated that you could almost set a stopwatch by them. Always precisely the same grip, precisely the same two seconds before release.

Ed reached around their mother to shake his hand. "Will, you're looking bloody fantastic this season. Congrats."

"Clarissa and the girls couldn't come?" Ed's wife, Clarissa, was pretty humorless and uptight. Missing a visit with her wasn't the worst thing in the world, but he was genuinely sorry to miss Ed's two little girls, Sarah and Molly. He adored them, sticky fingers and all.

"Moll's got the flu and Clarissa's worried they're both contagious. She sends her love."

"Who's your friend?" Jem asked, eyes raking over Mira with interest. Jem would be worse than a dog with a bone if she sensed he was involved with Mira. Which meant he had to play it cool.

"Oh, um, this is Miranda, the team principal's assistant."

At the wall of blank stares, he elaborated slightly. "The principal is like the CEO of Lennox Motorsport."

His parents nodded in vague understanding. He'd only been racing professionally since he was a teenager. You'd think at some point they'd have bothered to learn something about it.

"Well," Mira said brightly. "I'm just here to hand off your VIP passes. Someone will come over to Will's motor home before the race starts to escort you to the VIP suite."

"Thank you, dear," his mother said perfunctorily, an endearment she used when she didn't know someone's name and didn't care to learn. The moment he'd uttered the word "assistant," his mother had erased Mira from her consciousness, relegating her to the category where waitstaff and cleaning people existed. This was about as bad as a first meeting with his family could go.

He could see from Mira's expression that she felt the sting of that dismissal and he itched with frustration. He wanted to introduce her properly, but if he did, he'd be outing their relationship in a pretty public way, and *she* was the one who didn't want that.

"It's very nice to meet you all," she said. "Enjoy the race."

She was being the brisk professional she was with everyone in the paddock, and he didn't like it. But it was too late, because she'd already turned and disappeared into the crowd.

Up until today, he'd been okay with keeping them under wraps. There was a lot on the line for both of them. If they were going to crash and burn, better to do it out of the public eye. But he wasn't comfortable with hiding anymore. If Jem knew they were dating, she'd go mad. She'd *love* Mira. Mira would love Jem. Ed would have a field day relaying all the details to Clarissa. If they went public, they could both stop lying to Violet. Paul Wentworth wouldn't send his daughter on fruitless cockblocking missions.

Did all this mean he was ready for more with her, whatever that meant? He didn't know, but one thing was certain, he wasn't going to figure it out in a bunch of late-night hotel hookups, no matter how fun they were. He needed more time with her. He *wanted* more time. That alone told him plenty. He'd never wanted more with anyone.

"Will?" Jem said quietly. "Is everything okay?"

He smiled at his sister. "Yeah, everything is fine. Come this way, guys."

As they made their way through the low-key chaos of the race paddock, his mother was making that face of hers, and Will could feel himself already getting defensive.

"She's been in a mood since we left London," Jem muttered, falling into step beside him. "Spoiling for a row, if you ask me. So don't give her one."

"Why do you think *I* would, Jem?"

"Because I see that look on your face, baby brother. Watch it, mate."

"I'll be fine. She's the one who needs to watch it. Her and Dad both."

He ushered all of them up the steps and into his motor home, where his parents glanced around in confusion.

"Can I get you a drink?" he asked almost desperately. "Ed? Jem?"

"A beer would be brilliant," Ed said.

"Have you got something fizzy?" Jem peered over his shoulder as he opened the fridge.

"Is champagne fizzy enough for you?"

"Ooh, champagne is *perfect*!" He passed her a bottle of Moët, a sponsor gift.

"Jemima, it's not even lunch time," his mother admonished.

"That's why I'm drinking *champagne*, Mum. Much more appropriate for brunch than whiskey, don't you think?"

Will snorted in laughter and his father scowled at him. "Mum, Dad, anything?"

"No, thank you," his mother huffed, answering for the both of them.

"This is rather posh, Will," Jem said, running her fingers over a glossy wood table. "Quite a step up from last year." Jem and Ed had come to watch him drive in a few of his Formula E races, but not his parents. Not after that fight three years ago.

"This is just a Lennox perk, and only for the European races. Not complaining though. It's nice to have some privacy on the track."

"Do you *live* in here, then?" his mother asked, askance.

"Of course not, Mum. My hotel suite is in Buckingham. I've also got my flat in London, but I'm not there much during the season. I stay in hotels on the road."

His mother shook her head. "Still living out of a suitcase, like some refugee, at your age."

"Mum—" Jem sighed, but Will cut her off before she could continue.

"I'm not living out of a suitcase, Mum. I'm *traveling* for my *work*, which is racing."

"Mum," Ed interjected, "Will's one of the best drivers in the world. Have you picked up a bloody paper this season?"

"This is *sport*. This is not a proper job," his father growled.

Will's temper, only barely tamped down, flared up like dry tinder. "*This* is a multibillion-pound industry." He pointed to a stack of promotional material Velocity had just sent over. "I'm about to sign one of the largest sponsorship deals in Formula One history. I'd think even *you'd* be able to appreciate the money involved, Dad."

Unfortunately, the infamous shirtless black-and-white Velocity ad lay on top of the pile. Not showcasing him at his most professional, but Will was past the point of caring. Mira was right—that sponsorship deal was huge, and *he* was the one making it happen. That was nothing to be ashamed of.

His mother glanced at the Velocity ad and slammed her eyes shut. "Good heavens, it's that horrid photo. I can't believe you're proud of that."

"Nine generations of Hawleys have handled the finances of some of the finest families in England," his father said in that stupid House of Lords voice of his. "All the way back to King George the Third. But that legacy wasn't enough for you. You had to throw it all away for this. Your name in all the scandal rags, taking your shirt off like a *Page Six* whore, and using our good family name to sell *trainers*."

"Those ads are going to fund an entire season's research and development and help pay the salaries of four hundred employees. Yes, I *am* proud of that. And when I'm not selling trainers for Velocity, I'll be behind the wheel of the most technically advanced car on the planet, driving it better than anyone alive. It's not bloody Hawley and Sons banking for fossilized British families, but I'll be damned if I apologize for it. Not to you or anybody else."

"Hey—" Jem reached out to touch his arm but he yanked it away.

"Sorry, Jem. I know you meant well, but this was always going to be a disaster. Look, I've got a race," he said, heading toward the door. "I know that means bugger-all to you two, but it's important to me and every other hardworking person out there, so I don't have time for your fucking judgment."

"Will—" Jem tried again, but he was already out the door.

The post-race reception after Silverstone was packed. It was Lennox's home turf and Will had won, so tonight was a celebration. Her dad and Natalia were making a slow circuit of the room, shaking sponsors' hands, accepting congratulations on the day's success, and toasting the team. He didn't need Mira, so she retreated to the upper balcony overlooking the floor, where she could brood in peace.

Meeting Will's family today had bothered her. He'd been doing exactly what she'd asked of him—keeping what was happening between them private. She knew she had no business having hurt feelings that the meeting had been so brief and impersonal. But she did anyway.

It wasn't until she was standing in front of them being dismissed like the help that she realized she wanted more. Well, maybe not from his parents, because they seemed like assholes. But his sister and brother seemed nice. She wished she'd been able to meet them as Will's . . . what?

The midseason break started tomorrow. She kept telling herself they needed to discuss it, but every night she chickened out, afraid of what she might hear. So now Will was off to New

York and she was heading back to Essex, where she'd hang around, obsessing over him and what he might be doing without her. Ugh, how had she wound up here?

She could see him down on the floor below with his family. His parents looked miserable. They must have had him late, because they were older than she'd have guessed. Generational differences didn't account for their shitty attitudes, though.

Predictably, Will looked wretched. Her hands tightened on the railing, wishing she were down there to tease him a little, and coax him back into a good mood. But even if she could, maybe he wouldn't want her to. After all, she could see women all over the room below eyeing him with interest, ready to move in the moment there was an opening. Maybe he was fine with what they currently were—late-night secret hookups. But she didn't think she was anymore.

"Here you are."

She spun around as Violet approached. "Oh, hi."

"You're missing all the toasting downstairs." Violet was holding two champagne flutes and passed one to her.

"Thanks," she said, taking a sip.

"So why are you lurking up here alone? You look like you're plotting an assassination." Violet joined her at the railing and looked down at Will's parents just below. "On the other hand, if you wanted to assassinate those two, no one would blame you. What a couple of puffed-up wankers. How did a pair of such insufferable toffs produce Will Hawley?"

"Classic rebellious youngest son."

"His sister is mad cool, though."

"I didn't really get to meet her."

Violet turned to eye her. "You know, if he's sleeping with you the least he could do is introduce you to his family."

Having her secret exposed triggered a familiar flush of panic, but she kept her eyes on the party below. "What are you talking about?"

Violet rolled her eyes. "Please. Leave off the valiant denials."

She bit her lip, debating. After seven years, here she was, back to keeping secrets and lying about a guy, and she *hated* it. She was desperate to confide in someone, especially after today.

"How did you guess?"

"Aside from the fact that you two have wanted to climb each other since the moment you met?"

"I did not—!"

"Yes, you did. I was there. Now you're trying so hard *not* to notice each other that your necks are about to snap. It's painful to watch."

"Is it that obvious?"

Violet shrugged. "Not to anyone but me, who has a prurient interest in other people's sex lives. So it was Melbourne, right?"

"Melbourne what?"

"When you started fucking."

"Will you keep your voice down?" She cast a panicked glance over her shoulder, but the balcony was empty aside from the two of them. "No. Well, we kissed in Melbourne but that was a mistake. And then there was Singapore. Also a mistake. But it happened officially in Austin."

"But that was only a month ago!"

"It's really new."

"So why all the secrecy? If he's making you sneak around like some dirty secret, I swear, I'll kill him and hide him where they'll never find his body."

"No, *I'm* asking *him* to sneak around." That sounded terrible. Because it *was* terrible. All of this was terrible. Why had she ever started something she knew was so wrong? And for what? So she could beat herself up constantly, wondering where she stood? Why was she taking this enormous risk, imperiling everything, for what might be just some meaningless fling? Was he really worth it?

"Why?"

She eyed Violet. "You know why."

"Fuck all that. You like him?"

"Yeah, I do," she admitted quietly, watching him below as he ducked his head to hear something his sister was saying to him. He was right there in the room with her but he might as well be on the moon, and she *missed* him.

Violet leaned in and dropped her voice. "I'll let you in on a little secret. I think he likes you, too."

"You think so?" She hated that desperate note of hope in her voice.

"I do. He does that sad little thing where he thinks he's being chill but he manages to bring up your name in almost every conversation. 'Did you ask Mira about that?' 'Do you think we should check with Mira before we schedule this?' 'Have you seen Mira? I have to ask her this random question that is in no way part of her job.' It's honestly disgusting how into you he is. I can't believe everyone isn't onto him at this point."

"Don't say that," she groaned.

"You know you can't keep it secret forever, right? People always find out."

"Yeah, I know."

Violet tossed back the last of her champagne. "I need another drink because I am volunteering to be your beard for the evening. I'll go insert myself in Will's family so you can come with me and have an excuse to talk to him. That means I'll have to make conversation with his insufferable Tory father, so I hope you know what a huge sacrifice I'm making for you here."

"Violet, you're a hero, but that's okay. I think I'm just going back to the track."

"What, *now*?"

"Yeah. I'm worried some of my files ended up in the advance pack out for Monza, and I need to make sure they go back to Lennox."

"But I think the Awful Hawleys are leaving soon. Will might be looking for you."

"It's okay." She glanced back at Will down below. "I just need to think about this a little bit. Alone."

Will stood in the front entrance of the reception room gritting his teeth while his mother griped at his father about something.

"I don't understand why they even came," he muttered under his breath to Jem.

"Because the plan was to attend the reception after the race, and Mother isn't going to deviate from the plan, even when the day goes to shit and everybody ends up loathing each other." She downed the last of her champagne in one gulp. Jem had dealt with their mother's sniping by drinking her body weight in champagne. God, how he envied her.

To be fair, neither of his parents had said anything particularly offensive at the reception. There were a lot of people there, some they even judged to be marginally important, so it wouldn't do to make a scene like the one in his motor home.

The Mira situation was still eating at him. He'd wanted her with him today. Dealing with his parents' bullshit would have been a lot easier if she'd been there. That was the whole point of relationships, right? He'd thought they were trying to have one, but he'd had to deal with today on his own, so what the fuck did he know? Maybe he was wrong.

"All right, Mum," Ed said. "The valet has just brought the car around, so why don't we shove off?"

"Language, Edward," she muttered under her breath, and Ed rolled his eyes.

"Will, good luck at Monza!" he called over his shoulder as he propelled their mother toward the door.

"Thanks, mate."

"William." His father turned back to him briefly, then looked away again. "It was good to see you."

Then he left as well.

"So much for that," he sighed.

Jem squeezed his arm. "I'm sorry. I should have known they'd blow it."

"It's nothing less than I expected."

Jem opened her mouth to say something, then stopped, which was totally out of character. Ordinarily she said whatever was on her mind without hesitation. It's what he loved most about her.

"What?" he prompted.

"I know they were horrible, but they're not in a great place right now, if that makes any difference. Especially Dad."

"What do you mean? What's going on?"

She shook her head. "Nothing you need to worry about."

"Jem, don't do that. I'm not your baby brother anymore. Tell me."

"You will always be my baby brother. Look, it's just . . ." She blew out a breath, ruffling her dark fringe. "The firm is in a bit of a sticky spot at the moment," she finally admitted. "And Dad, being Dad, would rather blame anyone but himself. You're the only one not around, so I'm afraid he's decided it would all be different if you were."

"The bank is in trouble? How?"

She waved a hand in the air. "The banking world has modernized. Hawley and Sons . . . hasn't. That's all."

Will rolled his eyes. "That tracks. Dad wouldn't embrace modernity if it was all that stood between him and a fiery death."

"Yeah, well, he's going to embrace tradition right into insolvency, if he's not careful."

"It's that bad?"

"I keep telling him we need to diversify. Maybe accept some clients whose families didn't come over in 1066, but he won't listen."

Figured. Of the three of them, Jem was the one with vision. But she was a daughter, not a son, so she was the last person their father would listen to.

"Well, diversity of any kind has never been Dad's strong suit." Jem barked out a laugh.

He grasped her hand and squeezed. "Listen, are you going to be okay?"

Ed poked his head back in. "Jem, she's ready to go, and you know she gets testy if you make her wait."

Jem rolled her eyes. "And I get testy when she acts like a right bitch." She turned back to Will. "Don't worry about us. We'll be fine. You just keep yourself safe out there."

Jem would be fine. She'd always land on her feet. But Ed's whole life was Hawley and Sons. And Clarissa and the girls were relying on him, too. But Jem was smiling brightly at him, probably sorry she ever said anything, so he let it go. For now.

"If I'm meant to stay safe then I'm definitely in the wrong line of work."

"You know what I mean. Now shove off and go find her."

He startled. "What do you mean? Who?"

She gave a shrug of exaggerated innocence. "Don't know. But you couldn't stop looking around the room tonight. It was obvious you were on the hunt for someone. And since you ordinarily can't be bothered to look for the ladies but let them look for you, I'm guessing this one, whoever she is, must be special."

He stuffed his hands in his pockets and looked down at his feet. "Maybe? I dunno. It's tricky."

"Well, any girl who's got you feeling a little unsure of yourself gets my vote." She reached up to pinch his cheek and he swatted her hand away. "You and this pretty face of yours have had it too easy. You need to work for it a bit. It'll be good for you."

"Jem!" Ed called in desperation from behind her. "The longer she waits, the worse she gets!"

"Coming! Take care, Will."

She hugged him and he squeezed her back. "You, too."

He watched them go, still thinking about what Jem had said. She was right. In the past, he'd never had to exert much effort if he wanted someone. But he'd been pursuing Mira since the first day he saw her, which had to mean she—this—was different. Important. If he wanted more with her—and he did—he was going to have to suck it up and be brave.

Pulling out his phone, he sent a text to Violet.

Do you know where Mira is? I need to ask her something.

She texted back immediately.

Your *girlfriend* is back at the track. Next time text her directly.

Well. Seemed Violet had figured it out. Now it was time for him and Mira to figure it out, too.

33

Usually the crew would have had almost everything struck and loaded out this many hours after a race, but since they were heading into the midseason break and the Lennox factory was just a couple of hours' drive away, her father had given everyone the night off. There was no one in the Lennox garage to even wonder why Mira had shown up there at midnight.

She hadn't been lying to Violet, exactly. Even though the teams weren't allowed to work on the midseason break, she knew she'd go crazy if she didn't have access to her most critical paperwork. She retrieved her files, then headed to the garage to be sure everything going in the advance shipment to Monza was properly labeled. But now that she was here, she was standing between the two cars, clipboard in hand, and staring into space instead of working.

She needed to talk to Will, but she was terrified. What if she told him she wanted a real relationship and he . . . didn't? That would hurt. Actually, it would be devastating, because no matter how hard she'd tried to keep a handle on her feelings, she had to admit, at least to herself, that she was crazy about him. And if he didn't want her back—

"Hi."

She shrieked and spun around.

Will was standing just inside the side door to the garage, hands in his pockets.

She flattened her palm over her pounding heart. "What are you doing here? You scared me to death."

"I could ask you the same thing. What are you doing here alone at this hour?"

"Just going over some stuff." She gestured to her ignored list.

He eyed her in that way he did when he knew she was bull-shitting. "Really?"

She dropped her eyes to her checklist, fiddling with the frayed corner of the paper. "I wanted to check a few things—"

"Mira."

She looked up at him. "Yeah?"

"I missed you today."

She blinked, surprised. "You did?"

He took his hands out of his pockets and rubbed them together. He was nervous, she realized. Will was *nervous*. "I did. My parents were being assholes. I mean, no surprise there. But maybe it wouldn't have been so bad if you'd been there with me. They'd still be assholes because—"

"Will."

"Yeah?"

"I missed you, too."

He exhaled and smiled. Then he ran a hand through his hair and crossed the garage to stand in front of her. He was still wearing the fitted charcoal suit and black dress shirt he'd been wearing at the reception. When he was with her, he was either dressed for a race at the track or undressed in her bed. Seeing him dressed up and hot was making her feel all flushed and fluttery.

"Look," he said. "I'm sorry about how that went with my family today. We haven't really discussed—"

"You're right. We didn't talk about it. It's fine." If her feelings were hurt, that was nobody's fault but hers.

"It wasn't fine, Mira. That was fucking awful."

"You were just doing what I asked you to do."

He nodded slowly, looking down at the floor. "I was. But I don't think I want to do that anymore."

Her heart stopped beating in her chest. Didn't want to do *what* anymore. *This?* Him and her? He'd said he'd missed her, but maybe he didn't mean it like—

"You'll like Jem and Ed," he continued. "When you get a chance to meet them properly."

She blinked, trying to halt the panic spiral she'd been falling into. "You want me to meet them?"

"I did today. I do. Listen, Mira . . ." He stepped closer, reaching out to snag her fingertips with his. "We're off for the next two weeks, yeah? I was thinking . . . maybe we should spend some time together outside a hotel room. I'm heading to New York. I wondered . . . I mean, maybe you'd want to . . . Will you come with me?"

Relief flooded through her, so intense she felt almost weak-kneed. But as much as she wanted to fling her arms around him, cover him in kisses, and say yes, she still needed to proceed with caution. They were in the middle of a minefield, and things could explode around them at any moment if she fucked up.

"Traveling together is not exactly keeping a low profile," she pointed out.

"But it's America. Nobody knows who I am there."

"Americans do watch racing, you know."

He reached out and took her other hand, squeezing them both with his. She was shaking with nerves, hanging on to him like an anchor. "Look, I don't know what it will be like. I can't promise anything. But know I want you there with me. Will you come?"

She was still terrified. Terrified of everything that had gone wrong in her past, and terrified of everything that could go wrong in the future. But she could see in Will's eyes that he was scared, too. This was new territory for both of them. And in the end, she wanted him. That was more powerful than her fear.

"Yes," she finally said. "Yes, I'll come."

The grin he unleashed nearly washed away every reservation she had.

He pulled her into a tight hug. "Thank you."

"Why are you thanking me? You invited me," she murmured into the crook of his neck.

He squeezed her tighter. "Because I get you all to myself for two weeks."

"You've always got me all to yourself." He could have her, body and heart, for as long as he wanted her, as long as she got to have him, too. As long as she could hold him like this.

"Always?" She'd heard that shift in his voice enough at this point to know when Will was thinking filthy thoughts. "Like now?"

She leaned back enough to see his face. "Are you kidding? We're in the garage."

"There's no one here."

"Someone could come."

"It's the middle of the night. No one's coming. Except you, if you want to."

His hand slid down the small of her back to her ass, where he squeezed. She was wearing the black dress she'd bought in Barcelona, and the thin silk was barely even a barrier between the warmth of his palm and her skin. Despite the less-than-romantic surroundings and the chill of the night air, she felt her body heating in response. She was so shamelessly easy when it came to him.

"I'm not getting down on that floor. It's filthy and freezing." She might want him, but not that badly.

His dark blue eyes lit up with mischief. "I wasn't thinking about the floor." Oh, she knew that look. When she saw it, she knew he was about to do something outrageous and heavenly to her.

"Then where—?"

He tilted his head toward his car, right behind her.

"Are you insane? It costs millions of pounds!" She pushed on his chest, but he didn't release her.

"We'll be careful."

"And we wouldn't even fit. You barely fit."

He rolled his eyes. "Not *in* it."

"Then what are you suggesting?"

Without looking away from her, he lifted his hands to the straps of her dress. "Let's start here."

She felt the tiny straps slide over her shoulders and she licked her lips apprehensively. Was she really going to let him do this here?

"God, I love you in this dress," he said lowly, his eyes roaming over her. "And out of it." He dragged the straps down her arms and she felt the silk slither down her chest. It caught on her nipples, because they were hard and pebbled, already aching for him.

"I'm not—"

"Not all the way off." He leaned in and captured her mouth in a kiss. His mouth was warm and drugging. She forgot everything when he kissed her.

"Just this far off," he murmured against her mouth, dragging the silk down to her waist. Her arms were pinned to her sides, still caught by the straps. He wrapped his arms around her and lowered his mouth to her breast.

"Will . . ." She sucked in a breath as he took her nipple in his mouth.

She swayed in his arms, getting hotter by the second, moaning every time he sucked her. By the time he lifted his head to kiss her again, she was so wild for him that she'd have let him do anything he wanted, even if the entire pit crew was here watching.

She managed to free her arms from the straps so she could reach for him, digging her fingers into his hair as she kissed him.

"I've always wanted to do something . . ." he said between kisses, beginning to walk her backward. "To try this . . ."

"What?" she whispered eagerly. She was already so wet for him. He could bend her over the nearest table and she'd be there in seconds.

He kissed her again. "Call it kind of a fantasy. For as long as I've been driving."

Suddenly her calves hit the low nose of his car, right in front of where he sat when he raced.

"I told you," she mumbled in between kisses. "We won't fit."

"Just trust me."

Grasping her hips, he pushed her back until she sat down. She braced herself with her hands, unable to stop calculating what the carbon fiber body cost, even now when she was sitting on it half naked.

"What are you—" She bit back the rest of her question as he started shrugging out of his suit jacket. Her mouth went dry as he tossed the jacket to the side and got down on his knees. *Oh.*

"I've always wanted to do this." He set his hands on her knees and spread them apart, leaning in between her legs. His hands slid up her thighs, pushing her dress up, and then he grasped the backs of her thighs, coaxing them farther apart as he kissed her. He had her nearly naked in the middle of the garage and she absolutely did not care.

"Lie back," he commanded.

She did as he asked, leaning back, reclining across the front of his car. His expression was rapt as he looked her over. He caught the sides of her thong with his fingertips. "Can I take this off?"

She licked her lips and nodded.

He slid it down her legs and off, and then he leaned down and put his mouth on her. The moment his tongue touched her she arched up and gasped. With one hand, she fisted his hair, flattening the palm of the other to the cool glossy surface of the car, trying desperately to ground herself as he licked her core. She heard her own moan echo off the steel walls of the garage, but self-consciousness had become a foreign concept. All she wanted was him, his mouth, this moment.

Her release was already bearing down on her when he slid two fingers inside of her. "Will," she breathed.

"Right here, on my car," he whispered against her.

That was all it took. She was arching up off the car, gasping for air, shaking all over as her body was consumed with pure, aching pleasure.

New York,
New York

"I can't believe we just did that."

"Did what?"

Mira momentarily lost her train of thought, watching as Will carefully licked a trail of melting ice cream off the side of his waffle cone before it could reach his hand. Maybe she could drip melted ice cream on herself and he could—

"Did what?" he repeated. He took another swipe at his ice cream and she couldn't decide if she was glad he'd decided on a cone or not, because watching him lick it for the past ten minutes was getting her really worked up and they were a long way from their hotel room. His lips, his tongue . . .

"Oh. Dinner. We just went out to dinner. Together. In public."

He shrugged. "We can do it all the time, if you want. And not just at little no-name restaurants in Brooklyn, where no one is going to recognize me."

She poked at her own ice cream with her spoon. "Will . . ."

"I'm just saying, we've got two more nights. Let me take you out someplace nice tomorrow. Who gives a fuck who sees us?"

"Will."

"I'm serious, Mira. This whole week, all these lunches and receptions I've had with sponsors . . . I really hated that you weren't with me."

"I know."

This trip hadn't been exactly the romantic getaway of her dreams. His days had been full of meetings with sponsors, none of which she could go to, so she'd spent most days knocking around the city on her own. Every time he had to leave he asked her to come. And every time, she'd said no.

She was so happy with Will. Every minute they'd managed to steal together in New York had been blissful. But when she imagined the world finding out about them, she was gripped with an elemental terror that she couldn't talk herself out of.

They tossed out the wrappers from their ice cream. "Just say the word, Mira, and it's Jean-Georges tomorrow. Or Per Se. Or whichever is the best right now. We'll get dressed up and do it right."

"You know I don't need stuff like that to have fun with you, right? Tonight . . . in that back garden of that restaurant in Brooklyn was perfect."

"It was." He smiled at her, but it didn't quite reach his eyes. "Come on. Night's not over yet. Let's walk over the bridge."

They'd already taken a big risk, going out to dinner tonight. If they were smart, they'd grab a cab back to the hotel now. But she could never seem to hang on to her smart, sensible side around Will. It was a beautiful, warm summer night and he was right here in front of her looking absolutely edible in jeans and a T-shirt, and she wanted to enjoy him as much as she possibly could for as long as it lasted.

"Let's go."

The pedestrian walkway was crowded with people, and Will, a baseball cap covering that gorgeous head of dark hair, barely stood out. The sun was low over the horizon, setting New York Harbor afire with colors. At the center of the bridge, they stopped and found a spot along the railing, staring out across the water.

"It's so beautiful," she sighed.

When she glanced at him, he was facing her, and the look in his eyes made her heart tumble over in her chest. He reached out to tuck a curl behind her ear, his fingers lingering on the side of her face. His expression shifted, and he licked his lips. Her chest tightened, feeling like something momentous was about to happen, like he was about to say the words that had been fighting to burst out of her all week. "Mira—"

"Hey, you're Will Hawley! I can't believe it!"

She startled, jerking around. It was a young guy, maybe sixteen, and British. She cursed herself silently. Some anonymous restaurant in Brooklyn was one thing. The Brooklyn Bridge was packed with tourists from abroad, and a lot of them probably watched racing. They'd been so stupid.

Will tugged the front of his baseball cap down instinctively. "I, ah . . ."

The kid raised his phone. "Can I take your picture? My mates'll never believe I saw you here!"

She reached out for Will's arm in a panic. "No!"

Immediately, he stepped in front of her and reached for the kid's phone. "Here, we'll do a selfie."

"Seriously?"

Will turned the kid the other way, angling his phone at their faces and away from her. She finally exhaled, turning her back to them and keeping her head down. Will exchanged a few words with the starstruck racing fan and then sent him on his way. He came to join her, leaning his elbows on the railing.

"Sorry about that."

"No, *I'm* sorry."

"What are you sorry for?"

"You shouldn't have to do this. The sneaking around, the subterfuge, the lying. I mean, my dad thinks I'm in Thailand with Violet!" She swallowed hard around the lump in her throat. "You wouldn't have to do any of this if you were here with anyone else."

He was quiet for a minute. Then he shifted closer until his shoulder was pressed against hers. Slowly he reached out and took her hand in his, threading their fingers together. "You know I don't want to be here with anyone else, Mira. Just you. But I want all of you. The daytime hours, too. I'm tired of pretending you don't exist when . . ." He exhaled hard, staring out over the water. "When I'm thinking about you all the fucking time."

It was just what she wanted to hear, but the way he said it— defeated and mad—made her feel *terrible*.

"You know how complicated this is for me."

"I get it. You've been through shit I can't even imagine. But—"

"I know. Hiding isn't going to make everything magically better."

"Look, what if you just start with your dad?"

She sputtered a laugh, imagining Will coming to meet her dad before a date, like some old TV show from the fifties. Her dad would be the *hardest* place to start. "You're ready to face my dad? Really?"

"Yeah, I'm ready." He paused, looking at her uncertainly. "Unless you're not? If you don't think—"

"No." She grabbed at his forearms. "It's not just my dad, Will. It's everyone. A lot of ugly stuff is going to get stirred up again the minute my name is attached to yours. Are you ready for that?"

He scoffed. "Ugly press is my specialty, remember?"

She squeezed his hand with hers. "But you shouldn't have to deal with it. It's not fair to you."

"Hey." He took her face in his hands, heedless of who might see them. "It's not fair to you that you ever had to deal with it at all, especially when you were just sixteen. I'm a grown-up. I can handle it. For you, I want to."

How could she keep denying him when he was looking at her like that? When he was telling her how much she meant to him? She didn't want to hide anymore either. She wanted to tell the world she was in love with Will, because she was. *Hopelessly* in love with him. What she had with him was worth whatever she had to face. The time for fear was over.

"Okay, when we get back, I'll tell my dad."

He grinned, pulling out his phone and holding it up to her. "Hang on. Say that again so I can record it as proof."

"I can take one of both of you, if you want." They turned to look at the smiling older woman who'd been passing by.

Will looked at her in question.

Mira took a deep breath. "That would be great. Thanks."

Will handed the woman his phone and slipped his arm around her shoulders. After the woman had left, Will showed her the photo. She stared down at the glowing screen, at their faces pressed together and their wide smiles, with his arm around her and the sunset over the harbor and the Manhattan skyline behind them. They both looked so happy, just a guy and a girl out having fun. Just a guy and a girl, falling in love.

"**M**ira, what's this dinner you've got me scheduled for on Sunday night?" Her father was staring at the calendar on his phone in confusion.

Mira froze, turning to face him. "Um, that's with me, actually."

His eyebrows furrowed together. "You?"

"I've got something I need to discuss with you."

Will. She was going to tell him all about Will.

She'd returned from New York head over heels for Will and ready to tell her father all about it. But in the chaos of packing the team and traveling to Italy after the break, there simply hadn't been a good moment. It wasn't fair to distract her father or Will with a bunch of personal drama in the run-up to a race.

But by Sunday night, the race would be over and she'd tell him everything. She'd considered bringing Will along for the dinner, but that was probably too much, too fast. She'd tell her dad about them herself and give him a minute to adjust to the idea before he saw Will again. Once he had a little time to process it, she was sure he'd be okay with it. After all, Will was on track to win the world championship. Her dad *loved* Will.

"You're with me all day long, Mira. What do you need to talk about?"

"Not before the race. I don't want to distract you."

"You're worrying me."

She leaned up to kiss his cheek. "It's nothing to be worried about, I promise. All good news. But it can wait until after the race, okay?"

He smiled and shook his head. "Whatever you say. Actually, I've got to get over to the race bay—"

She laughed. "See? Go. I'll catch up with you in the pit lane."

Once he'd gone, she checked her phone. If she hurried, she could make it over to Will's motor home and wish him luck before he had to get ready for qualifying.

But inside, he was nowhere to be seen. Now she wouldn't see him until after he'd run qualifying and finished up his strategy meeting with Tae, Harry, and her dad. She fired off a good-luck text to him as she clattered back down the motor home steps, so she didn't see who was waiting for her there until she nearly ran into him.

"I thought that was you."

Brody. Wearing his green race suit, arms crossed casually over his chest, he was leaning against the side of Will's motor home and grinning down at her in a way that sent a pang of dread straight through her. He'd always deployed that boyish grin with such ruthless effectiveness. The years had been kind to him and probably always would be. Those tiny laugh lines around his eyes lent his face a sort of open friendliness that probably came in handy. He wore his reddish blond hair a little long, giving him a windblown surfer look he could still pull off. It made him look younger than he was, and Brody had never looked—or acted—his age.

She'd tried so hard to avoid this—*him*. But now he was here, and he was looking at her in a way that set off alarms in her head. Why, why, *why* was he seeking her out now? Why couldn't she just erase him from existence, like blocking a contact on her phone, never to see him or hear from him again? But there was no blocking a real person, and after seven years, Brody McKnight, in the flesh, was standing in front of her, demanding her attention.

"I saw you scurrying past. How have you been, gorgeous?"

His familiar lazy Australian accent sent a wave of revulsion slithering down her spine. And that generic "gorgeous"? She'd bet money he didn't *quite* remember her name, which after *everything*, was so insulting she wanted to scream.

How had she let this asshole wreck her life the way he had? He was *nobody*. Just some arrogant, semitalented piece of shit. Her nerves were making her feel shaky, but she refused to let him see that she was upset. No way would she give him the satisfaction of an emotional reaction.

"Brody." Nothing about her body language or tone of voice was giving out any sort of invitation. But when had her wishes ever mattered to Brody? He'd always just taken what he wanted, when he wanted it.

"Nice to see you back on the track, doll. You're looking great."

"What do you want?"

He had the audacity to look surprised at her frosty tone, like he had no idea why she could possibly be angry with him. His golden eyebrows raised and he chuckled. "I just wanted to catch up, darling. To see what you've been up to."

She flushed with anger, from her feet to the tips of her hair. It boiled up like a volcano in her chest, making her incandescent with rage. "It's *Miranda*! And I'm not your darling or your doll or any fucking thing else! I think you know damned well what I've been doing with my life, Brody. I've been putting it back together after you took a sledgehammer to it."

Brody paused, a tiny hesitation in his slick game of seduction. His eyes, those twinkling green eyes she once thought were the clear, bright windows to his generous soul, flicked over her, assessing. The Prince Charming expression slipped for an instant before he recovered, grinning wider than ever. How had she ever fallen for this bullshit act of his?

"You're still mad about that?" he said teasingly, like all he'd done was steal her parking space, not that he'd seduced her as a teenager, convinced her she was in love with him, and then tossed her out with the trash when the game stopped being fun. Her hands were shaking with the effort it took not to reach out and smack him.

"Mad?" She sighed, and raked her eyes down him in judgment. "I'd have to give a shit about you to be mad, and I don't. If I'm mad at anyone, it's me, for letting you take up so much fucking room in my head. You don't deserve it. You never did. Everything about you is just a sad fraud, and I think you know that."

He straightened up, all traces of that charming smile gone. He looked furious, which was good, because that's exactly how she felt, and for once, he was going to hear it. "That's why you always need a new girl, a younger one, because the young ones are easier to fool, right? They can't see through you to what you really are, just a shell of a human being, filled with nothing but your own desperate, needy ego."

His jaw clenched as he stared down at her. She willed herself to stare straight back at him. "You seem to have a lot of bruised feelings there, sweetheart."

If she stayed another second, she was probably going to start crying, and she'd never let him see that. "I'm not your fucking sweetheart," she spat, then she turned to make her escape.

"Hey." He reached out and snagged her upper arm, his grip tight enough to jerk her back around to face him.

"YOU'D BETTER GET YOUR HANDS off her, McKnight, before I rip your bloody arm off."

Brody slowly released Mira—the sight of his hand gripping her arm had Will almost nuclear with rage—and turned to examine him. When he'd rounded the corner and seen Brody talking to Mira, seen how obviously upset Brody had made her, he'd been furious. But he wasn't going to intervene. He was going to let her handle him herself—until the bastard touched her.

"Do you have a problem, Hawley?"

"I have a problem with you pressing yourself on a woman who clearly wants nothing to do with you."

"She and I are old friends, so how about you step aside, mate?" Brody's broad, drawling Aussie accent was just as annoying as his smug, shit-eating grin.

"How about you get your bloody ass out of our paddock . . . *mate?*"

Brody's smarmy grin faltered, temper flaring in his eyes. "Look, keep your overtaking confined to the track, Hawley. Off the track, they're all fair game."

Will's tenuous hold on his temper snapped. Reaching out, he grabbed a fistful of the front of Brody's race suit. "She's not some fucking *game*, asshole!"

Brody shoved at his arm and Will released him, breathing hard, teeth grinding in his fury. He felt Mira's touch on his shoulder.

"Will, don't. Just let it go."

Brody's eyes flicked from Mira, to his motor home behind her, and back to Will. "Ah, I see. I was poaching another man's turf. Don't blame you. I've sampled myself. Well worth it."

It was impossible to tell if the roaring in his ears was his blood surging to a boiling point, or if it was his own shout of rage. All Will knew is that he lunged and his fist made loud, satisfying contact with Brody's jaw. A sharp stab of pain radiated through his hand and up his arm, but he didn't care, reaching for Brody, fisting his hands in his race suit again, hauling him forward. Brody swiped at him. Will dodged, but not quite fast enough, and Brody's fist glanced across his cheekbone, snapping his head back. Before Brody could get in another one, Will drove forward, planting his shoulder in Brody's chest and propelling him back against the side of the motor home.

Mira screamed, and the air around Will erupted in shouts as people rushed in from all corners of the paddock. Hands were grabbing at him, seizing his arms and shoulders, pulling him back away from Brody. A couple of Deloux mechanics had shown up, shoving themselves between him and Brody, and holding Brody back when he tried to come at Will again. Beyond thinking clearly, Will struggled against the hands restraining him, desperate to get at Brody and plant his fist in that fucker's face, to wipe the smug smile off it once and for all.

"Will! Will, stop. Not here, not now." That was Omar, shouting in his ear. Tae was there, too, on his other side.

"Leave him!" Mira said, planting a hand on his chest and putting herself in his line of sight.

As his eyes met hers, the rage ebbed. He was still shaking with unspent adrenaline, but he could think again. And this wasn't great.

A cluster of Deloux mechanics were huddled around Brody. Several more Lennox guys had also shown up. Violet had materialized, too.

"Oh, my God," she was muttering, "everyone's recording on their fucking phones."

"Get your boy out of here!" Omar shouted at the Deloux mechanics, still keeping one arm braced across Will's shoulders to hold him back.

"Just who do you think you are, calling me a 'boy,' boy?" Brody shouted. Now Will was the one restraining Omar, who made a lunge in Brody's direction. But the Deloux guys were pushing Brody back, dragging him out of the paddock before Omar could get to him.

"Stop," he said to Omar. "I've already fucked up enough. Don't make it worse."

"Brody started it," Mira said.

"Yeah and Will threw the first punch," Violet snapped. Then she glanced at Will. "Sorry, but it's true."

"You've gotta go," Tae said, taking him by the shoulder and turning him away. "You're almost up."

Fuck. Qualifying. He had to go out there and fucking drive. *Now.* His hands were still shaking.

Tae started dragging away Will, who stopped and turned back, looking for Mira. Every head in the paddock turned to watch as he crossed back to her. Well, fuck it. It was all out of the bag anyway—no saving that. So he wasn't leaving without checking on her.

He took her by the shoulders, crouching slightly to look her in the eye. "Are you okay?"

She was pale but she nodded tightly. "I'm fine. I'm sorry. He just—"

"Stop. The only one who should be sorry is Brody fucking McKnight."

She reached up and touched his face, the spot on his left cheek where Brody's fist had caught him. "You're hurt."

"I'm fine. You're sure you're okay?"

"I've got her," Violet said, stepping up to Mira's side. "You just go run quali. We'll talk after."

After. There would be consequences for this. He didn't know what they would be, but he was sure they were coming. No time to think about it now, though. He had to go get in the car and drive.

"I'll see you after?" he said to Mira, brushing a couple of curls out of her face and tucking them back behind her ear.

She nodded. "Just go. Good luck."

Will walked between Omar and Tae back to the race bay. He shook his hands out, trying to dispel the stiffness. His whole body still felt wired with adrenaline.

"That fucking asshole," Omar muttered.

"He's probably already in the FIA offices filing his fucking complaint," Will seethed as the enormity of his fuckup began to register. A fight. A physical *fight*. He'd fucking *punched* Brody McKnight.

"Forget it," Tae commanded. "The place to kick his ass properly is out on the track. Nothing else matters."

Will nodded, but that was easier said than done. He did his best to put himself on autopilot as the well-oiled Lennox crew got him geared up and into the car.

A few minutes later, Tae's voice crackled in his earpiece. "Okay, you gotta shake that off, Will. It doesn't matter now. You're okay to start the engine."

Somehow he fired the engine and got out onto the track, running through the usual routines to warm up the tires and check the systems, even though his head was a million miles away. He could still hear Violet's voice. *Everyone's recording on their fucking phones.* By now it was out there. His gut hollowed out, that same feeling of pressing dread he used to get three years ago, waking up hungover and checking his phone to see just how bad the news was from the night before. None of that had been as bad as this was about to be.

But then he thought of Mira's face, remembered Brody's hand on her arm, and the rage flared up bright and hot, and for a moment, the only thing he was sorry about was not pounding Brody straight into the fucking pavement.

"Denis is pushing behind. Watch for traffic with Denis. You're clear behind him." Tae's voice jerked him back to the present. The very important present.

So far he'd been running through the out lap pretty much on instinct. Weaving, slowing, gradually speeding up, letting the tires heat up until the engineers were satisfied with the specs. But qualifying starts were staggered and other drivers were out on the track already running at full speed, or in the middle of a cooldown lap. All he needed now was to stumble into someone else's path and pile on yet another penalty on top of whatever was coming.

He held up on the weaving, allowing René Denis to scream past at full speed. As soon as the engineers gave the all clear, that would be him, and he couldn't afford to be less than one hundred percent on his game. As he entered the last turn, he could feel it. The tire grip was perfect. He didn't even need Tae's confirmation that they were in the sweet spot of the engineers' target window.

"All clear for your push lap," Tae said, and Will smoothly applied the throttle as the car swung wide to the exit of Turn Eleven, starting his push lap.

On the straight, he opened the car up to the maximum, well north of three hundred kilometers an hour, and felt himself unclench slightly now that he was back in the zone. There was no traffic headed to the first turn, and he smashed the brakes and dropped down the gears, navigating the slow and clunky chicane. He smoothly applied the throttle on the way out, and then full energy as he headed toward the next turn.

It was an easy one and he found the absolute limit on the exit, trying to maximize the time on throttle as he eyed the traffic around him on the track, now on cooldown laps. It had become a game with some drivers to wait till the last second to get out of the way, or to casually narrow the entry and exits for those on push laps. Not enough for a penalty, but more than enough to steal a tenth or two from a competitor, which was sometimes all it took.

Before he knew it, he was flying through the straight, flanked by trees, and coming up on the high-speed chicane. Tae was barking stats in his ears, which just confirmed what he already felt in his gut. Despite the shitty start to today's qualifying, he was dropping the hammer, laying down a time that would once again secure him pole position in tomorrow's race.

There was a slow-moving car ahead and to his right, in the midst of its cooldown lap, but he'd pass it easily well before he had to swing out for the approach to the final turn. As he gained on it, he registered the flash of the car's green livery. Brody. Of course.

But then the gap between him and Brody wasn't narrowing at the pace he'd expected. Was that fucker actually *speeding up* on his cooldown lap, just to get in his way? Fine. He wanted to play it like that? Will would turn it around on him, and draft in his slip stream all the way up to the turn, using him to claw back a few more tenths of a second.

With the two-hundred-meter board in sight Will pulled out from behind him, but then, milliseconds before he began to pass, Brody twitched his wheels ever so slightly to the right. It was tiny, a wobble so slight it was impossible to say if it was there or not. But Will felt that wobble in his gut, as surely as if Brody had just thrown another punch at him. His body registered Brody's movement even before his head did, and he moved to the outside edge of the track to avoid a collision. Motherfucker. But it was done now, he'd passed him. He could still save this. In his mind, he envisioned his best approach to the turn from his current, less-than-ideal starting position and angled the car into it, still flying at three hundred kilometers an hour.

That's when he felt it.

Tink.

The sound of his back tire clipping Brody's front end, because the motherfucker was *still accelerating.*

It all happened so fast. A shudder. A shriek of rubber on asphalt. A bank of flashing lights from the control panel. Just enough time to register a blown tire, and then he was spinning out, straight toward the wall. The sound was deafening: screeching tires, Tae shouting on Race Radio, and then the collision, the impact rocketing through his body as it slammed through the car, metal and fiberglass crumpling all around him. His head snapped hard against his HANS device as the car spun again, slammed against the wall again, and finally came to a stop. And then there was just silence.

36

"**W**hy is it taking so long?" Mira gripped the sides of her chair to keep herself from exploding into hysteria.

She and Violet were sitting side by side on hard plastic chairs in the medical center waiting room. Will was in the back, still being examined.

She might never recover from the horror of that moment, watching Will's car spin into the track wall, the sparks, the flying debris, the smoke and flame, and then the awful stillness after. It had felt like an hour, but it was just seconds before she'd seen him moving inside. Still alive. In that moment, that was the only thing that mattered.

He'd climbed out of the car by himself, which was a good sign, but his in-ear accelerometer had gone off, which meant he'd sustained a serious impact and required a mandatory medical workup.

Now he was off in back and her father was in there with him, and there was no way any of this was going to end well.

"I'm sure he's fine," Violet said. "You know they have to check him out if the accelerometer goes off."

"I know," she muttered numbly.

In her initial panic about Will, she'd forgotten all about the fight with Brody and what it would look like to her dad. To everyone else. Now it was all coming back and panic of a new kind threatened to overwhelm her. But she didn't have time for that now, not until she knew that Will was okay.

"I'm sure they're just being really cautious," Violet said again. "X-rays and CAT scans and all that. You know that stuff takes forever."

"Yeah, I know."

They sat in silence for several more minutes, Violet scrolling through her iPad, Mira staring at a scuff on the opposite wall and trying not to cry.

"Shit," Violet muttered.

"What?"

"Shit shit shit."

"Violet, what is it?"

Wordlessly, Violet handed her the iPad. The article was from a British gossip website. The British ones were always the worst. Right at the top, there was a slightly blurry photo of Will and Brody, Brody pinned to the side of Will's motor home and Will's hand gripping his race suit.

Underneath it screamed the headline "Formula One's Bad Boy Champ Takes Out Rivals on and off the Track!"

Part of her had known the second she'd come face-to-face with Brody that her hiding was done. Her past from seven years ago was about to come screaming back into her present. And now Will was right in the middle of it, too. It had nearly killed him. She felt sick . . . cold and shaky with dread. She didn't want to read the story, but her eyes moved over the text against her will, every word hitting her like a physical blow.

This season's Formula One sensation, Will Hawley, seems to be just as aggressive off the track as he is on it. Just moments before taking to the track for qualifying, Hawley took a swing at fellow driver Brody McKnight when he caught his lady friend chatting up Brody in the paddock. Team members for both drivers broke up the fight, but not before Hawley unleashed his rage and landed several blows on McKnight.

The woman in question, Miranda Wentworth, is not only the daughter of Lennox Motorsport's principal, Paul Wentworth; she's also got a bit of a past with Brody McKnight. Several years ago, she lured McKnight into a torrid affair just weeks before his marriage to actress Lulu Heatherington.

Wentworth returned to America after that scandal broke, but it seems, on her return to the sport, she's wasted no time snagging herself another driver. Or maybe two?

She fought back a swell of nausea and thrust the iPad at Violet, but the damning article still glowed on its surface. There was no escaping it now. Apparently, there never had been.

Violet surged to her feet, pacing back and forth across the tiny waiting room. "They're going to go crazy over this. It feeds right into Will's bad-boy narrative, and you know how much they love flogging that."

"It's bullshit, Violet! I told Brody to leave me alone and he wouldn't. He was harassing me and Will just—"

"Will threw the first punch," Violet said quietly.

"He was provoked."

"Doesn't matter in stories like these. It hits all the right selling points. Two hot superstar athletes fighting on the track and now fighting over a woman."

"I was *not* flirting with Brody. God, he disgusts me."

Violet stopped her pacing and came back to sit beside her. "Mira, you know I'm on your side. You were involved with him once, though."

Mira swallowed hard and dropped her eyes to the floor. "Yeah, I was."

"That's all these bloodsuckers are going to care about. They're going to have a field day with this. With *you*. They always try to paint the woman as the bad guy in these things. It's not fair, I'm sorry. But it's probably going to get a lot worse."

Right now, it was hard to imagine how things could possibly get worse. The last seven years of her life—her perfect grades at UCLA, her nonexistent personal life, all her hard work this season with Lennox—it was all washed away, deemed irrelevant because she'd once been stupid enough to sleep with Brody McKnight and was now audacious enough to get involved with Will Hawley. None of this was her fault and yet she couldn't help feeling frozen with shame.

Violet's phone rang, startling her out of her shock. Violet looked at the face and her expression grew impossibly grimmer.

"It's Ryan from Velocity. This can't be good."

Her heart sank. Will's major endorsement deal with Velocity, the new label they were supposed to roll out . . . Things had just gotten much, much worse. He might lose his endorsement. He'd been in a crash that could have killed him, one that might still end his entire season. Her father might get hauled in front of the FIA to answer for another scandal, and once again, here she sat at the center of everything.

As Violet turned away and accepted the Velocity call, Mira closed her eyes and folded in on herself, pressing her forehead to her knees. It was all too awful. There had to be something she could do to fix this, to keep it from getting any worse.

She lifted her head and blinked. Of course there was. There was *one* thing she could do. The thought of doing it made her feel like she was cutting out her own heart, but really, she had no choice, did she? Maybe she never had.

WILL HAD BEEN TRYING, unsuccessfully, to convince the Italian medical staff that he was fine, but no one seemed to be listening to him. Whether it was due to their rigorous commitment to his well-being or to his terrible Italian, he couldn't be sure.

The doctor and nurse were still prodding at him, shining a light in his eyes, taking notes in his chart, when the exam room curtain was ripped open to reveal Paul, Tae, and Mitchell, the team physician. Paul's expression was impossible to read, somewhere between panic and rage.

"Hi, Paul." He glanced over Paul's shoulder but couldn't see any sign of Mira.

Paul's eyes raked down Will and then cut to the doctor. "How is he?" he asked in perfect Italian. Will didn't understand the words, but he didn't miss Paul's gesture in his direction.

"Doing okay?" Tae asked him as the doctor, Paul, and Mitchell proceeded to have a discussion in Italian. Was he the only one who failed languages in school?

"I'm fine. They're just being cautious," he told Tae. "Is Mira out there?"

Tae cast an apprehensive glance at Paul. "She is."

"Can you go get her? I need to tell her—"

"How's the head?" Paul said to him.

"Head's fine. That's what I keep telling them. The stupid sensor triggered, but I'm fine." Mira must be so upset. He needed to see her.

"They said you don't have a concussion," Mitchell said. "Which is good news."

"I *know* I don't have a concussion. Honestly, I'm fine. Can you just get them to sign my release and—"

"And the hand?" Mitchell's eyes had fixed on his right hand, hidden under an ice pack. "The doctor said you've got some damage."

Will fought the urge to hide his hand behind his back. He'd managed to crash into a wall at three hundred kilometers an hour and walk away unscathed, but apparently smashing his fist into Brody's fucking face did some damage. He'd felt fine when he climbed into the car, but he'd still been buzzing with adrenaline. And then there was the shock of the crash. It was hard to feel anything in the midst of that. But the longer he sat here, the worse it felt.

"It's nothing." He held it out, and Mitchell and Paul leaned over, examining his red knuckles. "Just a little sore. It'll be fine by tomorrow."

Mitchell frowned forbiddingly. "This swelling's not good."

"It's fine." As proof, he flexed his thumb for Mitchell, but had to stop when a sudden flash of pain shot up his arm. He hissed through his teeth. Paul and Mitchell glanced up at him.

"Not so fine," Paul muttered.

Mitchell ran his fingers along his thumb, prodding at the obvious inflammation. "It hurts?"

"A little," Will conceded.

"A little?" When Mitchell rotated his thumb, Will winced again.

"A lot."

"Hmm." Mitchell was still scowling. "You've got a sprain."

"No. I'm sure it's just a little swollen. Give me a shot to bring down the inflammation and a little something for pain and

I'll be fine." Mitchell flexed his thumb again, and Will's face crumpled. Besides hurting like a beast, his range of motion was diminished. Like, nonexistent. "Fuck. Mitchell, you have to fix it."

Mitchell straightened, rubbing a hand over his short-cropped salt-and-pepper beard. "It's soft tissue damage, Will. There's nothing I can do for that."

Paul let out a tired exhale, his eyes falling closed. "Ah, bloody hell. That's that, then."

"What are you saying?"

Mitchell stared at him. "Will, you know what this means."

Yes, he did know. It took a million constant adjustments to operate a Formula One car and almost all of the controls were on the steering wheel—and they all required his thumbs. A sprained thumb. What a stupid fucking injury. But it was about the worst injury a driver could have. He had walked away from that crash unscathed, but this—his bloody fucking *thumb*—was going to put him out of the race.

"So he can't race?" Paul asked, sounding as if he already knew the answer.

Even hearing the words made Will feel sick.

Mitchell shook his head. "Not in Monza, for sure."

"And Spielberg?" Paul pressed. "That's in a week."

Mitchell heaved a sigh. "Ice and heat to bring down swelling, anti-inflammatories . . . we'll keep a close eye on it. And we'll just see. That's all we can do."

"Paul," Will pleaded, "come on. Mitchell can give me a cortisone shot. I'll ice up all night. I'm sure it'll be fine by tomorrow."

Paul shook his head, arms crossed over his chest, looking as cold and forbidding as a glacier. "I can't take that chance, Will. You know I can't. You're out for Monza."

At Harrow, when he was fourteen, he'd been playing a pickup game of football with some friends. He'd taken a wrong step into a divot in the grass and sprained his ankle. He'd ended up on crutches for six weeks. Mitchell was right— there was no predicting these things. Best-case scenario, he'd be back behind the wheel in Austria. Worst? His season was over and so was his fight for the world championship.

The instant her father emerged from the back with Mitchell and Tae, Mira was on her feet. "How is he?"

Her father met her worried eyes with his own steely gaze. She fought the impulse to squirm or hide. A nightmarish conversation with her father was right around the corner, but not until she knew Will was safe.

"No concussion," Paul finally said. "But he's sprained his thumb. He's not racing this weekend."

"Shit," Violet said.

Mira groaned and wrapped her arms around her midsection. There seemed to be no bottom to this well of terrible news they'd fallen into. Will's race this week—maybe his whole season—was in jeopardy. He'd fought so hard, accomplished so much, and it might all be ruined, all because of her.

"He'll be back for Spielberg, though?" Violet asked.

Paul shook his head. "No telling."

She closed her eyes and swallowed hard, battling a swelling sense of nausea as she forced out the words. "When can he leave?"

"He's finishing up now. We'll drive him back. You girls head back to the hotel."

She shook her head. "No, I need to talk to Will. I'll wait."

Silence greeted her statement. She couldn't bear to look at her father to see his reaction.

"Violet," he said quietly. "I'm leaving my car and driver for Will. Can you arrange cars for us? I'll be right out."

Violet glanced between Mira and her father, then she nodded and ducked out of the room with Mitchell and Tae.

"Mira," Paul said lowly.

Her eyes started to water, the emotional toll of the day combining with the relief of knowing Will was okay and her need to see him herself. Her throat closed up and she couldn't speak.

"Mira," Paul said again, "do you know why Will went after Brody McKnight today?"

She swallowed hard, unable to look at her father. She kept her face averted, eyes on the floor, and nodded. He sighed heavily and she broke, the tears streaking down her face.

"Was this what dinner on Sunday was going to be about?"

She nodded again.

"I suppose I should be grateful you were planning to tell me this time." The bitterness in his voice was unmistakable.

"Dad, I—"

"Miranda, how could you?" The anger and disappointment in his voice nearly broke her in two. "After everything we've been through . . ."

"I know, Dad. I know. This is awful. I'm so sorry."

"You should leave with Violet. I'll handle this."

She started at the suggestion. As if she'd leave her father to clean up her mess again. "No, I did this. I'll fix it. Please, Dad."

"You've done enough, Miranda."

That hit her like a fist to the chest, but she dragged in a deep breath around it. "I have to try. Just let me try."

"Well, it certainly can't get any worse." With another heavy sigh, he turned and left, leaving her alone in the waiting room with her devastation and dread.

After what felt like hours, footsteps echoed in the hallway outside. She could tell from the cadence that it was Will. Taking a deep breath, she raised her head to look at him.

He stopped at the doorway, looking rumpled and exhausted. A red mark traced the top of his cheekbone and his right hand was wrapped and splinted.

"Thank fucking god," Will said on an exhale. "Are you okay?"

That his first thought was for *her* well-being brought tears to her eyes. "I should be asking you that." Her voice was coarse with strained emotion. "You crashed."

He shrugged. "I'm fine."

"You could have *died*, Will."

"Mira, I'm fine. No head injury. It's okay."

"You're out of the race. That's not okay."

"It's one race."

"One race that could end up costing you the championship. And it could cost Lennox the Constructor's . . . God." She stopped, her hands shaking, and drew another deep breath. "I'm sorry, Will. I'm *so* sorry. That's all I seem to be able to say and it's not enough. Not for anybody."

"Hey." He was at her side in a moment, reaching for her hand. "This isn't your fault. You know that."

She couldn't bear it, his affection in the face of this wreckage. Turning away, she crossed the room, needing to put a little distance between them as she said what came next.

"Will, look what's happened to you because of me. Last week, nobody on that track had a chance of taking the world championship away from you. Now you're out of a race, maybe two. Everything you've accomplished this season is about to be wiped away, because of me."

"Mira—"

She turned back to face him. "Ryan from Velocity called Violet."

He scowled. "Ryan? Why?"

"They've seen the fight online. They might kill your sponsorship, Will."

He shook his head and waved his good hand dismissively. "You think I give a shit about that?"

He came toward her, reaching for her, but she batted his hand away. She couldn't bear it if he touched her with those gentle fingers, pulled her into that warm embrace. She was already certain that when she left the room, she'd be leaving an irreplaceable piece of her heart behind. His tenderness would only make it worse.

"You have to save that contract."

"Did you just hear me? I don't care about the contract."

"I do! Will, do you remember what you told me after your first press junket in London? You told me—you *swore* to me—that you'd never do something to harm Lennox."

"Of course, but—"

"Don't you get it? *I'm* that thing! You and me, *we're* the thing that's harming Lennox. And I won't do it. Not to you, not to the team, not to my dad. Not again."

Will looked like she'd punched him, his eyes stricken and his mouth gaping. "So you're saying we're over?"

She dropped her head. She couldn't look at him. Not now. Her hands started to shake involuntarily. She balled them into fists. "Yes," she said. "Take me out of the mix and it's a little track rivalry that got out of hand. I'm taking myself out of their damned story, so you get a chance to write your own ending to this."

"Don't tell me you're doing this for me. You're doing it because you're scared." Will eyed her, like he was just now coming to see her clearly, and it felt awful, like she'd been stripped down to just her ugliest, smallest parts. "They're going to talk about you again and instead of standing with me, you're going to run and hide."

His anger hurt worse than anything had so far.

"That's not fair," Mira whispered.

"Oh, I know what you're scared of. You're scared of disappointing your father. You're dumping me just to spare his feelings."

Anger of her own flared in her chest. She refused to let one more person pay for what she'd done, not when she had the chance to fix it. "It's not about his *feelings*! It's about his *life*! It's about *your* life. It's about this team! Don't you get it?"

Will stared at the floor, his shoulders heaving as he dragged in deep breaths. When he spoke, his voice was hard and icy, shaking with rage. "Got it. So I'm good for sneaking around with and fucking, a little forbidden fun, but when shit gets real, you drop me cold. 'Just go drive, Will. That's all you're good for.'"

"That's not—"

He lifted his chin and the look in his eyes froze the words on her tongue. "You know, you made me think you believed in me, and stupidly, I was starting to do it, too."

"Will—"

"You'd better go. Someone might see you with me, and we can't have that."

She'd known this would hurt, but never did she think it could feel like this, like she'd just pulled her own beating heart out of her chest. She wanted to beg him not to hate her, but cutting him loose meant cutting herself out of his life completely, no matter how ruthless she had to be to do it. She couldn't begrudge him his anger, even if it killed her to face it.

In the end, she didn't say anything. He was sending her away, so she went, slipping out of the room. Before someone could see.

Will had thought the sprained thumb was the worst fate that could possibly have befallen him.

He was so wrong.

It turned out that losing Mira hurt a whole lot more than sitting out Monza.

This morning, Paul had called at an ungodly hour. Not that the hour mattered. Will hadn't slept all night, unable to get his conversation with Mira out of his head. Being ordered to attend an emergency team meeting—a *real* one—at the crack of dawn didn't even faze him after that.

Everyone was here—Paul, Simone, Violet, Mitchell, Matteo, both reserve drivers, Connor Meade, who was the head of Lennox communications, and half a dozen suits from Lennox's legal department. Mira was conspicuously absent. Paul didn't comment on it and Will didn't dare ask about her. Currently, Paul wasn't making eye contact with him. That was a problem he'd have to face later.

"You're sure the sprain will put Will out of Monza?" Connor asked Mitchell. "What about beyond that?"

Mitchell nodded. "Monza definitely. Beyond that, I can't say. You never can predict how fast these things will heal."

Paul cursed under his breath, but Connor raised a steadying hand. "This might actually be for the best."

"We're missing a bloody race. How can that possibly be for the best?"

Connor, in his fifties, tall and good-looking in an expensive, corporate way, leaned forward on his elbows, looking over the tops of his titanium-framed reading glasses at everyone around the table before focusing back on Will. "Deloux is kicking up a fuss about this with the FIA, calling for you to be banned for the rest of the season."

"What? That's bullshit!"

Connor motioned for his silence. "They're just grandstanding. They know the FIA won't take that kind of action about the fight, which seems to be a personal matter."

"What about the crash?" he pressed. "Can we go after him for that?" Brody was so far down in the rankings that a penalty wouldn't even matter, but it would sure as fuck make Will feel better.

"We can't prove he did that on purpose," Paul said.

"But we all know he did," Matteo said quietly. Will looked to him. Matteo shrugged. "I saw it. He jerked his wheel, and then he accelerated into you. Every driver out there would agree."

While he was grateful for Matteo's backup, it wouldn't matter in the end. Paul was right. It would be extremely difficult to prove without a doubt that Brody caused his crash.

"Your injury will shut down any speculation that you're missing the race because they've barred you from driving," Mitchell said. "At the moment, that's good news."

Will rolled his eyes. That definition of good news was a stretch.

Now Simone spoke up. "Now, the bad news is that Deloux isn't just talking to the FIA. They're talking to the media—anybody who will listen. And unfortunately this thing has gotten away from us a bit. Violet? What's the story on social media?"

"The big F1 media sources were all over it fifteen minutes after it happened," Violet said, casting articles from her iPad to the flat-screen in the corner. "It's all framed to favor Brody, not Will, and Will threw the first punch, which doesn't help."

Of course Deloux was pumping the story out to the press. That wanker Brody probably did it himself. He had loads of experience with that game. "Violet," Will protested. "You were there. You saw—"

"Will, what I saw and what I know doesn't matter. There's only how the story is being perceived. And right now, everyone seems to think this is you showing your true colors."

Will scoffed. "I have never gotten into a fight with another driver in my life." Before yesterday he hadn't even thrown a punch since he was thirteen. And just like Brody, that little asshole had deserved it, too.

"The good news, if there is any, is that in the comments, where the fans debate, reaction seems to be pretty split. Plenty of Lennox and Hawley fans have come to your defense, but as these things go, no one's changing their minds. If they weren't a fan of yours before, they certainly aren't now."

"What about the sponsors?" Paul looked to Simone.

Simone pressed her palms to the conference table. "I think I've put out the fires with Rally Fuel and Archer Autoparts. They're not too spooked. I've got conference calls with Compendium Banking, Marchand Timepieces, and Helix this afternoon. I'll see what I can do to smooth this over." Her eyes flicked up to Will's and then away again. "Velocity is another matter."

Will stifled a groan. He already knew the bad news from Velocity. They were having an emergency meeting in New York this afternoon to discuss shutting down the new line and possibly dropping their sponsorship altogether. Personally, he didn't give a shit if his name was never slapped on a single pair of trainers. But now that his initial fury had subsided, he had to acknowledge that the loss would be a serious financial blow to Lennox. Mira wasn't wrong about that part.

"Are they pulling the plug?" Connor asked.

"That remains to be seen. It's a major deal, lucrative for everyone involved, so they won't want to jettison it unless they determine Will to be too much of a liability."

"Up until yesterday, they couldn't get enough of me."

"And then you pummeled a fellow driver and crashed your car into a wall," Simone said. "You came into this season with a reputation"—Will started to protest but Simone spoke over him—"earned or not. And I know you've walked the straight and narrow all season, but it doesn't take much to stir up old talk. On many fronts."

A moment of tense silence stretched out as Simone's meaning sank in. Mira. They were talking about Mira and what that bastard Brody had done to her years ago. Except that's not how it was playing out in the press. Violet had shown him some of the articles right before the meeting and they made him sick. She was being portrayed as some sort of racing groupie, a siren luring unsuspecting drivers to their doom. They implied that she'd flirted with Brody, her ex-lover, until Will, her current lover, was out of control with jealousy. Not one of them brought up the fact that Brody had been thirty to her sixteen when they'd been involved, or that he'd been engaged and lied to her about it. However, as he'd learned personally, facts didn't matter much when the media had its own story to tell.

She'd been dragged through the mud once before, and she clearly had no intention of being dragged through it again, not even for him. Seeing what was being said about her already, he wasn't even sure he blamed her. Who was he to force her to stay and face it all over again? Maybe she was right. She needed to get away from this mess and stay away. Not for *his* own good, but for *hers*.

"Okay," he said, slapping his good hand on the table. "I get it. I fucked up. Tell me what to do to fix it. Whatever it is, I'll do it."

"It's not that easy, Will," Simone said. "We don't want to get involved in a mudslinging press war with Deloux."

"So we let them just say what they want about me with no pushback?"

"No, we counter, carefully, strategically. I'll be looking for an outlet for a sit-down interview, someone who'll be favorable to you. We'll be cautious and discreet about what you say and how you say it. Too many details could come across as unpleasant or lurid."

He could read between the lines. There was a way to play this and come out clean. He could throw Mira under the bus, just like Brody had, let the press think he'd been lured into trouble by an untrustworthy woman. But despite the easy out it presented, no one in the room wanted that, especially him. He'd never turn on her, even though she'd just dumped him. Brody might have hung her out to dry, but he'd never do that to her. *Never*.

"Okay, find me an interview, tell me what to say, and I'll do it. I'll be perfect."

"Good." The word was positive but Simone's expression was still grim. "Until we come up with a strategy, your instructions are to lie low. Don't give anyone any reason to talk about you. No one even catches sight of you buying a coffee. Understood?"

The warning wasn't necessary. Maybe in the past he'd have coped with a setback by going on the mother of all benders, but those days were done. Now all he wanted to do was fix this. "Done."

"We might even send you back to London until you're cleared to race again, just to avoid the scrutiny of the track press." Simone eyed Will across the table. "Is that a problem?"

Running back to London like he had something to hide felt all wrong. Leaving Mira behind to weather everything without him also felt wrong. But she'd already walked away from him, hadn't she? All he'd ever wanted to do was protect her. But when he'd tried to do that his way, he'd set off the chain reaction of disasters that had led them all here. So maybe he needed to try it her way. Maybe the right thing to do was to let her go. For her sake. For everyone's. He felt sick just imagining it, but he was just going to have to get used to that, because she was already gone, wasn't she?

Simone stared him down, waiting for an answer.

He didn't have much choice. He'd started this. Now he had a responsibility to every person in the room—hell, to the hundreds of Lennox employees there and back in England—to do whatever he could to fix it. So he was leaving.

39

Mira's first instinct was to go back to LA. She knew Violet was right and the drama surrounding her would only get worse, even if she stayed away from Will. But she'd already caused her father enough grief. There was no way she could leave him stranded without an assistant in the middle of the season on top of it.

Her eyes burned and her head felt fuzzy. After she'd left Will the night before, she'd gone back to her hotel room, locked the door, and crumpled into a heap on the floor, sobbing until she didn't have any tears left. Now all she wanted to do was hide out in the dark and cry some more. But like it or not, she had a job to do, so she was at the track to do it. If she just kept her head down and worked her ass off, this would pass. It had worked for her once before. It had to work again. Maybe if she stayed busy enough, she wouldn't break down and find Will and beg him to forgive her for what she'd done.

He wasn't in Monza anymore, anyway. Violet told her this morning that they'd packed him off on a plane to London to wait out his injury and the media firestorm. Gone. He was gone. The ache was relentless, this terrible feeling of wrongness, like she was moving through a twisted dream instead of reality. Perhaps Will had been the dream, and this ugliness was what she was left with again, now that she'd woken up.

Walking over to hospitality, she kept her eyes on her notepad, pretending to be engrossed in her work. If people were staring or whispering, she didn't see them. She didn't want to. Safely through the crowds, she slipped inside and made her way to the back, where guest services had an office.

"Hi, Dom. I know it's last minute, but we've got the head of Marchand Timepieces and his wife flying in for the race. Can you help me out with some VIP passes?"

Dom, the guest services assistant, leaned back in his chair and grinned. "Well, if it isn't Mira. Where have you been hiding?"

Guess she'd been too naive, hoping that the people she worked with would be sensitive enough not to mention any rumors they might have heard. "Busy day," she said with a bright, forced smile. "Is it going to be a problem? The passes?"

Dom eyed her for another moment, then turned to his computer and typed in a few things. When he'd finished, he slid two VIP passes on lanyards across the counter to her. She moved to take them, but he held on to them.

"I'd ask you for a little favor for those, but it seems you only hand those out to drivers."

She froze, mouth hanging open. Her face flamed with anger, mortification, or some bubbling mix of both. She *knew* Dom. She'd been working with him all season. They'd joked around and chatted. And he thought he could say something like that to her?

Suddenly Violet was there, slapping her hand down over Dom's and shoving it away. "A, she doesn't have to do you a fucking favor for doing your *job*, and B, being a driver has nothing to do with it. The problem is, you're a sad fucking asshole. And a lousy lay, from what I've heard."

Dom's face colored, but he said nothing. Violet tugged her out of Dom's office, and Mira stumbled after her, still in shock.

"I can't believe he said that to me."

"He's an idiot," Violet growled.

"God, if people who know me are going to believe all that crap . . ." Mira closed her eyes and shook her head. "I'm never getting out from under this. I should just go back to LA. I'm making it worse by staying." Her heart folded in on itself just thinking about leaving, but maybe her name was just too tarnished in the small world of racing. Maybe she'd always be branded as that slut with a thing for bad-boy drivers.

"Hey." Violet stopped, swinging around to face her. "None of this is your fault."

"I don't know, Violet. If bad things happen because of you, even if they're not your fault, maybe they're still your responsibility."

Violet blinked. "That's why you broke up with Will, isn't it? You think you're saving him or something."

"I *am* saving him. Being with me was only going to hurt him."

"He can handle it. He's done it before."

She shook her head. "No. He's worked too hard this season to blow it because of me." Violet opened her mouth to protest, but Mira cut her off. "The one thing I could do was to get out of the way, so I did."

"Just be careful, Mira. Don't let them decide who you are."

"That's not what I'm doing. I'm just trying—"

"To do the right thing. Yeah, I get it. I'm just not entirely sure this is it. Listen, I have to go. Are you okay?"

"Yeah, I'm fine. Thanks for that back there with Dom."

Violet gave her a light punch in the arm. "Anytime. Fuck the patriarchy, remember?"

When Mira opened the door to race command minutes later, she heard her dad's voice. She hadn't seen him since last night. When she'd arrived at the track this morning, he'd been busy putting out fires in the emergency meeting that now had Will on a plane back to London. She'd been avoiding him on purpose, too. But she knew she'd have to face him eventually and apparently time was up.

Steeling herself, she peered through the open door. He and Harry were studying the video monitors of the track, deep in debate.

"Tae thinks Rikkard is in great shape," her father said. "Good simulator times and he's backing it up in practice. We could probably finish the season with him, if it comes to that."

"Will's coming back before the end of the season," Harry grumbled. "The boy's got fire, Paul, and you know it."

Oh god, they were talking about Will. She shrank back, intending to retreat the way she'd come and wait until they were gone. But her father's angry outburst froze her in place.

"I'm not sure I know anything about Will anymore, Harry. I thought all that nonsense from three years ago was behind him. I trusted him. Then it turns out the bastard seduced my own daughter behind my back. Of all the women he could have had, he targeted *her*. What was he *thinking*?"

"It's a shame he's such a handful. Never seen a better driver."

"Maybe he's just too much of a risk, no matter how bloody talented he is. I have to think of what's best for the team, and maybe that's not Will anymore."

Cold sweat prickled along the back of her neck as Mira gripped the doorframe until her knuckles went white.

"You need to do what you feel is right, Paul," Harry said with a weary sigh. "I'd better get back to the garage. The team's got their hands full putting Will's car back together."

Without making a sound, Mira scrambled back out of the office and ducked around the corner, waiting while Harry left.

She felt like she couldn't breathe. Walking away from Will hadn't fixed a single thing. In the vacuum she'd left, people filled in their own story—about him and about her—and they were all wrong. They'd been wrong about her years ago, and they were wrong about Will now. Her father was about to abandon him, thinking the worst of him.

Silently she let herself into the office. No one else was there, just her dad, pensively staring at one of the monitors. The camera was trained on the garage, where the mechanics were hard at work repairing the damage to Will's car. Except it might be Rikkard's car soon if she didn't fix this.

"He didn't target me."

Paul whipped around, startled to find her there. "Mira? What are you talking about?"

"Will didn't target me. And he didn't seduce me. He's not some predator. He's been so good to me, so kind and support-ive. I think . . ." She had to pause to draw a deep breath, to stop the shaking in her voice and summon the strength to get the rest of the words out. "I think he loves me. You're wrong about him."

Will was not Brody. She hadn't gotten involved with him as an act of reckless rebellion. She'd fallen for him, for all the right reasons. The only mistake she'd truly made was trying to hide it, and all because she didn't want to disappoint her father with more ugly gossip.

And now here she was, destroying her own happiness to placate him, and somehow destroying Will's future, too, all because she was scared of losing her father for good. Well, if loving Will meant she lost her dad, then she had to take that risk, because it was time to take a stand for Will, and for herself.

Her father watched her, first with skepticism, then with a sort of pitying sadness. "Mira, if he cared, he wouldn't have kept you a secret. You should know that better than anyone at this point."

"Yes, I *do* know better! And that's not how it happened. It was *me* hiding and keeping secrets, because I was so afraid of disappointing *you*. Again."

Paul dropped his head forward and pinched the bridge of his nose. "I am disappointed, Miranda. I thought you'd outgrown all that recklessness. But here you are, involved with the worst man you could have picked. And look what's happened as a result. You've been dragged back into this nightmare after all these years, after you'd finally put it behind you."

She shook her head firmly. "No. *He's* been dragged into this nightmare because of *me*. Look! Here you are, about to kick him off the team, and all because of me!"

Paul's voice was thunderously loud in the tight confines of the room. "I'm about to kick him off the team because he's a reckless liability! A fight with Brody McKnight, over my own daughter."

"A fight Brody brought on himself! If you want to be angry at someone, Dad, be angry at him. Or be angry at me for lying to you. But Will's done nothing to deserve your anger. He's worked his ass off for three years to prove himself and you know he has."

"Yes, he's good, but that's not enough . . ."

"If you want to kick someone off the team, kick *me* off! I've earned it, right? I know you're sorry you ever brought me back here, because look . . . I've just proved you right. You can't trust me."

Paul's head snapped back as if she'd struck him, and his eyes went wide. "Mira . . . of course I trust you."

"No, you don't. You haven't trusted me since I screwed up seven years ago. Do you think I can't see it every time you look at me? I get it . . . I really do. I ruined your life and you had every reason to send me away—"

"I didn't send you away. It seemed better for you to be at home, with your mother . . ."

"I wanted to be *here*, with *you*. But you said I should go home. So I left. And I never came back, because you never asked."

His face creased in confusion and pain. "I didn't think you'd *want* to come back and face this again. Face *him*. I was trying to protect you. You thought I didn't want you here?"

"You said you were sorry you ever brought me here, Dad. Believe me, that's not something I'd ever forget."

"I was angry, yes, but not at you. I was angry at myself. I wasn't . . . I'm not . . ." Paul paused and took a deep breath. "Mira, understand . . . fatherhood wasn't a natural fit for me, and with you so far away, I didn't get much practice at it. You were growing up in LA with your mother and it felt like I barely knew you. When I started bringing you on the circuit with me, I finally felt as if I was your father, properly."

The anger that had been fueling her began to ebb, and in the shaky, emotion-drenched aftermath, tears filled her eyes. "I felt that way, too. I loved being here with you."

"I loved having you with me. But when that happened . . . the mess with McKnight . . . Ah, Christ, Mira. What sort of father lets his teenage daughter wander about alone in this place? That bastard never should have been allowed to get near you."

She blinked at him in confusion, as his meaning, as the real reason behind his anger became clear. "Dad, it wasn't *your* fault. I was the one who got involved with him."

"You were just a girl. A girl who'd been left on her own too much. And that was my fault. I never should have brought you on the circuit with me when I was so ill-equipped to properly care for you."

"That's why you sent me home?"

"I was not a proper parent for you."

"Dad . . . I wasn't a baby. I was sixteen. I made those choices. The blame for that is on me, not you."

Her father's face was aghast. "Mira, tell me you're not blaming *yourself* for what happened with that bastard?"

"There was a price to be paid for what I did. I get it. It's okay. I understand why I couldn't stay. I'm sorry you finally took this chance on me again and it blew up in your face. But I'm—"

"Let's get something sorted. I never blamed you. Not once. And I wasn't angry with you. That bastard Brody, yes. That was a kind of rage I've never felt before, and I let it get the better of me. It had nothing to do with you."

"Dad, it had everything to do with me."

"My actions were my own, and so were the consequences. And if I seemed mistrustful . . . Well, I've been worried, that's all. I didn't want the same thing happening to you again. And now it has—"

With a forceful shake of her head, she cut him off. "This is not the same at all. I'm a grown adult, Dad. I chose Will. And I'm not sorry about that. Not even a little bit. You might have your doubts about him right now, but I don't. He's the best man I know. And now you're the one making him pay for something that's not his fault."

Paul sighed and shook his head. "What's the right thing to do here, Mira? I'm lost. I thought I did the right thing seven years ago by sending you home with your mother, but clearly it wasn't. But Will being here on the team is going to cause you—us—problems."

"Don't kick Will off the team. He's not the problem."

He gave her a stern look. "Neither are you, so don't you dare suggest it."

"No, maybe not, but I am the solution." All her pain and anger from the past twenty-four hours—from the past seven years—was finally beginning to coalesce in her head into something new. A resolution. Something she could do that finally felt good, felt strong.

"What do you mean?"

"Seven years ago, I didn't handle this right. I let Brody's lies about me stand as the truth, and it's been an anchor around my neck ever since. I've been trying to live down a story someone else told about me. I'm not doing that this time. I'm telling the truth. I'm sorry for you and for Lennox if it makes things more difficult than they already are, but I have to do this. If you need me to leave the team, I understand, Dad. I really do."

Her father looked at her as if he hadn't been properly seeing her in a very long time, which might have been true. They'd both been seeing all the wrong things. He sighed deeply. "You're not going anywhere, Mira, and neither is Will."

The relief left her nearly weak in the knees. "Thank you, Dad."

He pulled her into his arms for a fierce and all-encompassing hug, and Mira felt some small, wounded part of herself—a piece that had been hiding in the dark for seven long years—finally start to heal.

After that long-overdue conversation with her father, Mira went in search of Violet. The race was underway, but Mira didn't have time to watch.

Violet was outside the press center, scowling at her iPad as she flipped through news sites.

"Violet, I need another favor."

"Am I bringing matches or a shovel?" Violet replied without glancing up.

"Neither, I hope. I have a story to tell and I need the right person to tell it to."

She paused and looked up. "This sounds serious."

"It is. And I'm going a little rogue here, so you might not want to help me. It's okay if you decide to steer clear."

Violet leaned against the side of the press center. "Maybe you'd better tell me this story first and let me decide."

Mira took a deep breath and swallowed hard. "That might require a drink. Are they serving alcohol in the press center?"

Violet snorted. "This is Italy."

Violet ducked inside and emerged a few minutes later brandishing a bottle of wine. "Nicked it from a crate in the back.

Sorry, no glasses. We'll have to rough it. Come on. Let's sit back here. The last thing we need right now is other people."

Perching on a set of shallow metal steps along the back side of the press center, Violet took a hefty swig of the wine straight from the bottle. "One perk about Italy is that even the crappy free wine is still pretty good."

She passed the bottle to Mira, and she took a long drink of her own.

"So," Violet began. "I've already sorted the main points of this little tale, but I'm guessing I don't have the whole story, do I?"

Mira took another drink. "Nope." Then, for only the second time in her life, she confided in someone, telling Violet everything, from the start to the bitter end.

"Goddammit," Violet muttered when she'd finished and they'd downed half the wine. "I'm going to castrate that motherfucker."

"I think there's a line forming."

Violet's expression turned shrewd. "You know, he doesn't have the same PR people now."

"Who? Brody? What's it matter?"

"It matters because he *fired* the last guy. And *that* matters, because I know him. PJ Anders. I slept with him once."

"What?"

Violet waved her hand in annoyance. "Not the point."

"What *is* the point?"

"If Brody really did instruct him to purposefully smear the reputation of the sixteen-year-old girl he seduced, PJ might be bitter enough to rat him out. Or at least help me plant some equally damning dirt on Brody."

Mira shook her head. "I'm not looking for retribution."

"Speak for yourself."

"Whatever. I just want to tell my side of the story—someplace where people will see it."

"You know that it won't change everyone's minds."

"I know. But I'm tired of hiding from this, praying for it to go away. He doesn't get to own the narrative anymore."

Violet nodded sagely. "I know the right person. She writes for the sport. She's smart and kick-ass. She'll make sure it gets done right."

"That's all I want."

"Then hang on." Violet pulled out her phone and started typing out a text. "This is about to become a bumpy ride."

Within a few hours, it was all set up, and right on time, there was a brisk knock on Mira's hotel room door.

"There she is." Violet got up to let Alison Rodgers in while Mira swallowed down her fear. Years. She'd been hiding from this for years. That was over.

Violet brought Alison over and made the introductions. The reporter was in her early thirties, in jeans and a fitted leather jacket, and with a streak of silver in her dark hair that made her look like a badass seventies rock star. Mira liked her immediately. They made small talk for a minute, then Alison got to work setting up.

"Are you sure about this?" Violet asked.

Mira looked at her and let out a nervous laugh. "No? But I'm doing it anyway." She was definitely still scared, but when she got past that she felt . . . powerful. For the first time in forever, she was going to tell her own story, and the whole world was going to hear it.

"She's cool. I promise."

Mira nodded.

"Want me to stay?"

Mira nodded again. What would she have done without Violet this season? She was more grateful for her friendship than she could possibly express. She grasped Violet's hand and squeezed. "Thank you, Violet."

"No problem. I'm going to relish taking down that asshole."

"Not about Brody. Thanks for everything you've done for me. Maybe if I'd had someone like you seven years ago, I'd never have made that stupid choice with Brody in the first place. Thank you for being my friend."

Violet's face screwed up in discomfort and she waved her hands in front of her. "You know I don't do well with human emotions."

"I won't do it again, I promise."

With an awkward shrug, Violet squeezed her hand again. "You're welcome."

"Okay, Miranda," Alison said, when she'd started recording, "where do you want to start?"

Mira inhaled deeply, running back over all of it in her memory. "Well, I guess it all started right after I turned sixteen . . ."

Will sat in the back of the black sedan, watching through the tinted glass as the teams set up their race bays on the track. A day before practice, thing were relatively quiet, just team workers and press. His eyes scanned endlessly for a glimpse of Mira. Tae had told him she hadn't gone home, which was a huge relief, even though it didn't change anything between them. Still, she was here somewhere. That's all that mattered. She wasn't gone forever. Not yet.

He hadn't seen or heard from her since that night at the hospital. No phone calls, no texts. Done meant done. At least he still had racing. His thumb had healed fast, in time for him to make it to Austria. His massive points lead had evaporated when he missed Monza, but there were still enough races in the season for the championship to be within reach if everything fell perfectly into place. He could still win it all.

That didn't set his blood pumping the way it would have three months ago. Who knew falling in love would color everything else in your life this way? When he'd been with her, every victory had tasted sweeter. Now a world championship would be, at best, a consolation prize, since what he really wanted was out of his reach.

The last morning they'd spent together—the one he hadn't realized would be the last—he'd kissed her goodbye as she'd slipped out of his room, and the words had been right there on the tip of his tongue. *I love you.*

He hadn't said it. Now he supposed he never would. It didn't matter that he'd never told her, though. His heart was still hers, no matter that she'd left him. He hadn't expected that. Seems that once you fell in love, you stayed there, even when the other person was gone.

A security agent in a dark suit rapped on his window and opened his door.

"This way to the press conference, Mr. Hawley."

Team press conferences were mandatory before every race. Facing this one felt like facing a firing squad. In there, he wouldn't be able to outrun the media shitstorm he'd so steadfastly avoided for the past week. Simone would instruct the media to stick to racing, but inevitably someone would ask about Brody—about Mira. He sighed, willing the patience, the energy, the smile, to come from somewhere. One press conference and then he could hide out again until practice tomorrow.

When he stepped out of the car, Violet was waiting, wearing a solid black suit and looking as severe as a head of state in mourning. "Have you been online since you got here?" she asked, with no preamble. Before he'd left for London, Simone had recommended staying away from news sites and social media while things were, in her words, "at their most volatile." He'd been happy to oblige. Instead he'd spent the last week working out in his home gym and watching old races online.

"'Hi, Will. Welcome back. How are you feeling?'" he asked sarcastically. "I'm fine, Violet. And how are you today?"

Violet rolled her eyes and handed him her iPad. "You need to read this before you go in there."

"I really don't need to read yet another story about how I'm a hotheaded wanker, thanks."

She pushed the iPad into his chest. "Read it."

Sighing, he took it and began to skim the article she had open. His heart stopped. He didn't read it all. He didn't need to. The important parts leapt right off the screen at him.

. . . one of us was sixteen and one of us was thirty. I would ask yourself, who should have known better? I can tell you for a fact, it wasn't me . . .

. . . my father was the one who ended up being sanctioned. I'll never forgive myself for that, but I don't blame him for going after Brody . . .

Mira had talked to the press. Oh, god. She hadn't just talked, she'd dredged up that entire ugly spectacle from seven years ago and told them *everything*. She'd poured out her secrets, her past, her heart and soul, to this reporter for the whole world to see.

Then he got to the final passage.

. . . this time, Brody's actions affected the man I love, so I'm telling my side of the story . . .

Stunned, he read and reread it until the words blurred together on the screen as his eyes burned with tears.

"Why did she do this?"

"I don't know, maybe because she was tired of being called a whore in the press? Or maybe because she's still being all noble and trying to clear your name. Maybe it was some of both. Either way, this dropped this morning, so as you can imagine, that pack of wolves inside is in a frenzy, and—"

"Where is she?"

"Avoiding that pack of wolves, no doubt."

"*Violet.*"

"I think she's in the garage, but—"

"I have to go."

"But you have a press conference!"

"I can't. Tell them to read this and go ask *Brody* some fucking questions, for once."

"Will!"

But he didn't hear the rest of her screeched protest. He was already pushing through security personnel, dodging around satellite trucks, jumping over piles of cables, and climbing steel barricade fences to make it to the Lennox garage.

Crew members stopped to stare as he ran past. Some called out in concern, but he didn't stop to explain himself. He couldn't explain it yet, because he didn't know exactly what was happening. But he was determined to find out.

In the garage, he found her, standing between the twin Lennox cars with Harry, scribbling something on her notepad as Harry rattled off instructions. Harry trailed off as he spotted Will coming to a stop, breathing hard.

"Will? Something wrong?"

Every mechanic in the garage stopped what they were doing to watch, too.

Mira whipped around, eyes going wide at the sight of him. Seeing her face again after this miserable week without her was like coming up for air after having been underwater for too long.

"Not sure yet," he said to Harry without looking away from Mira's face. "Can I get a minute, Harry?"

"Sure, Will. What's the issue?"

Now he did look at Harry, shooting him a look he hoped the older man could interpret. "I meant a minute with Mira. Alone."

Harry scowled, looking from Mira to Will as if he was considering arguing. Then he turned to address the mechanics. "Quit gawping and get back to work!" he barked at them, before stomping out of the garage.

Every pair of eyes immediately swiveled away from them.

"I read the interview," he said with no preamble.

"Oh."

"Mira, why did you do it?"

She sighed, dragging a hand through her loose hair. God, how he'd missed that hair. He'd missed every single thing about her, from her dimples to her ankles, from the way she chewed on her bottom lip when she was nervous to the way she whispered his name when she was close to coming.

"I got tired of hiding from it. So I put it all out there. If people are going to judge me, then at least it can be on the truth. My version of it, for once."

His chest ached with a mix of pride and pain. What she'd done was brave. Reckless perhaps, but brave. "You know some people are still going to think the worst, no matter what you do. Trust me, I know."

She let out a huff of laughter. "Oh, I know. Read the comments section if you want a little taste of the worst of humanity. But lots of people have been really kind, too. A few people have reached out to me, to make sure I'm all right, and plenty of people think Brody is a scumbag. Even more think you were totally justified in kicking his ass. So mission accomplished, I guess."

He shook his head. "No, Mira. I would never want you to put yourself out there like this on my account. It's not right." In truth, it made him feel sick to think she'd done this for him. Ever since she'd told him the whole story in Austin, he'd wanted to protect her from getting any more hurt and now, because of him, she'd offered herself up as some sort of sacrifice.

"It wasn't for you. Well, not *just* for you. At the end of the day, it was about me. I've been living my life like I was ashamed. Like everything they said about me seven years ago was true. But I'm done believing it or apologizing for something I didn't do."

"You never should have had to."

She dropped her eyes to a patch of concrete just in front of her feet, and she hooked her hair behind her ear. "Did you read through to the end of the interview?"

"I did."

"So you know what I said at the end. About you."

His heart ached, but not in misery this time. Not so long ago, this feeling would have scared him, but not anymore. He'd learned that love was worth the risk—that *she* was worth the risk.

He moved forward, until his feet were inches from hers. "The part where you said you loved me?"

She looked up and nodded, eyes bright with tears. "I thought I was doing the right thing, to protect you. But now I know I was just running away, like I've always done. I'm sorry I left you."

A hard lump formed in his throat. He didn't realize until this moment how desperately he'd wanted to hear her say those words.

"I'm done being scared." She blinked and a tear broke free from her damp lashes and slid down her face. He reached up to brush it away and spread his palm over her cheek.

"Good. Because I never got to tell you that I love you, too." Cradling her face in his hands, he took another step, closing the small space between them. "I can't seem to live without you anymore."

Mira beamed up at him. He could look into those green eyes for the rest of her life. "God, if there's one thing worse than you being an arrogant ass, it's you being a hopeless romantic."

He grinned. "You know you love it."

"I do," she murmured.

"I'm going to kiss you now."

"We're outside. Someone might see."

He leaned in, until his lips were just a breath away from hers. "Who cares? Let them look. Because it's going to be a really good one."

Abu Dhabi,
United Arab Emirates

The sun had set an hour earlier and it was still ferociously hot, but Mira wouldn't have retreated to the air-conditioned comfort of the offices if her life depended on it. She stayed right behind her father, next to the track, watching the race on a bank of monitors over his shoulder. Behind her, nearly every other member of the Lennox team stared at the monitors as well, in rapt, anxious silence.

At her father's side, Harry chomped on a gnarled plastic coffee stir stick. Now and then, Paul spoke into his headset microphone, consulting with the two race engineers or the team strategist, but mostly, he just stared motionless at the monitors as if he was willing himself inside.

Out on the track, an hour into the race, Will's championship still hung in the balance. Despite the points lost in Monza, Will had come back strong in the following races, but he was still stuck in second place.

He'd dominated in qualifying, pulling pole position. But his gearbox failed at the end of the day, requiring an unscheduled replacement. It led to a five-spot grid penalty, putting him at a disadvantage right from the start. He was driving masterfully, fighting like hell, but so was everyone else, in this, the last race of the season. In the end, his best might not be enough to make him *the* best.

Even without the world championship, the season was already an unqualified success for Lennox. Two races ago, Lennox amassed enough points to ensure they'd be awarded the Constructor's Championship for the best car of the season. That was a triumph for everyone. They'd gone into today's race with Matteo ranked seventh and Will ranked second. No one could argue with those results.

But Mira wanted this world championship for him so badly. He *deserved* it. And after the incident with Brody had nearly imperiled his whole season, he'd clawed his way back to the top of the heap. He was almost there. Only five points back.

Violet came to a stop beside her. "Well, I've laid in enough champagne to fill a swimming pool. Either we'll be celebrating a victory with it or drowning our sorrows. How's it looking out there?"

Mira nervously tapped two fingers against her bottom lip, watching the sleek blue of Will's car bank sharply around a curve, just behind another car. "Seven laps to go. He's just caught René Denis but Liam O'Neill is still out in front."

René, the reigning world champion, had come into the season strong, but Liam had been the surprise, sneaking up the rankings and ahead of René while everybody had been paying attention to Will. After Will missed Monza, Liam had shot into the season lead.

"Hmm." Violet's grim hum echoed everyone's mood. Thanks to that penalty, Will had started in sixth place. Even though he'd carved his way up to third, he needed to win the race to take the championship. He'd have to ask the car for the impossible to pass both René and Liam.

It didn't matter, she told herself. Will was young. He had many years of racing ahead of him, and so many more opportunities to win this. If it didn't happen this year, he'd just go for it again next year. He'd shown everyone in the sport that he was already a champion, with or without this win.

But it still didn't stop her from wanting it. She wanted it so badly.

HE WAS SO CLOSE he could taste it. Despite the penalty, Will had a great start, and he'd ruthlessly worked his way back onto the podium. Now the world championship dangled in front of him, so close and yet still just a little out of reach. He'd passed René. Now Liam O'Neill was the only one left between him and the win.

Up ahead, Liam's gearbox taunted him as the laps ticked down. As they approached Turn Five, Tae delivered the good news. "Four laps to go. Reminder, you're clear to use your overtake anytime until the end of the race."

Great. But *where* to use it? Because it wasn't unlimited usage. If he took the classic dive bomb into Turn Six, it would give Liam the opportunity on the exit out of Turn Seven to retake. And if he somehow held Liam off, the DRS down to Turn Nine would be fatal to Will's chances. Even worse, it would drain the battery and he'd lose time letting it recharge. So at best he had two shots to make it work before he ran out of time. As he rounded the painfully slow Turn Five he could see Liam's car twitching on exit, a sure sign he was putting it absolutely on the limit. It was time to set the trap.

"I think my tires are going. I'm starting to lose the rears," he told Tae in his headset.

"Affirm," Tae replied, instantly catching on. "Let's try to increase lift and coast into Turn Six."

Every radio transmission was being monitored by everyone out on the track, so Liam and his team had just heard that. But there wasn't exactly a rule against bluffing.

He engaged the DRS on the long run down to Turn Six. As they approached the braking zone, Liam braked a couple of meters earlier than he'd expected. Clearly his team had taken the bait and they were into "get it home in one piece" mode. He'd hooked him.

He barreled toward the turn with as much speed as the car could bear, using the grip he'd just told Tae his tires didn't have. Liam, who'd been counting on Will's worn-out tires, was stuck, forced off the racing line entering Turn Six and compromising his exit of Turn Seven. But with the inside Liam was able to maintain the lead, which was exactly what Will wanted. For now.

"Am I good to use overtake yet?" He knew the answer, but he prayed that Tae would still get what he was trying to do.

"You're better off waiting until two laps from the end, Engine Eleven position six," Tae said, fully on board with the bluff.

Time to roll the dice.

As he began closing the gap to Liam once again, he shifted slightly to the inside. Once again, Liam took the bait, moving to the inside to defend his position. Will made a show of following him to set the hook deep, and then when he was running at full speed into the turn, he swung fast to the outside, blasting past him. He'd left Liam no time to widen his turn and block him.

But it wasn't over yet. Even though he'd pinned his rival to the inside, he was left fighting for his life around the outside, struggling to keep the car on the track. Liam was still there on his left. But if he could hang on through this turn, he'd have him. Just as he began to fear he'd asked too much of the car, it was done. The track straightened out ahead of him and all he had to do was accelerate, mashing the overtake button he'd been saving and burying the throttle.

"Got him!" Tae shouted in his ear as he nosed ahead of Liam.

That felt good, but this wasn't over. He had to hold Liam off and grow that lead as much as he could in the remaining laps. He'd faked Liam out, but that wouldn't work again. And he'd counted on Liam's car being maxed out. There was always the possibility that Liam was faking, too.

"Three laps to go," Tae said. "I believe you owe everyone on the pit wall a new pair of underwear."

"I just need a list of their favorite colors. How am I for these laps?"

"You're good on fuel to the end."

"What's the gap?"

"One point four."

Just over a second between them with three more laps to go. Too close for comfort.

Paul suddenly broke into the channel. "Stellar job, son, let's bring this home in one piece."

Oh, so now he was "son"? Paul had thawed a lot since the nightmare of Monza, but he was still uncomfortable whenever he encountered a reminder of his daughter's relationship. Maybe if Will won today, every last reservation Paul had would magically melt away.

"Just have champagne waiting for me in my hotel."

"That's what I like to hear from my world champion."

He held Liam off for another lap, but only just. He was still nipping at his heels. The fucker might still manage to sneak around him in the last lap. Time to make that impossible.

"Gap?" he asked Tae.

"One point seven."

Better, but not good enough. Not for him. As he entered the straight, he opened up the car and gave it everything he had. He had the best car on the track, without a doubt, and now it showed. He focused on controlling the speed as Tae barked times into his ear.

"Just a reminder, Will," Tae said. "We don't need the point for fastest lap."

"Yes we do," he said between gritted teeth. He was leaving it all on the track today. Everything the tires could give him, every ounce of fuel, every bit of strength left in his body. Then, while he was gritting his teeth through the last turn complex, his head still full of tire pressures and brake temps and hydraulic pressure, he rounded Turn Sixteen and suddenly there it was, waving in front of him, filling his vision—the checkered flag.

He won.

He'd just won the world championship.

DIMLY, MIRA WAS AWARE OF SCREAMS, of Natalia kissing her cheek before Paul snatched her up in a hug, of Violet shrieking in her ear and throwing her arms around her neck. The Lennox paddock was pandemonium.

First, Will had to do the obligatory victory donuts with the car, burning up the tires and sending up a curtain of smoke as the race fans screamed their appreciation. But finally, the crew pulled aside the barricades and the sleek blue car coasted into the waiting crowd. He was swarmed, an army of pit crew guys and mechanics rushing to pull him free, everyone shouting and laughing. Eventually his head rose above the crowd, his hair sweaty and tangled where he'd yanked his balaclava free. As if there were no other person in the paddock, his eyes went straight to hers, and he grinned, wide and triumphant.

"Go," Violet said, shoving her through the crowd toward him. "He doesn't want any of them. He wants you."

She wound her way through the crew, until they seemed to realize she was there and fell back enough to make space. Will was standing on the seat of the car, helmet still hanging from his left hand. He reached the other out to her. Planting one foot on the edge of the car, she let him pull her up, until she was standing next to him, his arm banded around her waist.

She reached up to touch his flushed face. "I'm so proud of you, Will. You won," she said, her voice barely audible over the rising din.

He glowed with triumph, and her heart felt about to burst. The smile he gave her was a private one, something intimate that had nothing to do with winners' podiums. He pressed his palm to her cheek. "Yes, I won," he said. "We won."

And she knew he wasn't talking about the team or racing. When she answered him, neither was she. "Yes, we did."

EPILOGUE

Onetahi,
Tahiti

Mira's eyes were closed, but she felt the dappled sunlight dancing across her eyelids. In the distance, she could hear the gentle sound of the ocean surf. The warm breeze was scented with sea salt and some tropical flower that was blooming in the jungle ringing their private villa. Cool water lapped at her shoulders and chest as she reclined her head on the lip of the plunge pool. Perfection. This spot, right here, was the most perfect spot on earth. Well, it would be, except Will wasn't there enjoying it with her.

"I'm serious, Jem. It's you or I'm out . . . uh-huh . . . well, put him on, I'll tell the old man myself . . ."

Mira cracked an eye open and twisted around in the water. Will was pacing back and forth just inside the open sliding door of their villa, phone to his ear, in just his board shorts. Actually, *this* was perfection.

"Ed agrees with me, Jem," he continued. "You're the brains here."

With Will's world championship win, the Velocity sponsorship deal had come together even better than before. Will had decided to sink a portion of the money into Hawley and Sons to keep the business afloat. But his money came with strings attached. Namely that his father let Jemima run the expansion and diversification necessary to stay competitive. Mira had recently spent a few evenings in London with Jemima. It was definitely a smart move.

Will wandered deeper inside the villa, his voice now muffled by the surf. Closing her eyes, she soaked up the glorious sensation of the sun on her shoulders. Finally she heard him saying goodbye to Jem.

"Are you coming out?" she called. "This water isn't getting any more perfect."

"Coming," he called.

He emerged a moment later with a bottle of Moët and two champagne flutes.

"What's this for?"

"I don't know if it's exactly something to celebrate, but after avoiding it my entire life, I'm officially a partner in Hawley and Sons."

"That's definitely something to celebrate, because you're doing it on your terms."

Will grinned as he popped the cork. "The old man is gnashing his teeth about it, but yes, I am." He poured the champagne and passed her a glass.

They touched glasses. "Congratulations on your entry into international finance, Mr. Hawley. Now get in here with me so I can do wicked things to you."

"I'm all yours."

He settled into the water next to her, and she shifted over onto his lap, looping her arms behind his head.

He pushed his fingers through her wet hair. "Come here and kiss me. It's been an hour since I've had my hands on you. I'm desperate."

Leaning in, Mira kissed him, slow and luxurious, because they had four days in paradise to do nothing but enjoy each other. She planned on having sex with him here, and then maybe later down on their private beach, and again tonight in that gorgeous big four-poster bed, romantically draped with netting.

He shifted underneath her and she could feel him grow hard against her. He'd just slid a hand up her back and started tugging the ties to her bikini top when *her* phone started ringing from the foot of the chaise longue next to the pool.

He groaned, dropping his head to her shoulder.

"I'll be quick," she whispered in his ear.

The season might be over, but that just meant *last* season. Back at the Lennox factory, they'd been working on next year's car since the midseason break. And now, with just four months left until testing, they were operating at a fever pitch to get it done. It wasn't the best time to be away, but if they hadn't taken a vacation now, they wouldn't have been able to do it until *next* winter.

Reaching out of the pool, she snagged her phone off the edge of the cushion, answering without even looking at the screen.

"Now, I'm moving to my new office this week, but they'll start repainting my old one right after the holidays, so you'll have to work out of your father's office until they finish up."

"Hello, Pen." She rolled her eyes at Will, who rolled his eyes and slipped under the surface of the water.

Once Pen's baby had finally arrived, she'd decided she couldn't handle being on the road for months at a time. She was transferring to another department, which allowed her to work full-time at the factory. Mira had been thrilled beyond words when her father had offered her a permanent position as his assistant.

By then, Natalia had brokered a dinner with them and Will, so her father could start acclimating himself to the idea of Will as Mira's boyfriend. He'd been prickly to start, still afraid of Mira getting hurt, but once Will declared his love for her over the appetizers, Paul had thawed. Will's world championship trophy sitting in a place of pride at the Lennox factory probably didn't hurt.

She zoned out a little as Pen rattled on about everything else that had to happen in the transition. Then she felt Will slip up behind her underwater. She bit her lip as his hand moved up her rib cage to her breast.

His head emerged from the water and he leaned into her back. "Be very quiet," he whispered in her ear. His other hand slipped below the edge of her bikini bottoms. "I'm going to make you—"

"Hey, Pen, I have to go!" she blurted into the phone. "Email me that list and I'll call you tomorrow. Give Toby a kiss for me!"

She ended the call and gripped the edge of the pool with her free hand, gasping as Will stroked along her sex.

Her phone rang again.

"Give it to me. I'll tell Pen you drowned."

She glanced at her phone and swiped to answer. "Hi, Mom."

In a flash, Will was on the other side of the plunge pool.

"Hi, baby girl!" her mother said. "Now, you guys are flying in on the twentieth, right?"

"Yep. We land at LAX at six."

Will cupped his hands and splashed water on his face, then leaned back on the edge of the pool, staring at the blue sky overhead.

"Great. I'll come pick you up."

"No, you don't need to. Will's getting a rental car."

"Make sure you let me know if there's anything I can get for Will before you get here. Oh, hey, did you see?"

"See what?"

"Deloux finally dropped that piece of trash."

After ignoring racing for over twenty years, her mother was now obsessively following racing news. Well, following one specific story in racing news—the destruction of Brody McKnight's career. She hadn't intended for her interview to be a weapon, but it seemed to have had that effect. In the weeks after it dropped, so did Brody's sponsors, one by one. Without them, it wasn't at all surprising that Deloux had pulled the plug. And without sponsors, it would be impossible for him to get a ride anywhere else in auto racing. He was toxic, and now everyone knew it. Violet had been hard at work making sure every shady thing Brody had ever done . . . and there was a lot . . . was getting maximum press attention.

"What happens to him isn't my concern anymore."

"That's what mothers are for, baby girl. Now it's *my* concern. I'm loving every minute of this."

Mira laughed. "So is Violet. Give her a call and you guys can cackle about it together. Hey, Mom, can I call you later? We were about to head out for lunch."

"Sure thing, baby. Love you!"

Mira tossed her phone back on the chaise and turned back to Will. "Now, where were we?"

When they left Tahiti, they were heading straight to LA for Christmas with her mother. Then she'd pack up the rest of her stuff for her permanent move to Chilton-on-Stour. Will had just signed a new contract with Lennox, so he was looking to buy a place there, too. On the flight to Tahiti, he kept showing her real estate listings, hinting not too subtly that he was hoping she'd be living there with him. She was hoping that, too.

Leaning in, she kissed the corner of his mouth. "I'm done," she whispered.

His eyes slid closed and his hands came to her hips. "Good, because if your dad called next, I was going to walk into the sea."

She kissed the side of his neck, then nipped at his earlobe. "No more phone calls. Just you and me."

"I like the sound of that."

Lifting her head, she looked into his face. His gaze met hers and she felt it all over again, an overwhelming rush of love for him—love for his patience, dealing with her past and all the complexities that came with her; love for his generosity, making the people who were important to her important to him as well; love for his passion, because it woke up the passion in her, too, the passion that had nearly been snuffed out. And she loved him for loving her, for holding her as tightly in his heart as he held her in his arms.

She took his face in her hands and looked into the blue eyes that had possessed her from the minute they met her own. "I love you, Will. I love you so much."

The soft, wondrous smile that spread across his face was one only she ever saw. It was his smile when he looked at her. "I love you, too, Mira. I didn't know I could love anyone this much until I met you."

There were moments when it all seemed too good to be true, more happiness than she ever dared hope for. But perhaps she didn't need to hope for it anymore. Maybe her happy future was already unfurling from this blissful present. All she had to do was to keep living it and see where it led her. Where it led *them*, because Will was going to be at her side for every moment of it.

ACKNOWLEDGMENTS

My husband, Matthew Ragsdale, has always been my biggest supporter, cheerleader, and unpaid research assistant, but this is a book I literally could not have written without him. He researched racing incidents for me, explained the minutiae of automotive engineering in words I could understand, and never once got exasperated when I interrupted him yet again to ask about some small detail of Formula One. This book is his as much as it's mine. Thank you, Matt.

I'm deeply grateful for the assistance of Bradley Philpot, professional race car driver, who made sure my racing lingo was accurate.

Any remaining mistakes are entirely mine, not theirs.

A huge thank-you to the entire *Missed Apex Podcast* team, especially Richard "Spanners" Ready, Chris Stevens, Kyle Power, Alex "Jeansy" Vangeen, Steve Amey, and also Matthew Somerfield of Motorsport.com, Dan Drury aka "Engine Mode 11," Scott Tuffey, Jules Seegers, Hannah Hassall, and Antonia Rankin. It's thanks to all of you that Formula One has become such a big part of our lives, and the reason I chose to write about it.

Anne Forlines has been the first to read my new work for a dozen years now, and she was particularly instrumental in seeing this one into the world. Thank you for the friendship and support, Anne!

Mira's tentacle phobia is courtesy of my good friend Rocky Cataudella. The fear is real. Trust.

This writing business can be a long, rough road, and it helps to have friends to vent to when the going gets tough. Thank you to Micki Knop, Sara Dariotis, Lucy Smythe, Jennifer Pickard, Sue Bartelt, Jennifer DiMaio, and Adele Buck for being there to lean on along the way.

Thank you to Hayley Wagreich, Sierra Stovall, Nicole Otto, and the whole team at Zando Projects for choosing to make this book one of Slowburn's inaugural publications. It's an honor to be a part of this.

And I owe a huge thanks to my agent, Rebecca Strauss. Without one extremely well-timed email from her, thinking about my career when I wasn't thinking about it myself, this book might never have happened. Thank you for your professional guidance and support on this journey!

ABOUT THE AUTHOR

AMANDA WEAVER has written everything from steamy contemporaries to swoony historicals and can now add sports romance to that list, after her husband's job as a Formula One journalist sparked a whole new obsession. In her "other life," Amanda is a costume designer working on Broadway and in opera. Born and raised in Florida, she now considers New York City home, and she lives with her family and cats in Brooklyn. Find her at amandaweavernovels.com and @amanda_weaver_author.